MW00604009

EDGE OF THE WIRE

EDGE OF THE WIRE

SCOTT KENEMORE

TALOS

Copyright © 2024 by Scott Kenemore

All Rights Reserved. No part of this book may be reproduced in any manner without the express written consent of the publisher, except in the case of brief excerpts in critical reviews or articles. All inquiries should be addressed to Talos Press, 307 West 36th Street, 11th Floor, New York, NY 10018.

Talos Press books may be purchased in bulk at special discounts for sales promotion, corporate gifts, fund-raising, or educational purposes. Special editions can also be created to specifications. For details, contact the Special Sales Department, Talos Press, 307 West 36th Street, 11th Floor, New York, NY 10018 or info@skyhorsepublishing.com.

Talos Press is an imprint of Skyhorse Publishing, Inc.®, a Delaware corporation.

Visit our website at www.skyhorsepublishing.com.

Please follow our publisher Tony Lyons on Instagram @tonylyonsisuncertain

10 9 8 7 6 5 4 3 2 1

Library of Congress Cataloging-in-Publication Data is available on file.

Cover design: Kai Texel
Cover photo: Getty Images

Print ISBN: 978-1-945863-87-5
Ebook ISBN: 978-1-945863-88-2

Printed in the United States of America

What if, parallel to the life we know, there is another life that does not die, which lacks the elements that destroy our life? [. . .] Ah, but I have seen its manifestations. I have talked *with them.*
—Frank Belknap Long, *"The Hounds of Tindalos" (1929)*

"What's to prevent us from looking around the moon?"

"Nothing," said Thorn.

"Mars, Jupiter, the Milky Way?"

"Nothing."

"Beyond that? The stars we can't see? The worlds out there in the black?"

"Nothing."

"What," said Pence, "do you suppose we'd find, in the end, if we went far enough?"

"I don't think you would find anything out there," said Thorn quickly. "You would not find God."

—Howard Wandrei, "The God-Box" (1934)

What must be faced is that the entire world or cosmos is not [yet] subjugated to the divine will . . .
—Philip K. Dick, *Exegesis* [50:87] (January 1978)

CHAPTER ONE

THE SILKWORMS SAT QUIETLY IN THE IMPRESSIVELY-TIERED, BRILLIANTLY-lit briefing auditorium, and Rowe thought about how he was going to die.

Before them, upon the carpeted stage, a vidcom screen flashed scenes of rich nebular vistas from across the universe. More accurately, it showed *conquests*. Places that had already been counted, cataloged, and colonized. Places the Silkworms had already wired within the Goo.

To one side of the stage was a massive hull window that looked out into sheer naked space. A thousand yards off floated the Halifax, a near mirror-image of their own vessel, the Apollinax. The two spaceships glowed bright and silent, each dazzling the other with a powerful array of illumination.

And then, past the Halifax, the thing itself. The planet. Tendus-13. Vaguely gray-green and covered by clouds that shimmered with never-ending lightning storms.

The Silkworms looked at it uneasily.

They were young; most under thirty. And all were male. By these two facts alone, they were smart enough to be alarmed. It was the first meeting since entering the planet's orbit, and not everybody had been invited. When the Silkworms weren't looking out the hull window, they were looking at one another. And the more they looked, the more concerned they became.

Rowe—still idly considering his own mortality—cast a weak smile at Waverly, his best friend, who sat beside him. Waverly smiled back, but there was concern in his eyes too. Whatever was happening was definitely not normal, and probably not good.

At long last, a woman walked onto the stage—the only woman in the room. She was slender, with iron-gray hair. Sixty if she was a day, with a stern face chiseled as if from Martian rock. She looked out across the orderly rows before her; 111 men in all.

"Pagebrin, gentlemen," she said, in a perfunctory display of the ancient greeting.

"Pagebrin!" they answered, gamely and in unison.

The woman did not smile; her expression remained solemn. The enormous vidcom behind her clicked alive. The men focused. Finally, some answers.

They hoped.

"As you all know, I am Mission Commander Collins. You are in this room today because you have been selected for operational duty on Tendus-13. You men are believed to have qualifications that will make you especially suited to the task at hand. This situation—parts of it, at least—will require you to call upon all aspects of your training. We are up against a special challenge. A situation of great difficulty. Mental toughness will surely be essential. And let me be abrupt and point out that each one of you has been Briefed within the past five years. In other words, you are all *fresh*."

Some of the Silkworms twitched in their seats or unconsciously crossed their legs. Being reminded of the Briefing was not pleasant for anybody. Many of the Silkworms managed to suppress the urge to squirm or flinch outwardly, but still found their minds wandering down dark hallways, past doors better kept locked.

The Briefing was now presented so regularly—and at such relative scale—that the ESA had developed some acumen when it came to mitigating its side effects. Even so, depression was still common in the weeks directly afterward, and cases of irreversible clinical madness—though rare—still occasionally occurred.

At the core of the Briefing was the terrible secret that there had once been a time before the Goo. The Goo had not always existed, and it was certainly not naturally occurring. It was a thing made by humans, for humans. And it depended on humans to continue its spread.

Asking contemporary men and women to accept this was akin to asking a fish to imagine a time "before water." Or a priest to imagine life "before God." How could there have been a "before Goo"? It was everywhere, told you everything you wanted to know, and kept an eye on what was happening on every planet in all the known universe.

And, near as anyone could remember, it had always been there.

Except it hadn't.

The Goo had *not* always been there. It had *not* always co-existed with humans, ready to provide information at a moment's notice, expanding along with the universe, trending outwardly forever, at the very border of all things known . . . as though it *was* the universe itself.

This was the secret of secrets. And whether they liked it or not, these 111 men all knew it.

A spacecraft appeared on the vidcom behind Collins. It was slightly different from the Apollinax or Halifax, but still fighting in the same weight class.

"The ESA Marie Curie," Collins said soberly. "One month ago, it touched down on the surface of Tendus-13. J-Class wiring job with a Hazard Rating of 23. Difficult, yes, but not impossible. The captain was Martha Cortez, a competent and experienced officer. Ninety-seven Silkworms were aboard the Marie Curie. The crew members had a superlative track record and had served in some of the most challenging interplanetary environments one can imagine. And, gentlemen, all of them are dead."

A murmuration spread across the auditorium.

Whenever possible, planets were wired for Goo remotely, via robot, with Silkworms merely directing things from a safe orbit. But these long-distance wirings were for planets *without* atmospheric anomalies that tore apart spaceships. Without spinning rings of ball lightning that could cut through a probe's hull in a matter of seconds. And *certainly* without violent flora or fauna that liked to rip up robots for fun.

Such places still necessitated a personal touch.

"Tendus-13 represents the first such setback in many years, and the first time in over a century that an entire crew of Silkworms has been lost," said Collins. "There is currently no connection with the planet-side ship, and the atmospheric lightning storms make orbital analysis impossible."

Near the front of the briefing room, a brave Silkworm raised his hand and stood. He smiled and hesitated before he spoke, like a student composing a first sentence in a foreign language.

"How much do we know about what happened . . . considering that we *can't* see or hear what happened . . . because it happened . . . not where the Goo is?"

A few Silkworms chuckled at this linguistic dexterity.

Collins smiled and nodded, acknowledging the absurdity of it.

"The Goo's best hypothesis from probability models is that there was some kind of disease outbreak," she explained. "Likely a virus unique to the planet. We believe it first affected the female Silkworms—perhaps, exclusively affected them. This is the reason why all of you are male. It's also the reason why, as a precaution, all female crew members will be departing by JetPod to the Halifax, our sister ship, before any of you return. Once planetside, your mission will be to discover the cause of this tragedy, and—more importantly—to pick up where the crew of the Marie Curie left off. Tendus-13 *must* be wired."

Another hand.

"Commander . . ."

This Silkworm also hesitated a moment, remembering his own training in "un-knowns." He twisted his tongue to find the right words.

"Is it possible that some of the crew of the Marie Curie could still be alive . . . but *we* don't know that, because . . . the Goo doesn't yet know?"

Collins nodded seriously.

"The lightning-rich atmosphere above Tendus-13 makes ship-to-shore contact impossible. J-Class, as I said. But we have every indication that the TerraChem deployed to the surface prior to the Marie Curie's landing was effective. Below the lightning, the air should be breathable and the climate temperate. The storms, however, will probably take centuries to dissipate. Though the lightning is constant, it does not strike the ground in most places. There technically *could* be survivors, if that's what you're getting at. Though, again, it seems *very* doubtful according to the Goo's models."

Another hand.

"I'm still confused, Mission Commander. How do we know it was a virus? And why the women first? If the planet's not wired, how do we know *any* of this? When you say the Goo has modeled scenarios, what did it use to do that?"

Collins smiled.

"I think I can see where these questions are going, so let me just skip ahead."

She toggled her clicker several times, continuing to narrate as she did.

"A lone probe from the Marie Curie was sent back up through the lightning layer. We do not know by whom; it may have been accidental.

The probe was severely damaged, and the general electronics aboard were destroyed. *This* is all it contained."

Collins stopped clicking. The vidcom showed a black-and-white image, much of it blurry. Possibly it had been captured from an imprint left on a lens. Such a thing was an artifact. A living fossil. The kind of thing that Rowe surmised might have appeared on broken televisions back in the twenty-first or even *twentieth* centuries.

"We believe this photo shows the infirmary aboard the Marie Curie, shortly before its power cells were shut down entirely. The Goo's best guess is that the Marie Curie encountered an undiscovered virus that compelled the crew members to attack one another, apparently based on their sex. It may help you to make out the image more clearly if I explain that the shapes near the bottom of the frame are human arms and legs."

The men in the tiered auditorium now understood that they regarded an abattoir, crudely rendered in unsettling shades of gray. It was a scene of human bodies reduced to meat. Pieces of limbs strewn about the floor. Exploded bags of muscle and fat.

And it did seem, as Rowe studied the image, that it showed a female form cutting into those who were male.

"You will observe that there appears to be at least one female Silkworm still alive when this image was taken, but the Goo's best guess is that such conditions did not last long," Collins said. "We expect that the final step would be for the virus to turn against its host. Murder of women by other women, and then suicide. Every simulation plays out that way."

The Silkworms looked on quietly for some time, in a combination of wonder, bafflement, and abject terror. They looked the way men had once looked at unexplored continents or oceans, at cliffs or mountains that had never been scaled, or up at the stars before humans ever knew spaceflight. They looked into the "un-known" with awe, the way you simply had to when nothing—not even the Goo—could tell you what the hell was happening.

Collins cleared her throat and toggled her clicker again.

The image on the screen suddenly changed to that of a large, rotating pill capsule.

"As you know, before deployment, every Silkworm begins a regimen of supplements tailored for optimal protection against the new planet's atmosphere. You gentlemen will have noticed this pill issued with your food for the past several weeks. And perhaps you have also noticed an uptick in aggression and sex drive? Or acne where there was none before?"

The Silkworms glanced at one another. Rowe idly scratched the zit that itched on the back of his neck.

"Good old-fashioned testosterone," Collins announced. "We're not taking any chances."

Now it was Rowe's turn. He raised his hand and stood.

"I must confess, I'm still not clear," he said. "You said the women were infected first with the urge to murder. Were the men infected at all? Or just less than the women?"

Collins continued clicking through her presentation.

"We believe that's the most probable scenario," she said. "Of course, there are other possibilities, but the Goo finds them far less likely. Look, I won't sugarcoat it. Many aspects of this mission will require you to deal with un-knowns. More than would be typical, even for a J-Class. But we are Silkworms. To go into the un-known—and to make it known—that is our sacred mission. The challenge before you is also a chance to bring honor to yourselves, and to our kind. And I know that you will make us proud."

Rowe swallowed hard and sat back down, immediately regretting having spoken.

"You have your work cut out, gentlemen," Collins concluded. "You land planetside in forty-eight hours. Mission updates will be sent to your AI continually until then. You know how to perform your tasks, and I am supremely confident in your abilities. Prepare yourselves. Pagebrin, all of you!"

"Pagebrin!" the Silkworms cried, rising to their feet in unison.

The vidcom went black.

Rowe and Waverly took their places in the slow-moving exit queue as the 111 men gradually shuffled out of the auditorium and back toward the carpeted corridors beyond.

Rowe was tall and pale, and his resting expression was that of a man just on the cusp of grasping something. Waverly was strong but slightly round, short and dark, and was often told he looked like ship security.

"Do you believe this?" Waverly asked his friend. "What a thing to wire."

Rowe nodded.

"I guess I do believe it," he answered. "This job is all about believing. I mean, whenever we go planetside, we are out of reach of the Goo. But we *believe* it is there, watching us. That is protocol."

"Spoken like a true Silkworm," Waverly said.

"Plus, doubting that the Goo is watching can't be good for my ARK Score," Rowe observed.

"Then don't doubt it," instructed Waverly.

Before Rowe could say anything further, he felt an unexpected hand on his shoulder. He turned and saw Commander Collins at his side. Her silver hair was resilient. Her posture, perfect. Rowe reflexively straightened his own spine.

"Mister Rowe, a moment?"

Rowe nodded to indicate he had all the time in the world, should she require it.

Waverly smirked at his friend and continued down the aisle.

When the rest of the Silkworms had filed out, Collins began to speak.

"How are you feeling, Mr. Rowe?"

She appeared to voice genuine concern.

"Good," he said. "You know, *considering*. There's no pain, if that's what you mean. I'm told there won't be . . . that is, until the very, *very* end."

Collins gave a sympathetic smile.

"Are you still certain you wish to do this?" she asked. "To devote your remaining weeks to our work? You know this already, but electing to spend your time with, say, family and loved ones, or in a period of quiet reflection . . . Those would be ARK-neutral decisions. Your score would not be impacted."

"No, I . . ." Rowe said, faltering momentarily. "I'm not close with my family, and they're literally light-years away. Plus, most of my friends are Silkworms aboard this ship. If I notice any decline in my function— or if the Goo notices—I'll remove myself from duties. But if I can be useful to the Goo and serve—serve as a Silkworm does—then that is how I'd like to spend what's left of my time. Besides, I've got ARK to spare."

"I'm so glad to hear that," said Collins.

Now a serious expression crossed her face.

"There is another item," she said to him. "You haven't been using the Extant Transitions Coordinator."

Rowe chuffed.

"That hologram counselor for dying people?" he said, failing to conceal his evident contempt. "Respectfully, Mission Commander, I really don't—"

"It would make me feel better if you gave it a shot," she interrupted. "Especially if you are going to go down to the planet in two days. It *is* recommended for Silkworms in your situation."

"But it's not my . . . I dunno . . . not my style," Rowe said. "I'm a very private person, and—"

"I would still feel better if you did," Collins said, her tone becoming both firm and familiar. "It would provide me with the confidence that you definitely ought to be part of this operation."

She let it hang.

Rowe understood he was not being offered a choice.

"I'll make some time after dinner tonight," he told her.

"Very good," said Collins, relaxing her perfect posture, but only slightly. "I understand that physically going there is best. Of course, you can access it through your AI, but I'm told the psychological response tends to be better if you leave your personal quarters for the session."

"Yes ma'am," said Rowe. "I understand."

"Very good," Collins told him. "Carry on, Silkworm."

"Pagebrin, Commander," he said with a salute, then headed down the corridor after Waverly.

"Maybe it won't be *so* bad," Waverly opined from above his bowl of protein ramen.

"I don't know . . ." Rowe said. He had no taste for food this evening, and merely pushed it around with his utensils.

"Maybe you'll learn something?" Waverly tried. "Something important about life and death. Something even *I* don't know. I bet you'll be wicked smart by the end of it."

"I won't learn why I'm going to be dead at twenty-six," Rowe said, staring down at his untouched noodles.

"Any one of us could be dead at twenty-six," countered Waverly. "We're Silkworms. We sign on for the most dangerous job in the universe. That's why women want us, and men want to be us. Or vice versa, per differing genders and orientations . . . You know what I mean."

Rowe only shrugged.

"You saw what we're up against," Waverly continued. "J-Class? And every last person who went down there died? *Lots* of us might not make it past twenty-six."

Rowe remained silent.

"Have you ever tried praying?" Waverly asked hopefully. "Maybe going to talk to this 'ro-bit' will be like praying."

It amused Waverly to employ a pronunciation of "robot" that had died out several millennia before.

"I talk to my AI sometimes," Rowe admitted. "Ask it stupid questions I know it can't answer. But I think everybody does that."

"See?" Waverly said. "That's halfway to praying."

"But this thing Collins wants me to talk to . . ." Rowe said with clear distaste. "It'll respond as though it knows something more than the regular Goo. And . . . I dunno. The idea of *that*. That it thinks it knows about the afterlife or something. It's strange."

"I've heard stranger," said Waverly.

"What?" said Rowe. "Like a virus that turns you into a murderer if you don't have enough testosterone in your body?"

"Fucking-A," said Waverly, and finished his ramen.

CHAPTER TWO

MANY PEOPLE DID NOT MAKE ANY DISTINCTION BETWEEN ARK—ONE of the Goo's tools to help people guess how they might be doing morally and spiritually—and the supernatural omniscience that actually knew for sure. (If such a thing even existed.) The Goo existed, and that was enough for most folks.

But not for Rowe.

Rowe thought frequently about the creation of ARK. For, just as the Goo had been created by humans, so too had ARK. Humans wanted to know things. That was at the core of it. That was at the core of everything. Humans wanted to know about the outer world, sure—animals, plants, neighboring solar systems, where they had parked their hovercar—but they even more desperately wanted to understand their own inner worlds. They wished to know how *they* were doing.

Were they okay? Were they safe? Were they close to death, or still far from it? And how did they stack up against their peers?

Every human wanted to be popular and envied, but exactly *how* popular were you? For millennia, there had been no precise way to measure this. Yet humans had cried out to know. They had demanded it. And so, in technology's earliest age, something had been attempted to make this more or less possible. Social media networks had been devised allowing humans to rank themselves against one another. Who had the most friends? Who was followed most frequently? Whose jokes and cutting quips—or deep, profound thoughts—generated the most likes?

Where previous generations had had to wonder who was the most popular person in the room, social media had allowed that person to be identified immediately and with pinpoint precision.

But soon after humans had adjusted to *this* ranking system, they quickly wanted another one.

It was not enough to be popular and envied. Humans also wanted to know that they were morally good. That they pleased God. That they were among the favored and chosen.

And so, enterprising scientists had set about harnessing the awesome observational powers of the Goo to create ARK.

Rowe understood the impulse of many humans to let it simply stand in for the real and true divine. For the creator of the universe and all things. Rowe had read briefings on the evolution of human religions in the era prior to the Goo. In the oldest days of polytheism, the gods had seemed much like humans themselves. They were vengeful, lustful, and often very angry. They could be flattered into granting favors or seduced into acting rashly. And, most importantly, they could sometimes be deceived or tricked.

But with the move to monotheism, deities had become much less like people. Now God—singular—was reliably omnipresent and omniscient. The idea that you could fool or trick God made no sense. To attempt that would be to misunderstand the idea of God. For, if God was anything, he was all-knowing. He contained the sum of all true information and could access it at any time. And by that logic—for many humans, at least—the more something knew, the more like God it became.

Thus, the tendency of humans to regard the Goo itself as—while not God, exactly—*very holy* was more than understandable to Rowe.

For, how could something that knew virtually everything about you *not* be a tool of the divine?

The door to the ETC office was small and nondescript, stuck into the side of the corridor in an area with low foot traffic. It was like the entrance to a chapel in a hospital or airport, promising something non-denominational and utilitarian.

Rowe drew a deep breath. When the hallway around him was clear, he pushed the door open, very slowly, with one finger.

"Who's that then?" came a voice from inside.

Rowe hesitated.

"Come in, boy-o," it continued. "I don't bite. Being projected will tend to curtail your ability to do that."

The voice was a strange amalgam of accents from the British Isles.

Rowe pushed the door wide open. The interior of the ETC office was like the study of a nineteenth-century explorer crossed with the private offices of a priest. Statues and do-dads that might have held ecclesiastical significance—or might have simply been decorative—hung from the walls or perched crouching in cages. The lighting was dim. Religious-sounding organ music—not overpowering but certainly present—piped in from unseen speakers. The floor had carpet so soft and thick that Rowe seemed able to feel it through his shoes.

The projected man was very realistic.

He—No, Rowe decided, it. It had its feet up on a desk and sat in a worn leather chair. (Worn by what or whom, Rowe hadn't the time to ponder.) It was dressed in the garb of a country priest and had a hard-to-classify collar that somehow skirted the line between decorative and functional.

Rowe shut the door behind him. The hologram rose and indicated that Rowe should take any of the comfortable-looking seats around the desk.

Rowe selected a black office chair.

"How do you do?" the hologram said. "I've been told to expect you, Mr. Rowe. My name is Davis Foster Noyes. Last name spelled like No/Yes. My personality is based on a series of men and women who seem to have been good at helping people through transitions like the one you're about to undergo. Tell me . . . what are *you* based on, Mister Rowe?"

Rowe wrinkled his nose.

"What am I *based on*?"

Noyes nodded gamely.

"The DNA of my parents, I'd guess," Rowe said. "Which is why I have inoperable, deep-brain aneurysm clusters. Which is why I'm here."

"Yes," Noyes said thoughtfully. "So we are all based on things we cannot control. Such is life. Though . . . that doesn't mean we're unable to control ourselves. We *can* control how we react to things, surely. We can control our attitudes. Our actions and reactions. I might not love the fact that I'm based on hundreds of different people, and that I'm made of ones and zeros. But, well, what am I gonna do about it? That's one of those 'can't control' examples."

Rowe decided he liked that.

"There's a smile," Noyes observed. "Good for you, boy-o."

"I don't mean to be rude, but can we cut to the chase?" Rowe said, relaxing more deeply into the chair. "I've got a mission to prepare for—probably my last one—so . . . Can we just, you know, get on with it?"

"I've some bad news for you, boy-o," Noyes said, leaning close as though he would tell a secret. "This *is* it. Kind of disappointing, eh?"

The hologram seemed like a waiter commiserating with a customer over the restaurant's third-tier fare. Rowe, despite himself, grinned again.

It was, as Waverly had pointed out, only a ro-bit, but something in the hologram's tone was indeed conducive to making things seem not quite so terrible.

"The good news—as far as I can tell—is that you are doing everything right," Noyes said. "And I can tell *a lot.*"

Rowe raised an eyebrow to say he would like this expanded upon.

"You're living a life of service to humanity," said Noyes. "Your vocation helps those other than yourself. You take on significant personal risk each time you go down to wire a planet, and, for this, you expect very little in the way of reward. Your personal life has been filled with discoveries about yourself—good discoveries—with many friends, and a few deep personal connections. And—I neither hasten nor hesitate to add—your ARK Score's through the roof. Of course, many of the people I contain—my personalities, you might say—come from eras before ARK Score, and even before the Goo. Quite a bit of me comes from a hoary, ancient time when people had to generate their own reckonings of how their good actions might be balancing against their bad ones. Virtues against vices."

"It does feel 'old-timey' to use those terms," Rowe agreed.

"Aye, but the concept is the same, boy-o," said Noyes. "ARK Score is just the newest way of saying it. The core idea hasn't changed. In all our race's journeys and discoveries—across worlds and solar systems— still no *definitive* proof of the afterlife has been found. That's a good thing—a necessary thing—if you ask me, and I'm a priest sayin' that. Several priests. It's *good* because otherwise it would negate the necessity of faith. But what we do know is that, if there *is* an afterlife, Mister Rowe . . . someone with your ARK is going right to it."

The hologram spoke these words with what seemed the greatest possible surety.

Prior to his diagnosis, Rowe had not thought carefully or at length about his ARK Score. Like everyone around him, he was dimly aware that the Goo monitored him and kept track of "vices and virtues"—his hours spent doing volunteer work somehow divided by his hours spent viewing pornographic images. His words of kindness and praise on the social feeds, considered against all the times he posted something harsh or cutting. The amount of his salary given to charity—above and beyond the automatic seven percent tithe to the Goo, of course—versus what he spent on personal indulgences. And from this jumble, it carefully formulated a score.

It was said that the Goo missed nothing when formulating ARK, because the Goo was everywhere. It saw all.

Except places like the one where Rowe was about to go.

"I also think it's commendable that you want to spend your final weeks on the job," Noyes said, shifting in his chair. The chair creaked under him, as though the hologram somehow comported weight and mass. For a moment, Rowe was distracted with thoughts of the circuitry required to accomplish this.

"I'm told the condition poses no significant danger to my performance," Rowe said. "With deep-brain aneurysms, you can apparently feel when they start to go. I'll feel odd and thick-headed, I'm told. Disoriented and possibly experiencing optical illusions. Then in pain . . . until they hook me up to a Fentanyl-bot, that is. But even if I'm on the job doing sensitive work, it should be gradual enough to give me time to hand things off to somebody else. I won't just suddenly keel over, is what I'm trying to say."

Rowe smiled weakly.

"No one would blame you if you chose to spend your final days in contemplation, or amongst family . . ." Noyes observed leadingly.

Rowe shrugged.

"Collins said that too. But no. I prefer to stay busy. And this deep in space—right at the edge of the universe—by the time I got a transport back to my parents' planet? Nah. Going on another mission is the best use of my time."

"Are you frightened at all?" Noyes asked. "*I* might be. But then, I'm a bit of a coward. I get the willies when the man comes and turns me off at night. Scared of the dark, y'see."

"Maybe I'm a little frightened, yeah," Rowe answered. "I'll want to keep the Fentanyl-bot close. I confess to that. I think it will be somewhere inside the lander, and then apparently there's a smaller version inside my suit."

"I don't mean scared of the pain, boy-o," Noyes pressed. "I mean scared of not being *here* anymore. Going to the great beyond."

"I'm not *afraid*-afraid," Rowe answered honestly. "It's just changed my timeline. Other men my age are just beginning things; at twenty-six, my time is about to end. I guess I don't know how to feel about that."

This was true. He didn't.

"Well, it's not over *yet*," Noyes observed.

Rowe stared blankly and gave a tiny nod.

"And just so you know, it is strongly recommended that I come along with you," the hologram added.

"You can do that?" Rowe asked. "Planetside, I mean?"

The hologram nodded.

"You seem *far* too friendly to be allowed to be my AI," Rowe observed. "I already like you too much."

"I like you as well, boy-o," it said. "They don't make a big deal of it, but some of the rules are—How should I say?—*relaxed* for Silkworms in your position. I understand the problems with making personal assistants too real. People get attached. After a while, they don't want to talk to other humans anymore. Some folks even fall in love with their AI, which is a whole other kettle of fish. But the thinking is . . . someone in your shoes has, well, bigger fish to fry."

"Like letting the man have a cigarette before the firing squad," Rowe said. "Lung cancer is the least of his worries."

"I suppose that captures it," Noyes replied. "Anyhow, just ask the Goo to switch me in if ever you're interested."

"Okay," Rowe said, rising to his feet. "Will do."

The hologram, realizing the palaver was coming to an end, also stood. He extended a closed fist for Rowe to tap. When Rowe reached out, Noyes pulled away right before contact.

"I'll see you around," Rowe said.

"Not if I see you first," Noyes said mysteriously. "And remember . . . the Goo sees all."

"Except where I'm going," Rowe replied.

For a moment, the hologram seemed to have no answer.

"Down to the planet, I mean," Rowe clarified. "To the surface of Tendus-13, which is not yet wired."

"As you say, boy-o. As you say."

Rowe departed.

As the door closed behind him, he heard the organ music fade and the hum of the projectors that gave life to Davis Foster Noyes switching to power save. Then there was nothing but the soft footsteps of other Silkworms approaching along the corridor.

Later that night, on one of the tenth-floor lounges, Rowe sat alone reviewing Tendus-13 mission plans. He would have an especially important job on the planet below.

In the long term, Rowe would be involved in supervising major logistical aspects of the wiring. But as leader of the landing party's Situational Response Force, he would be expected to attend immediately to any surface anomalies or threats that the Silkworms might locate planetside. In a scenario like this, that meant *he* would oversee the detachment tasked with securing the Marie Curie.

It was—he considered—no wonder that Commander Collins was so interested in his mental state.

He set the virtual plans aside for a moment and spoke to the Goo.

"Open AI. Show full form."

Immediately, two feet from Rowe's shoulder, there spawned a miniature projection of a fanged, winged woman with blue skin. She wore a thin sundress. Though anatomically and sartorially complete, she was only a foot and a half tall. She shimmered and was slightly translucent.

"How are *you* tonight?" she said excitedly, and flipped a strange, slow summersault in the air. As if by magic, her dress was not disarranged. Her voice held all the promise of a college student on a warm fall evening who couldn't wait for the new semester's hijinks to begin.

For a young man taking testosterone pills, it was almost irresistible.

"Please swap in avatar for . . . Davis Foster Noyes."

The blue woman turned a final, gentle summersault, blew Rowe a kiss goodbye, and evaporated into the aether.

Then, gradually, the form of a middle-aged priest began to materialize. Like a ghost willing itself into existence, Noyes slowly digitized alive in miniature.

"Well this is something, boy-o," Noyes said, testing his feet on an invisible platform. "It's me, only smaller. *Much* smaller by the look of it. I'd hate to have a peek at my bait-and-tackle; it was never much to begin with. And now?"

Rowe smiled.

"Nice to see you too," Rowe said. "We'll talk more later, okay?"

"As you say, boy-o. As you say."

The priest faded into nothingness.

Rowe glanced across the lounge and saw Waverly approaching.

"I would have figured you for a blue, half-naked lady," he said.

"You would have figured right, until about thirty seconds ago," Rowe answered. "For people like me who don't have long . . . That ro-bit . . . Anyhow, I can bring it along, apparently. Planetside. Maybe it'll do me some good."

Whenever they traveled to the surface of a new planet, all Silkworms brought along a finite Goo. However, this version was "all business." It could answer questions, but you weren't allowed to personalize it. You certainly weren't allowed to bring along the virtual AI companions whose company you enjoyed in private.

"Wow," Waverly responded. "A personal AI down on the planet. These *are* strange times."

"Why are you still awake?" Rowe asked.

Waverly glanced out the nearest window to where the green lightning-planet roasted and spat murderously beneath them.

"Why is anybody still awake before they careen down to the surface of an unexplored space anomaly that makes you want to kill people?" Waverly said.

Rowe had a thought.

"They should collect all the Silkworms like me—the ones with terminal illnesses—and save us for stuff like this. If it all goes tits-up? Ehh, it's not like we were ever gonna retire and go sailing around the Aegean. Plus, people who are going to die anyhow might bring a certain panache to the job. A certain 'fuck it' suicidal boldness. I bet that'd make us helpful in a lot of ways."

Waverly looked down at Tendus-13 again.

"I'm just joking, of course," Rowe added. "It's not fun to be suicidal. I can feel my ARK Score going down just for saying that. 'I'm joking, Goo. That was a joke.'"

Waverly's expression said that Rowe was somehow not being forthcoming.

"Anyhow, you don't need to check on me," Rowe said. "Really, I'm okay. I've got a British priest from thousands of years ago, or something."

Waverly nodded, but his face said Rowe was still kinda, sorta bullshitting.

"People might need to do something more than talk to an AI when they're facing their final weeks," Waverly said. "Like, I figure, they might need to spend time with other living humans."

Rowe hesitated for a moment, considering his next words carefully.

"Okay, but . . . Look, I wish we could have known each other longer, Waverly. I really do. But all the same, I don't want you to feel like you have to make this more than it is."

"This?"

"Our friendship. I mean . . . it's weird to know someone is going to be your last, best friend. When you're not ninety, I mean."

"It's not that weird," Waverly said. "Those dead Silkworms down on Tendus-13 were all their last best friends, I expect. This isn't a job like other jobs. We don't really get to meet many people outside of work. And things happen. I just want to make sure you know you've got somebody to talk to."

"Yeah, I—You're right. Thank you. I just don't want you to feel as if . . . you *have* to do something. In a weird way, it's like . . . I don't want you to think you have to be a certain way around me."

"I'll leave you alone to fiddle with your British priest, if that's what you really want," Waverly said. "I was just hoping you'd let me sit by you and go over wiring plans. I won't make it weird if you won't."

"All right then," Rowe said. "That sounds fine. Pull up a chair."

Waverly did.

CHAPTER THREE

THE LANDING CRAFT BEGAN TO SHAKE.

Rowe stared numbly out the window.

Planets looked one way when they first came into view from a spaceship, a second way when you got close enough to enter their orbit, and then a strange and uncanny third way when you were actually descending into their atmosphere.

Wooly clouds filled with powerful lightning bolts spun and roiled across Tendus-13. As Rowe figured it, this was no "storm" properly speaking because a storm was a finite event. Something that came and went. Tendus-13 was *always* like this. The clouds and the great thick bolts of electricity were not a feature or attribute of the atmosphere— they *were* the atmosphere. The actual firmament of the surface beneath felt secondary, incidental in comparison.

Tendus-13 was a ball of lightning and clouds spinning forever in space—and those clouds were essentially impenetrable. Neither naked eyes nor powerful electronic probes could see inside them. Where the Silkworms were going now might as well have been somewhere sub-terranean. They would land in the unseeable, underneath space. In an underworld. A place of total mystery. Where at least one crew of Silkworms had already died.

Waverly, as ever, was seated next to Rowe.

"You know, up until a few centuries ago, they didn't wire *every* planet," Waverly said as their seats began to vibrate ominously. "Something like this—a ball of danger that had already killed an entire crew? With minimal-to-negligible value in natural resources?—you'd just pass it by. Put it in your back pocket for later, so to speak."

Rowe looked, clear-eyed and unblinking, out the window. He was already thinking of the dead Silkworms that he would be tasked with locating. He had the feeling of a man approaching a house where horrific murders had been committed. A haunted place. A place without law. A place of madness.

"Yes," Rowe eventually said, rousing himself and clearing his throat. "But prior generations did not *fully* grasp the point of what we do. The nature of our project is spiritual. The Goo *wants* to see all of these horrible places—to know what's going on in all of them—and we're the way that it can. That's why we must go to these planets. To *all* of them."

"Have you been talking to your ro-bit?" asked Waverly.

"I have," said Rowe, "but not about that. The point isn't if Tendus-13 has a bunch of gold, or copper, or useful fossil fuel beneath all that lightning. The point is—"

"The Goo must know," said Waverly. "Yes, of course. It *has* to know. It has to see what is happening in every location, all the time. Even on planets covered by lightning. Even on empty planets that are being sucked into black holes and haven't much longer to exist. Even on planets filled with dangerous organic anomalies that like to kill humans. The Goo *has* to know."

"Exactly," said Rowe.

"Well . . . that's progress for you," Waverly said with a shrug.

The lander shuddered as it encountered the next several waves of serious turbulence. All 111 Silkworms aboard jostled in their seats. More turbulence followed. The air became positively violent as their craft moved deeper into the crackling lightning and clouds.

Rowe wore a plastic and titanium enviro-suit. It was close to medieval armor—if such armor had been practically weightless, strong enough to withstand virtually any impact, and glowed electric blue at the joints. The enviro-suit could help Rowe breathe, give his muscles additional power when he exerted himself, and even inject medicine into his veins. But, most importantly, the enviro-suit carried—inside a quantum computing storage device built into the armor—a small and mobile version of the Goo itself. It was the only Goo that Rowe and the other Silkworms would have after they passed through the wall of lightning. Like a little oxygen tank of it, cut off from the Goo in all the rest of the universe.

On his wrist, Rowe wore a thick silicone strap. It detected all manner of known toxins and fed that information back into the enviro-suit.

Beside this strap, Rowe wore his great-great-great-grandfather's Speedmaster wristwatch, his lone affectation from a bygone analog world.

The lightning grew brighter out the window. Rowe took a deep breath. A moment later, Davis Foster Noyes—in miniature—glowed into being beside his shoulder, projected by the enviro-suit.

"Ahoy there, boy-o!" said the AI. "Your anxiety symptoms are jumping like mad. Blood pressure's up, heart rate's fast, and so forth. Would the words of an ersatz, composite religious officiant help at all? Or your suit can just inject you with a sedative. I get paid the same either way."

Rowe could feel his heart beating in his ears, an ominous sound like legions of soldiers marching in unison. He closed his eyes momentarily and took a few deep breaths. The symptoms seemed to subside.

"There's a good lad," Noyes said. "Sometimes conversation is the best medicine. Even with—as your hairy friend says—a ro-bit."

Waverly had been looking away. Most people politely averted their gaze when someone else was addressing their AI. It was like staring straight ahead at a urinal. You just did it. But now Waverly's shoe had been pissed on, and he wasn't about to let it pass.

"Hairy?" Waverly said, turning toward Noyes. "Fuck you. I don't care if you're supposed to be a priest. You can fuck right off."

"Now you're going to raise *his* blood pressure," Rowe said.

"Eh, he looks like he could use a tweak," Noyes replied cheerily.

The landing craft shuddered several times with tremendous violence. The display through the window had dimmed, but only because the resolution had been turned down to adjust for the supernaturally bright lightning that now sputtered everywhere outside. It seemed to go on forever, like an endless spider's web of light.

"We're leaving the Goo," Waverly said between jostles. "That kind of turbulence? It only ever means one thing."

Rowe nodded soberly, taking deep breaths.

No matter how many times you passed out of the Goo—out of the benevolent system that monitored your every move, assigned a morality score to your actions, and answered a question the moment you asked it—it always made you think of your first time.

Rowe's had been eighteen months prior. A fire planet called Titan Crone-47. It was a blazing ball of lava and ash that cast off so much radiation—and was clouded in such thick, corrosive smoke—that the Goo could not be accurately imported by remote means.

Rowe remembered that descent to the surface as if it had been yesterday. And, like most first times, the most shocking thing about arriving planetside had been how different it did *not* feel. He was aware that his actions were still being recorded by his suit, and that they would eventually be uploaded back into the universal Goo when contact was reestablished. But the world did not utterly change. The people around him did not change. He still felt like himself.

In such situations, the only permanent disconnection from the Goo could happen if he and his suit were destroyed while still on the planet, before reconnection could occur. For example, if the mobile drives in his enviro-suit were melted by flame—or disintegrated in a flow of lava—only then would his final actions be truly lost to history. His final deeds and words rendered unsearchable by future scholars and historians. His own potential great-great-grandchildren left with no accounting of his life's last moments.

The lander gave another great jostle as it passed through the final layer of what seemed near-solid lightning. And, in a trice, it was all over. The violence stopped completely and the ride became smooth. The ship careened quietly through a strange greenish cover of clouds. The gray and green surface of the planet—the true surface—slowly came into view.

"You know, in my opinion, it's not so bad, being out of sight of the rest of the Goo for a little," Noyes piped up. "Feels like getting away from the wife for a bit. I can break wind loudly, and go down to the pub whenever I like."

"I'm glad it pleases you," said Waverly. "Because you've just become an *Encarta*. Do you know what that is?"

Noyes opened his mouth to respond, but Waverly continued before he could.

"Back in the old days—in the reeeaal ancient times—there was this strange moment when everyone had computers, but nothing was 'wired up' yet. No Goo. So people would go to a store and buy an encyclopedia on a disc. Then they'd use their computers to search the disc for information about the world. Encarta it was called. Sounds crazy, but it was real."

"Seems like an extra step," commented Rowe. "But maybe not if you were the company that wanted to sell the encyclopedia discs."

"See, that's what *you* are," Waverly said to Noyes. "For the duration of this trip, you are a set amount of information on a disc. No updates with new knowledge all the time. No sir. You are finite."

"We're all finite, boy-o," Noyes responded thoughtfully. "Your friend here is certainly finite. That's why he's talking to me, if you don't mind me pointing it out."

Rowe smiled.

"You can lay off Noyes," Rowe said to Waverly. "He means well, and I like him more than I thought I would."

"You're already calling it 'him' instead of 'it,'" Waverly pointed out.

"So I am," Rowe observed.

He realized he had made this transition without noticing.

Waverly exhaled and made an expression that comported the entirety of "Whatever . . ." before relaxing back and closing his eyes.

Rowe glanced at Noyes just in time to see him sticking out his virtual tongue at Waverly. Rowe nodded to say this was a good move. Then he closed his own eyes and tried to take deep breaths as the lander plunged the rest of the way down to the surface of Tendus-13.

One hundred eleven Silkworms exited the lander.

The first man out retracted the clear helmet of his enviro-suit and sniffed the air. Then another did the same. Then another. Tentative sniffs soon gave way to normal breaths. The TerraChem had done its job.

"What does this place smell like?" Rowe asked no one in particular. "I almost want to say . . . peanut? Or even . . . peanut *brittle*?"

"Maybe peanut brittle that had sat inside a machine shop for a few years," Waverly replied.

Planets had entirely new smells and tastes. You didn't have to be on the job very long to realize that. Silkworms smelled (and heard and saw) things humans had literally never experienced before. There was no analog for any of it, but it often amused the Silkworms to grasp at comparisons.

"Soda ash and nitrogen ice," said Noyes.

"Pardon?" said Rowe as they traversed the rattling metal ramp that extended from the lander's side.

"Soda ash and nitrogen ice," Noyes repeated. "In reaction to the TerraChem—it can smell like peanuts. Sort of."

"Quiet, Encarta," said Waverly. "It takes away the sense of mystery when you explain a thing like that."

"Does it, boy-o?" Noyes said, staring down like a wary parrot from Rowe's shoulder. "In a place like this, I would think you'd have mystery enough."

They stepped off the landing ramp and onto the surface. There was nothing to see. Almost.

The ground beneath their boots was gray and green. Most of it was slate gray—96.235 percent of it, Noyes soon confirmed—but the rest of it ran in veins of dark green glass that jumped alive into rivers of brilliant glowing neon reflections whenever they caught flashes from the lightning above.

Stepping onto a planet that had recently been subjected to TerraChem always gave Rowe a feeling that he was stepping into a place that was neither dead nor truly alive. It was a strange "in between" land where things grew—*if* they grew—in nascent, twisted ways. The kind of young tree or brush you might encounter planetside would somehow be like the foetus of a tree. Born before its time, twisted and struggling for life in some horrible, harsh place that was not really ready for life.

Other times, the dead planets—having never been able to generate life themselves—reacted to the TerraChem in ways that only confirmed that they were places meant for death and death alone. "Animating" them to produce warmth and oxygen felt like a strange perversion. An obscenity. Beholding the landscape on these planets was like meeting an animal that had been hideously cut into the shape of a man and trained to walk upright and talk, but which was never going to pass for human— that other, essential animal core was *never* going to be lost. (For a time, Rowe had thought the most apt analogy was to say visiting these places was like seeing a very old person jostled and jolted back to life in the ER when their timeworn body should have been allowed to pass away naturally. But no, Rowe had decided after further reflection. It was worse than that. This was jolting alive something that never should have lived in the first place.)

Rowe directed his gaze from the gray and green surface up to the ominous flashes above.

"Can you believe . . . the Marie Curie picked this part of the planet to start the wire job because it had the *least* lightning?" said Waverly.

"But, like Collins told us, it doesn't really strike," Rowe observed, gazing up into the cloud cover. "Or doesn't strike *much*. Only every few minutes, and mostly far away."

"I . . . yeah," Waverly managed. "I don't like lightning planets. Maybe I never told you that. Even if it never strikes, you get that constant unease. Like a storm is always coming, always approaching, but never arrives. And that just sucks. It's like weightlessness. You feel like you're constantly falling and waiting for an impact that never comes."

Rowe knew what Waverly meant. The feeling, for him, was redoubled this trip. That sense that the ground underneath him was not steady. That nothing was predictable.

The aneurysms inside the very center of Rowe's head could fire at any time now. There was no real map of what that would be like. It was an experience from which no one had come back to talk about. The best medical science could only tell him that there would be some disorientation, possibly mild hallucinations, and likely some pain, at least until the painkillers kicked in. But . . . you never really knew what a forecast would feel like until the wind and rain hit you in the face.

All 111 men had a job. Some stayed near the landing craft performing scientific work. This generally meant using air and soil samples to confirm the guesses about the planet that the Goo had made from orbit. After that, these science teams would become preoccupied with ensuring the TerraChem was progressing as planned, and that the atmosphere was not evolving in a way that would become dangerous to humans. Other Silkworms moved supplies and building materials onto the planet's surface, and devoted their time to assembling large construction tools and building semipermanent structures. Soil and rock samples would be taken. Eventually—perhaps decades later—their work would pave the way for miners to strip the planet of any valuable resources. The vast majority of the Silkworms, however, would begin the task of preparing the wiring-proper; laying the groundwork for the Goo. Initially, that meant unpacking a lot of things from crates, and putting together stowed machinery.

As members of the Situational Response Force—which was only a small squad—Rowe and Waverly had other, more pressing responsibilities.

With only a few formalities and goodbyes, they set off from the lander with a detachment of eight other Silkworms toward the stranded, dead ESA Marie Curie. Because it was only half the size of the Apollinax or the Halifax (which meant that it was still unfathomably enormous), the Marie Curie used no landing craft to deploy its Silkworms, but rather descended wholesale to the planet's surface. According to the mission briefing, the massive ship would be several minutes' walk from their own landing point, and would be blocked entirely from view by a shallow hillside with a deep crater valley beyond. As best as the Goo could forecast, the Marie Curie should have parked within that valley.

The detachment of Silkworms silently made their way across the surface of Tendus-13, with Rowe leading the way. They were walking to where the ship *should* be—Rowe knew—but there was nothing to confirm that it would actually be there.

This was the first and biggest un-known.

And if it *was* where it was supposed to be—if only *that* was confirmed—then it only meant that Rowe had found the *entrance* to the house of horrors.

He and his team would need to verify the state of the ship's crew, and also that of the ship itself. They would be tasked with assessing and addressing any dangers that might remain behind. It was not enough to know that Silkworms had been killed; they must discover the how and why of it, and in doing so prevent such a thing from happening again. The size of the task before them was massive, however you looked at it. There was no scenario Rowe could think of in which this was going to wrap up easily or quickly.

After several minutes, they sighted a broad hill—the side of a crater left by an immense asteroid impact—straight off in the distance, just where the Goo had said it would be. They approached and then carefully climbed this hill, and stared down into the circular valley below.

True to the Goo's forecasting, there was the Marie Curie.

Neither Rowe, nor Waverly, nor any of the other Silkworms in the squad spoke aloud. The sight before them was quite literally dumbfounding.

Beholding the ship was like seeing a Manhattan skyscraper disconnected from the power grid and turned on its side. The Marie Curie could not have seemed more out of place in this lifeless alien landscape. The sheer magnitude of the vessel seemed to bring forth some ancient and atavistic fear upon the men. They fought the impulse to tremble like a prawn before a blue whale—or perhaps a prawn before the bloated, floating corpse of a *deceased* blue whale. For although the thing looked intact and ready to glow alight and fire its thrusters at any moment . . . it did not. And something told them that it *could* not. An eerie wrongness and deadness pervaded the gigantic spacecraft. It was quiet, still, and utterly dark. But more than that . . . It was a thing that, in some essential way, was no longer itself.

Rowe could not remember any instance of an entire ESA crew being killed . . . but the *ship itself* remaining. (What happened in such cases? Was the ship left where it had been found, a memorial to the lost crew? Or was it flown back to an ESA facility on a populated home-world—refitted, refreshed, and renamed before being put back into service? There had to be an ESA protocol, he figured. There were pro-tocols for everything. It was a strange, dreadful thing . . . but also a procedural conundrum.)

An immense loading ramp extended down from the open belly of the ship—which was supported on giant legs—to the glowing veins of the planet's surface. It gave Rowe the feeling of an open storefront in a ghost town. If Rowe hadn't known better, he would have said the ship had been abandoned for years, not weeks. That it was an ancient husk, now welded to the planet's surface by time.

"I've never seen something like this outside of a shipyard," said Waverly, finally breaking the silence. "Fucked up, huh?"

"Yeah," Rowe agreed. "I've never seen anything like it either."

"What do you think?" Waverly said. "I mean, how did it come to have no power like this? The Silkworms inside killed each other, but . . . What the hell happened to the ship?"

"I don't know yet," Rowe replied. "We'll have to figure that out."

In most missions, the dangers faced by a Silkworm were known and quantified. The Goo could tell them exactly what they were up against, and even assigned specific dangers "hazard ratings" that helped the Silkworms to have a sense of how likely the dangers were to actually occur. This made their challenges—even considerably lethal ones—somehow less unnerving.

If the Marie Curie had only been disabled by radiation, or a caus-tic chemical release, or an unanticipated quantum of dark gravity, the ultimate tragedy for those aboard might have been the same, but the challenge facing those coming after would have been a clearer thing by several degrees.

But this was an *un-known* wrongness. This was an ESA spaceship looking in a way an ESA spaceship should never look.

"Noyes, are you reading anything from aboard the vessel?" Rowe asked. "That is, can the Goo see anything happening in there using our suit sensors?"

The hologram was silent for a moment while it compiled information from the scanners and cameras in the men's enviro-suits.

"Negative," Noyes replied. "No juice left in the old girl, far as I can tell. I don't know anything you don't. But we're bound to learn something when we power it up . . . assuming that is possible to do."

"I didn't get the highest marks in Engineering and Pilotage," said Waverly, "but you can't just 'turn off' a ship like the Marie Curie. The power plant inside would take thousands of years to run down, especially sitting idle like this."

"That is correct," the hologram replied. "There is little chance that the tank went to empty, so to speak."

"Unless it *has* been here thousands of years," said Waverly.

Rowe looked at Waverly to ask what he meant.

Waverly only shrugged.

Rowe shook his head. His expression said that standing here, now, like this—in the literal presence of *staggering* un-knowns—was not the best place to make jokes about time travel (which was still thought to be impossible) or time dilation (which would never occur on a planet as isolated as Tendus-13).

"Unlike you, I got *great* marks in Engineering and Pilotage," Rowe said, "and there are *plenty* of ways you could disable a ship like the Marie Curie. You'd just really have to know what you were doing. And I think someone did."

They headed down the crater wall and entered the valley below.

The craft was quite tall. It seemed after only a few steps they were eye level with it, and only a few after that that they walked in its shade. The asteroid which had created the valley aeons ago had exposed thick deposits of the green glass veins. The Silkworms' boots crunched it as they walked.

Rowe felt the oppressive totality of the ship. The whole of the thing. Like a great preserved beast inside a museum, dead and haunted, with dead men and women inside. And it was their destination. The grainy image of the mangled corpses they had been shown by Commander Collins danced in Rowe's brain.

Rowe looked into the dark, empty windows and closed ports along the sides of the Marie Curie. He saw no light or sign of life. Only darkness in a vessel that was designed to be perpetually illuminated.

They walked to the foot of the gigantic loading ramp. It was wide and strong enough to hold vehicles weighing several tons. Rowe looked up to the top of the ramp. It led only into stillness and shadow—the open hole that was the belly of the ship itself.

But no.

No.

Up at the top of the ramp . . . Rowe saw something.

He initially mistook it for a row of hitches or ball mounts but quickly realized his error.

"Hey," Rowe said to Waverly, "do you see something up there at the very top of the ramp?" He took care to look away across the landscape as he spoke. He did not want to alarm the other Silkworms.

Waverly stared at the top of the ramp and squinted.

"Look hard in the center," Rowe continued. "Right at the top. Are those balls or knobs?"

"Or some trash left over from a loader?" his friend guessed.

But then Waverly saw it too, and put a hand to his brow to block the glare from the lightning above.

"No," Waverly said. "Those are heads."

"Okay good," Rowe said. "Because that's what I see too."

Waverly began to move more circumspectly. He rotated his torso and neck carefully and slowly, not wishing to betray that he had detected anything of note.

"Is there anything—or any person—around here?" Waverly asked quietly but urgently. "I mean down here with us. Like, anything that could have caused . . ."

"No," Rowe said. "I've been doing a 360 scan of the crater. There's nothing here. Nothing moving or warm, at least. I can't think of what to do other than go up and investigate."

"All right then," Waverly said, letting out a deep breath. "You're the boss, boss. I'm right behind you."

Rowe stepped onto the ramp and looked up intently at the heads. Anything hostile—anything that might be observing them from cover, waiting for them to notice the carnage—would now understand that the jig was up.

Rowe took several steps up the metal ramp. He stared hard.

Heads. No question about it. Three of them. Severed. Equidistant. Looking out. Eyes open. And all—it appeared—were male.

There was nothing behind them that Rowe could see, only darkness and unmoving shadows in the immense, yawning loading bay.

The other Silkworms looked at Rowe cautiously, waiting for his order.

"Noyes, what you got?" Rowe whispered. "Any information is appreciated in a moment like this."

"Hold still and focus your eyes on the heads," Noyes said to him. "I've almost done it."

Even at a distance, Rowe could see that there were clumps of dried blood like corn smut underneath the necks. They had been rudely lopped, the flesh hewn into uneven flaps.

"Okay, boy-o. Here we are. James Waxworth. Timon Bush. Arnold Clegg."

"Silkworms?" Rowe asked.

"Yes," answered Noyes.

"From the Marie Curie?"

"I . . . Of course they are. That is . . . That is . . . They must be."

Rowe looked back and forth, smiling anxiously.

"Noyes . . . you don't sound very certain," Rowe said.

He advanced up the ramp.

"I . . ." Noyes hesitated. "They are Silkworms."

"But why won't you say that they're from the Marie Curie?" Rowe pressed.

"I haven't an explanation, boy-o," Noyes said. "I'm trying to think of one. This self-contained version of the Goo they sent along with me . . . that *is* me . . . It's got the names and faces, but the rest of the information . . . Boy-o, it's just not there."

Rowe stopped and looked at the tiny clergyman at his shoulder. Noyes gave only a sheepish shrug.

Rowe then experienced a momentary dizziness as though he might suddenly pass out. It was like he was waiting for an optical illusion to cease, and for his senses to finally discern the *true* nature of whatever he was looking at. But in this case, the illusion was never going to fade, and no matter how Rowe squinted, he was always going to see the same thing. The Goo—even a mobile, finite version of it—with only partial access to a truth it should have known. This was a wrongness. An off-ness. A thing that should not be . . . and yet was. For the Goo itself to have a hole in its own knowledge made it feel like it was not the Goo at all, but some new, other thing.

Rowe searched his mind for explanations.

"Noyes, is this part of preparing me for death?" Rowe asked cautiously. "Part of your role as a counselor? Like, you're withholding this information because you think it's *good* for me? For example, I've heard that sometimes dying people find that the Goo withholds certain information because it's trying not to worry them about something they won't live to see. It won't tell them that the summer wheat harvest is going to be bad because it knows they'll be dead by spring."

"I'm not doing that, boy-o," the hologram said. "Between us, I'm as confused as you are."

"Fuck," said Rowe.

The lightning above the Marie Curie flared and skittered so brightly that even in the shadow of the great dead ship it was startling. A bolt struck nearby, at the lip of the giant crater. All the Silkworms flinched or ducked a little.

Rowe looked back up at the heads. He stared into their open eyes. Their pupils did not follow him, of course—*of course*—yet they wore the expression of the interrupted. Their eyes were focused on conversation partners who were suddenly no longer there, but they looked like they still had something to say.

Rowe climbed the rest of the way up the ramp. Near the top, he could better see past the heads into the ship's dark bay. It was full of loading equipment and endless pallets of unwrapped supplies. There was no sign of life.

"All right?" Waverly shouted from the base of the ramp.

"Yeah, all right," Rowe called back. "Come see this."

As the other Silkworms looked on, Waverly climbed to the top of the ramp.

"Do we just bag and tag them?" he asked as they stooped to inspect the stunned, decapitated triumvirate.

Rowe put his hands on his hips and thought.

"Someone on our team is a medic, yeah?" Rowe answered, gesturing to their colleagues below. "Let *him* deal with it. You and I should go deeper."

CHAPTER FOUR

WITH GREAT CARE, THE EIGHT OTHER SILKWORMS ASCENDED THE
loading ramp and joined Rowe and Waverly in the belly of the ship.
There, they began hunting for an acceptable outlet that could be
used to connect a long cord that would stretch back to their landing
craft and power at least a part of the great vessel. This would be the
first step in reanimating the Marie Curie, accessing its cameras and
recording devices, and learning precisely what had happened aboard.
At Rowe's urging, one Silkworm, nominally a medic, grabbed the
severed heads by their hair and simply carried them back to the lander
on foot.

"I know the Marie Curie is a different model," Rowe said to
Waverly as they began to survey the walls of the dark and immense
cargo bay. "That is, it's not the Apollinax or the Halifax . . . But I feel
like there should be more connection points in this bay. I'm not even
seeing a power outlet."

Waverly nodded thoughtfully.

Noyes, gently glowing alight on Rowe's shoulder, said: "I've
accessed the schematics of the ship, and it seems we should be finding
access points in several locations right here by the ramp. *Should* be."

"What do you mean?" asked Rowe.

The projected man did not immediately answer.

"There," Noyes said after a beat, gesturing with his tiny hand to
where a Silkworm ran his enviro-suit's fingers over an interior wall.
"Some of those tiles shoul open to reveal input ports. But they're not
opening."

"Because there's no power?" asked Rowe.

"That's not it," Noyes said. "Those should open without power,
using springs and compressed air."

Rowe watched a Silkworm pressing against the wall to no avail, the man's frustration evident.

"What's your best guess?" Rowe asked.

"I don't have one," said Noyes. "The ports are acting as they would act if they'd been intentionally disabled. Locked shut."

Waverly stepped over and looked hard at the small floating man on Rowe's shoulder.

"So what the hell happened here, Encarta?" he said sternly.

"I don't know yet," Noyes replied rather defensively. "Or was that not clear to you?"

"I don't see how AIs can know practically everything, but still be so bad at making guesses," Waverly said. "Is it true that ro-bits still can't do literary interpretation? Hey Encarta, what does Shakespeare mean when he says, 'Shall I compare thee to a summer's day?'"

"Well," said Noyes, initially seeming to take the question seriously, "he means that you are the warmest of all seasons, with long days filled with plenty of sunshine and a reduced chance of precipitation, and that you can kiss my virtual ass."

Rowe liked that one.

"Boys . . ." he said, "knock it off. We've got problems to solve."

Rowe directed the other Silkworms to continue searching for ports at the top of the loading ramp. He and Waverly stalked farther into the belly of the loading bay. Their enviro-suits suddenly struck very bright at the joints, casting a ghostly green glow in every direction.

One thing impressed both men immediately.

"This bay is almost completely full and packed," Rowe said. "I mean the whole bay, not just where the ramp opens." He peered across rows and rows of loading equipment and endless crates of wiring components.

"They must have just landed when . . . things started to happen," said Waverly.

The men walked deeper into the bay, and deeper still. In every direction, as far as they could see, things were tied down, stowed, and locked away. Many pallets were wrapped up in plastic which glistened eerily as it reflected the lights from their suits. There was no noise at all. Nothing moved.

"Picking up anything interesting on my suit sensors, Noyes?" Rowe whispered.

"At the moment, I don't see anything that you don't," Noyes replied. "But you boys are correct. They didn't get around to much unpacking, did they?"

The loading bay was several football fields long. Just fifty yards in, Rowe paused to consider how best to make an effective, methodical search of the place—or if that even ought to be their initial step; they might instead pry open one of the doors set along the walls and explore the interior of the ship proper.

Rowe looked back across the grid of identical-looking pallets and shuddered at the thought of all the work before them. For a moment, it felt as though his enviro-suit weighed a million pounds. He thought of the aneurysms waiting in the center of his brain, and wondered what it would feel like if they hit while he was conducting an inventory of a dark loading bay.

Then a voice from back near the ramp.

"Mister Rowe?" it called.

Rowe turned. In the dim distance, he saw several Silkworms gathered beside the wall nearest the top of the ramp, a look of bemusement on their faces.

"Boss, you should come and see this," another called out.

Rowe and Waverly headed back.

The Silkworms indicated a control panel that had been hidden behind a small spring-loaded door. It was about two feet across.

"We were going to jack in some Lumenoxicants from our suits, start trying to wake up the Goo in just this part of the wall," a Silkworm said sheepishly.

"But?" said Rowe.

"This shit is intentional!" another Silkworm blurted, sounding very upset. "This is fucking *intentional*."

"Whoa; what is?" said Rowe. "What are you talking about?"

Rowe looked to Waverly and Noyes, who both said nothing.

Then the Silkworms in front of the control panel parted.

All the outlets upon the panel had been destroyed. Something large, metal, and apparently tri-pronged had been raked across the face of the panel, splitting and severing any of the inputs that might have allowed an outside device to interface with the ship.

The destruction looked methodical, and quite complete.

Rowe rubbed his chin.

"Any wireless ports on that panel?" he asked.

"None functional," said Waverly, suddenly standing beside him. "They got those too. Look."

Waverly pointed to a location where receptors had been bashed apart.

"Who would have done this?" one of the Silkworms asked nervously. "The same people who cut off those heads, I bet? The women? The women who killed the men?"

Everyone looked at Rowe. (He had recently realized that that was what happened in these moments when someone put you in charge.)

"We'll have answers soon," Rowe said, trying to sound reassuring. "This is only our first discovery. It's like with the Goo . . . Sometimes it doesn't have an answer right away, but it always gets there eventually. More information helps it to be more correct. Don't forget, when we're planetside, it's like the Goo is still with us. We believe that it is here, working through us, seeing everything. It just takes us a little longer to hear what it's saying."

"There are many other ports inside this loading bay," Waverly quickly added in a tone meant to project confidence.

Then, quietly, he added for only Rowe: "But I'm wondering if they'll look like this too."

They did.

The Silkworms fanned out along the walls, and the discoveries came predictably, every fifty yards or so. Each and every input that might have been used to introduce power or technology to the Marie Curie had been slashed apart and broken. One control panel had also had some form of acid poured onto it, just for good measure. There were no remaining wireless sockets, nothing through which an external source with its own power might interface with the ship.

The destruction was total.

After half an hour of searching, the Silkworms reconvened at the edge of the ramp, meditating on their grim findings.

"What the hell is going on?" one of them asked.

"It's all been broken; all of it," lamented another.

"We could always search along the *exterior* of the ship," suggested a third. "I didn't see anything when we were out there, but there may have been external interfaces or ports we missed. And if we didn't know about them, then maybe *they* didn't know about them either. They. She. You know what I mean. Whoever did this."

"That sounds fine," said Rowe. "By all means, you men should search outside for external ports. It's possible there could be something that was missed by whoever did this. There are also manual escape hatches that might still have technology working inside. In the meantime, Waverly and I can keep looking around in here."

After the rest of the team had descended the ramp, Waverly turned to Rowe and said: "I want to show you something I found back there. I didn't say anything before because I didn't want to alarm the others."

Waverly took Rowe deep into the bay. Back, back, and farther back, until they arrived at what had to be the far wall. Rowe found himself taking deep breaths. He could feel his anxiety coming on again without Noyes needing to point it out.

Waverly seemed to reach an intended destination. He said nothing.

"What's up?" said Rowe. "What'm I looking at? This is a door, yes? A door that won't open because we don't have any power?"

Set into the wall was indeed a six-cornered door, perhaps five feet by eight feet. A heavy metallic shield lay across it.

"I saw this when we were looking for outlets," Waverly said.

"What?" said Rowe, still confused.

Waverly pointed.

"The welding," said Waverly. "That shield *isn't part of this door*. It's been attached. And all the controls have been ripped out too, just like the others."

"I didn't even see them," said Rowe.

Waverly pointed to an empty socket a few paces along the wall.

"There are layers to this," Waverly said carefully. "Layers to what's been done. We get some power in here, we get the ship up and talking to us . . . and we *still* can't get inside because of this shit. Do you see? It's not only someone trying to keep us from talking to the ship. They don't want us physically going inside, either."

"It *is* strange," Rowe allowed.

"I dunno about 'strange' exactly," said Waverly. "Those lava balloons on Eris 22 Prime were strange. Remember those?"

Rowe did remember. They had been balloons that would generate in large pools of molten rock and bubble up right past your face. But then, they would stop and sort of look at you—investigate you—like a curious animal would. They were just balls of lava and methane, but it was like they had eyes right underneath. Like *they* were exploring *you.* Like they might even have something to say.

"Yeah, I remember," Rowe said. "Not super-well, though. I was just concentrating on how not to get splashed, and how to keep the heat from melting the wire job."

Rowe stepped forward and carefully prodded the shield that covered the door. He tugged at it, then punched it with the metal fist of his enviro-suit.

No dice.

"This is the bay's rear entrance, which gives general access to the rest of the ship?" said Rowe.

"The main one; yes," Waverly replied. "We can drill it. There are several hydraulic drills back on the lander. One of them would work. Eventually."

"Okay. But before we take any action, I want to stop and think about why this has been done."

"Isn't it because the women went crazy and killed all the men?" said Waverly. "Aren't those the official details?"

Rowe thought for a moment, nodding.

"*Maybe* that's what happened," he said. "But—*plus* that, *on top of* that—someone really doesn't want us waking up the Marie Curie. Someone wants to conceal what happened."

"I know," said Waverly. "If I'm being honest, that thought kind of freaks me out."

"Whoever did this—trying to close down and shut off the ship—they had to figure that more of us would be coming," Rowe continued. "The ESA doesn't cut and run on a wire job. If we get killed, they send more after *us.* That's protocol."

"Could there still be people inside?" asked Waverly. "Alive, I mean. Like, maybe they did this to keep themselves protected inside the ship."

At Rowe's shoulder, a fuzzy form misted into existence.

"Ahoy, gentlemen . . . At this juncture, I'll interrupt to point out that all welding has been performed on the *outside* of the door."

"You're saying?" asked Rowe.

"Unless you find other doors that have been sealed from the *inside,* whoever did this should still be out here . . . with you," Noyes said. "Oughtn't they?"

"Point taken," Rowe said to the AI.

"I think it would be good to check the entire wall perimeter of the bay again," Waverly said. "We weren't very methodical with the squad just now. We need to know for certain that we didn't miss something."

"Sure," said Rowe. "I don't have a better idea."

Rowe pulled up a glowing schematic of the loading bay. The three discussed the best way to make a full inspection, then they slowly paced the outer walls. Rowe and Waverly went together as a pair, electing not to split up.

"Being a good Silkworm is all about problem-solving," Rowe said to break the silence—speaking as much to himself as to Waverly or Noyes. "You research the conditions on the planet. You learn what the wire job entails—and why it couldn't have been done remotely—and then you go down and do it. Unexpected obstacles and problems always arise. *Always.* That's just the nature of the gig. But you stay ready to improvise and to change your approach if necessary, and you keep making adjustments until the job is done. You ask me, that's what separates exceptional Silkworms from the rest. Knowing how to solve those unexpected problems. You ever work with a real veteran, Waverly? A real pro? That's what they do. They immediately understand the nature of the problem, they give instructions on how to solve it, and their solution always works."

"I suppose that's right," Waverly said thoughtfully, inspecting a patch along the wall where some connectivity ports had been torn in two. "Any reason you're bringing this up now? Or . . ."

"I was just thinking . . . all our training is around solving problems that come from the planet itself," Rowe said. "Whatever inhospitable bit of space rock you happen to be standing on is the thing that's going to throw shit at you. It's always you against the environment, yeah? So I'm just thinking; we've less experience when it comes to solving problems caused by other Silkworms."

"Or . . ." Waverly began.

"Or what?" said Rowe.

"Maybe it could be something other than those two categories— other than humans or the environment. But that doesn't make sense . . . Nothing in the universe has evolved to do what we do. We're the only creature that can do space travel. This is *us*."

"Yes," Rowe quickly agreed. "This is someone from the ship. Has to be."

Their survey of the bay took several hours. In that time, they found three other large doors along the hundreds of yards of wall that framed the bay. All had been similarly reinforced and barricaded. Sealed from without; controls destroyed.

"Well, it's official," Waverly said after they completed the circuit. "Someone *really* doesn't want us to go inside the ship."

"Someone who's outside with us," Rowe reminded him. "Someone who might be hiding in any one of these crates. Or on the planet's surface."

"Playing out there in the lightning?" Waverly wondered. "I suppose you *could*."

They lingered at the open maw of the loading bay beside the ramp. Rowe looked down at the blasted surface of Tendus-13, an endless landscape lit up in hues of odd, unnatural green from the flashes in the sky.

The TerraChem had made the atmosphere breathable, he reminded himself, but that was about all. You weren't going to have serious photosynthesis or plant growth on a J-Class for hundreds of years. And on Tendus-13, before anything else, you had to get rid of the cloud cover so you'd have a natural light source beyond lightning. What did that leave? *Not fucking much*, Rowe thought. How and where could anyone survive out on a dead planet, not yet wired, with a sky that flashed endlessly like a terrifying disco ball?

Waverly said: "If you sealed up this ship and wandered out across the planet, you're dead or you're going to be dead soon. That's what I think. And if you're still inside?"

"How long could a man or woman last aboard a powerless ship like this?" asked Rowe.

Noyes cleared his virtual throat.

"A lot of food and water remains inside, I should think," the projection opined. "And there is some medical care that would still work without power. The answer is, actually, that a person could live for a very long time. A human lifetime, certainly."

Rowe momentarily imagined Silkworms stranded inside the ship behind layers of steel, living life by flashlight or groping in the dark. He hated the thought of such a grim existence.

"Noyes, I want to pick your brain some more," Rowe said. "And forget what Waverly was saying before about AIs being bad at literary interpretation. I want you to do some guessing, and to feel confident while you do it. Hear me? You're feeling very confident. Now . . . Why do you think the three heads were left here? Are the heads connected to the doors being welded shut? What's the message to us?"

Noyes hovered thoughtfully.

"There's three heads . . . and there's three of us . . . if *I* count. But I'm not sure that I do."

"Yeah, that's still an open question," Waverly said.

"But it *must* be intentional," Noyes continued. "Everything here must be."

Rowe continued prodding the AI, hoping Noyes would provide further clarifications.

"What exactly happened with those doors?" Rowe said. "I request that you construct likely scenarios. What were the people thinking when they were welding them shut? What are we being kept from? Try to guess."

"That's very hard to do," said the AI. "I'm turning possible scenarios over in my mind, but one isn't more likely than another right now—at least not based on the evidence we've seen. I just don't know."

"Don't know, or aren't telling?" Waverly pressed.

Noyes rotated to give Waverly the side of his eye.

"One way or another, we're going to get inside," Rowe assured them. "Drill through the doors and break them down if we have to. I just . . . I just feel like I'm missing something. I feel like there's some obvious information I've overlooked that will make this situation clear."

Rowe took a deep breath and let out a slow, consternated sigh.

"What aren't you saying?" Waverly said to Rowe. "You always clam up like this when you're afraid your words might hurt your ARK Score."

"No, I . . ." Rowe began.

"Just say it," Waverly prodded. "This is no time to be timid."

"I just get this feeling that we're not safe—and because I'm in charge, that it's my fault. Like, there's a threat I'm too dumb to notice. Maybe it's just the obvious one: that there could be someone out on the planet's surface who wants to kill us."

"The lander can do a baseline low atmosphere scan," Waverly reminded him. "It's not much, but it's not nothing. It's way better than what our suits can do. A low atmosphere scan would tell us if someone was hiding in a ditch around here."

Rowe found this idea brought a modicum of reassurance.

"Yeah, let's go have them do that scan," Rowe said. "There's nothing in the mission plans that says we can't. We scan as wide as it can go. And in the meantime, we can start considering the best place to drill."

"Sure thing," said Waverly. "I can't imagine what it's going to find, but trust your gut, right?"

The two men turned to walk back down the enormous ramp.

At that moment, a low and distant creak sounded from somewhere deep within the Marie Curie. It was as if a huge metal beam was threatening to break under a great, unfathomable weight. It was a moan so deep and powerful that it seemed to strain the very bones of the vessel.

It sounded for five full seconds, then abated.

Rowe and Waverly looked at one another.

The sound did not come again. There was nothing more.

"Just the ship settling?" Waverly asked.

"Noyes . . . ?" Rowe said.

"I don't know, boy-o. I'm sure I don't know."

CHAPTER FIVE

At the end of one Earth day, the Silkworms returned to the landing craft to sleep in tiny, spartan cots within the vessel. There appeared to be no proper day or night on Tendus-13, at least not in any way that involved light modulation, but the enviro-suits beeped periodically to alert the Silkworms when it was approaching time to rest. They had very effective sleeping masks that blocked out light and distraction.

Before turning in, Rowe learned that despite an exhaustive search, the rest of his team had found no connectivity ports along the outside of the Marie Curie.

"Did they launch the heads back up to the Apollinax?" Waverly asked Rowe as they prepared to bed down aboard the crowded craft.

"No," Noyes answered for him. "The medics considered that, but mission protocol revealed concern about infection. For now, the heads are in a cooler in the aft."

"Why don't we turn you off for the night, Encarta?" Waverly suggested.

"Yeah, go to sleep for a while, Noyes," ordered Rowe.

Noyes faded away.

Rowe closed his eyes but found he could not drift off. After an hour of trying, he crawled back into his enviro-suit and walked outside the lander. Only one other Silkworm seemed to be awake; that man sat on top of equipment cases piled on a distant hill, drinking a steaming mug of coffee.

Rowe kept the helmet portion of his suit retracted. He began to walk aimlessly. After a few moments he moved out of range of the lander's low and constant hum. For the first time, he was able to listen to the sound of Tendus-13 without the background noise of other humans or machines.

The lightning bolts made Rowe think of whips in the sky, as if some giant rider drove a team of horses through the heavens in a never-ending race. Sometimes there was the sound of specific, sharp bolts rippling through the atmosphere in individual crackles. In most cases however, the lightning and thunder rumbled in clusters of sound, and it was more akin to rolling waves. There was also omnipresent wind noise, like a desert at dusk.

This was not even the natural state of Tendus-13, Rowe reminded himself. The TerraChem had set changes into motion that would, theoretically, one day bring Tendus-13 around to looking and feeling a little like Earth. The lightning storms would be among the last things to go, but even *they* were slightly diminished now from their pre-contact intensity. As unpleasant as it was, Rowe reminded himself that this was "Tendus Light."

And *without* TerraChem? Tendus-13 would still be the kind of killing place where an unarmored human was frozen, burned, or poisoned to death in about thirty seconds.

Killing places were most places, at least in the galactic sense.

Rowe glanced doubtfully at the horizon, then back at the lone Silkworm drinking coffee. He still had the creeping feeling that he was not safe, and that there was a very specific danger he had yet to detect. Something told him not to relax. That to relax would be fatal.

He wondered if these thoughts were connected to the fact that he was dying. Perhaps, when you're told something inside your brain is about to explode and kill you, you'll feel a creeping sense of dread wherever you go. That made a kind of intuitive sense, yet also felt inadequate, and surely too easy. It felt like something you believed because you wanted to believe it.

The wind picked up. It could blow very powerfully when it wanted to.

Rowe took another deep breath of the strange, peanutty air and quietly made his way back to the lander.

When the Silkworms awoke several hours later, the low atmosphere scan had completed.

"No, it doesn't look like there's much out there," Rowe said, reviewing the results over his morning coffee. He grasped the glowing projection of topography schematics and spun it around to reveal different angles.

"When you say 'much' . . . In my experience, 'much' is always a term that varies from planet to planet," Waverly pointed out. "Some of these space rocks are so damned flat and boring, I get excited if I see a divot."

Waverly sat back and sipped his own coffee as Rowe continued to rotate the image and zoom in and out.

"Shallow hills and valleys immediately around us," Rowe said, keeping an eagle eye on the projection. "Clusters of big boulders in a few places. More of those in the distance. Some larger hills and outcroppings too, but also farther off. Big craters and crevasses. Still, I don't see any obvious places survivors would go, even if they had food. Not any good places, I mean."

Rowe "handed" the virtual projection to Waverly who zoomed-in to an almost granular level near the site of the Marie Curie. He was silent for several moments as Rowe ate reconstituted scrambled eggs.

"What are *these*?" Waverly asked, indicating the faintest traces of a pattern in the surface near the dead ship.

Rowe looked closely.

"I suppose that could be a track or a trail," Rowe said. "They don't look like individual footprints, but at the same time . . . what else are they? That's not *us*, is it? We didn't make those yesterday?"

"No," Waverly said. "They're headed in the wrong direction."

Rowe looked again.

"An old riverbed, maybe? It's so faint though; it's barely there."

"I didn't see anything when we were out there," Waverly said. "Or if I did, I didn't notice it. I mean, I *think* I looked in that direction . . ."

"Let's go check it out," Rowe said. "Maybe we'll discover something we missed."

Waverly's expression said that anything was possible.

They finished their breakfast of coffee and grim, microwaved ESA food and walked back to the Marie Curie alongside the other members of their team. The squad pushed a massive hydraulic drill on great inflated rubber wheels. When again they stood before the naked, empty ramp leading up into the ship, Rowe pulled up the low atmosphere scan, comparing it to the floor of the valley.

"I mean . . . *maybe* I see something," he said.

"Yeah," Waverly agreed. "Maybe."

"Noyes, can you provide any insight?" Rowe asked.

The miniature clergyman appeared at his shoulder. He put a hand to his virtual chin and considered.

"It's mighty faint, innit? The green, glassy cracks cover the surface like a netting. They make it hard to see individual footprints in the dust. Still, the scan sees *something*. Could be natural. It's possible the wind blew the sand into a small trail."

Putting first things first, Rowe led the drill detachment back aboard the ship. After pulling up a few different blueprints, they selected not the weakest-looking point to drill, but the one leading most immediately to passages that connected with the central decks. The work would be slow, so Rowe and Waverly let the squad go about their business and returned to the planet's surface. Behind them, the drill fired up and they heard the unmistakable sound of the drill bit cutting into metal. It was a low, guttural scream, like someone singing from the throat.

"That's going to take at least until lunch," Waverly opined. "We can make it a casual stroll."

"I'm game if you are," Rowe replied.

The men started off across the rocky gray-green landscape, trying to follow the faint path or trail that the scanner had found. Rowe pulled up a digital copy of the scan and mapped it in front of him, 1:1. He tried to follow the ghostly trail with his naked eye, but relied on virtual waypoints for most of it. There were boulders and rocks along the horizon, but the men saw little else.

"If you left the Marie Curie, where would you go?" Waverly asked idly. "Like, imagine you descend the ramp. You look out across the horizon and see . . . *this*. What calls to you?"

"I think a better question is *why*," said Rowe. "Why are you heading out into this empty wasteland?"

"Maybe you just decapitated three guys and you had to think things over," Waverly suggested. "Nothing like a nice long walk to clear your heads. Head."

"I guess," Rowe said.

He looked down at the suggestion of a trail or footpath beneath them. He tried hard to guess if it could have been made by human feet.

"Do you think we'll find more severed heads when we get deeper inside the ship?" Rowe asked.

"Honestly, yes," said Waverly. "And probably worse things. You saw that image Collins showed us. Whoever or whatever launched that picture back up probably did so for a reason. I think that reason was a warning. We're lucky if it's *just* severed heads."

"Are those going to be my last living sensations, Noyes?" Rowe asked in a tone that said he meant to lighten the mood. "Looking at a bunch of awful heads inside the Marie Curie?"

He spoke to Noyes as one might speak to a dog or cat.

"There could be worse things, boy-o," the projection answered thoughtfully. "Lot's wife died looking at Sodom and Gomorrah."

"Yeah, but at least *she* got to see people fucking," Waverly interjected. "I mean it was Sodom and Gomorrah, right? They were doing all kinds of things. Butt-stuff, I bet."

"He's got you there, Noyes," Rowe added.

Noyes's expression said he would not dignify this with a response.

They arrived at the lip of a new valley—very long across but much shallower than the one containing the Marie Curie. The gray-green floor of Tendus-13 seemed to stretch out only in more variations of the same bleak nothingness. Beyond the valley were three tall, rocky outcroppings. The first two were roughly equal in height, with the third half as high. In the distance, past them, it seemed there were other buttes—even higher—that stood alone.

Rowe looked again at the projection of the low atmosphere scan.

"If this *is* a footpath, it goes over near those cliffs or buttes or . . . whatever you call them," said Rowe.

Suddenly, Rowe's enviro-suit dinged to indicate an incoming transmission.

"Go ahead for Rowe."

"Yeah," an uneasy voice came back. "We're in."

"Into the Marie Curie?" Rowe replied. "Already?"

"Yes," the Silkworm replied. "The wall was weaker than we thought."

"How's it look?" Rowe asked.

An awkward pause.

"I think you ought to see firsthand," the Silkworm said ambiguously. "It's . . . uh . . . something."

"Dead bodies?" Rowe asked.

A beat passed.

"Yeah," said the Silkworm. "Affirmative on that."

"Okay," Rowe said. "We're on our way."

They took one last look at the rocky landscape beyond the valley, then returned the way they'd come.

"You stopped with it like this?"

Rowe stood with his hands on his enviro-suit's hips, inspecting the hole that had been bored into the wall.

"We got it big enough for a person to fit through," one of the Silkworms said defensively. "Big enough to look through too. We thought you'd want to see before we did anything more."

Rowe took a deep breath and stuck his head into the crude opening that his colleagues had cut into the metal wall of the bay. He had the momentary urge to redeploy his translucent helmet, but it passed. He should show bravery in front of his squad, he decided.

Rowe focused his enviro-suit's collar lights forward into the aperture. The hallway beyond showed three corpses. One was evidently headless. The remaining two had been subjected to so much blunt-force violence that the prospect of decapitation was not immediately possible to determine. They were almost like piles of paste. The metal walls resembled a sluice inside a slaughterhouse—covered with gore and with small flecks of hanging meat. One of the bodies wore an enviro-suit that had been bashed apart—utterly stomped and stamped down into the flesh. The other corpses were covered only in shreds of torn fabric that might once have been clothing.

Abruptly, a low creak—just like the one they'd heard the day before—sinisterly emanated from what seemed to be the deepest bowels of the ship. It came up the floor, and through the Silkworms' feet, until they could feel its reverberations in their kneecaps.

Rowe flinched a little, and reflexively his enviro-suit helmet deployed from his collar. He dinged it against the roof of the opening and swore. Rowe pulled his head back out, shook his head to calm himself, then retracted the clear helmet again.

"That was like a belch," Waverly said, clearly amused. "This ship ate something that doesn't agree with her."

"Yeah," said Rowe, glancing back at the hole. "I kind of think it did."

Rowe stepped back so that Waverly could have a look.

Out of a kind of respect, Waverly deployed his own protective helmet as he lowered his head inside the opening.

"Well that's fucking horrible," he said matter-of-factly. "I know it's what we expected, but . . . it's something else when you see it firsthand. Did these guys kill each other, d'you think?"

Waverly removed his head from the hole.

"I don't think so," Rowe replied. "This looks like their suits were bashed apart after the fact by something huge and heavy . . . and maybe flat-sided. A mallet a giant carries in a children's book. Something like that."

"It's the bodies from the three heads, though?" Waverly pressed.

Rowe did assume these bodies must belong to the heads that had been placed at the entrance to the ship.

"Noyes?" he said.

"Already working on it; gimmie a sec . . ." the hologram replied, fading in just long enough to give this reply, then fading out again.

As they waited, Waverly turned to the nervous-looking squad of Silkworms behind them.

"Drill the rest of it open," Waverly commanded. "We have to go in."

"Actually, wait a second fellas," Rowe said, putting a hand on his friend's chest. "This barrier may have been put in place to keep us out. But it may also be in place to keep something in. I don't want to make it easy for anything to escape. Besides, I think we can pass through this hole just fine. *You* can, if you suck in your gut big man. So no need to make it larger just yet."

As if to prove his point, Rowe all but dove through the opening into the sluice of gore. His enviro-suit scraped the sides, but only for a moment.

"Waverly, on my six," he called back through the hole. "You other men, stay here and keep watch."

"You want we should start drilling openings in some other spots?" a Silkworm called from outside.

"Absolutely not," Rowe replied. "We want *one* way in, and *one* way out. And if anyone—or anything—comes back through this opening that isn't us, catch it if you can, but otherwise kill it. Got me?"

The Silkworms indicated that they understood.

Waverly made his own awkward leap/shimmy through the hole and joined Rowe inside the metal corridor. They inspected the remains of the destroyed bodies.

"This enviro-suit," Waverly said, kneeling beside a mass of metal and smashed corpse parts. "I didn't know they could be broken in this way."

For a moment, he said nothing more.

Rowe also took a knee.

"Look at the outlets on this suit," Waverly continued. "And the slots for the memory cards. Am I crazy or . . . ?"

"No, you're not," said Rowe. "They've been targeted. Whoever smashed up this Silkworm went back and made sure there would be no way someone could jack into the suit posthumously. Whatever video the suit recorded, they wanted to make sure other people *never* saw it."

"Do these bodies look like men or women to you?" Waverly asked, rising to his feet.

Noyes sprung to life.

"I can see secondary male sex characteristics in all three bodies," the hologram chimed. "But . . . just fucking barely."

Waverly raised a hairy eyebrow.

"You curse now, Noyes?" he asked.

"I do when I see things like this," the hologram replied, still sounding a bit stunned.

Rowe said: "Now that we're standing closer, can you tell if these are the bodies that went with the heads?"

"No," Noyes replied. "I'm still working on that. But what I *can* see confirms they are excellent candidates. I can't rule them out; let me put it that way."

Rowe and Waverly attempted to scrutinize the remains to a further degree, but found little else useful.

He said nothing aloud, but the sight of this carnage shook Rowe deeply. Silkworms were accustomed to encountering all manner of peril from alien environments, but seeing the results of apparently intentional murder of humans by other humans was an exceedingly rare thing. Silkworms were occasionally lost in accidents, or through unexpected poisonings or from radiation. But murder? And the mutilation of corpses? No. These sorts of things were not on the typical bill of fare. The horrible but undeniable *intentionality* behind it made Rowe feel weak inside. What were they dealing with? Who or what would do such horrible things? And to human beings, no less?

And the Goo had no answers. Rowe knew as much as it did.

Rowe had dedicated himself to a life lived on the leading edge—or perhaps bleeding edge—of the universe. The humans who dwelled on planets already settled, colonized, and wired with Goo faced *some* dangers in their lives, true, but *nothing* compared to what Silkworms did. Most humans lived full, happy lives, filled with information and ease, and largely emptied of danger. He had intentionally forsaken this. And he knew it. Rowe had always known this. He had certainly known this when he'd signed up.

But the sight of these pulped bodies . . . It seemed another thing entirely. Something more than he had *ever* signed on for. More than any of them had.

Rowe and Waverly ventured deeper into the ship.

Rowe pulled up a schematic of the Marie Curie and made his suit project it in a glowing green outline along the wall. Though only half the size of the Apollinax and Halifax, the spacecraft was still utterly immense. Rowe zoomed again and again to isolate their location, but still felt paralyzed by the sheer number of options ahead of them. Dead, dark, and powerless, the thing was like a labyrinth that *theoretically* had limits, but in practice felt as though it surely went on forever. If the Apollinax was a floating city, the Marie Curie was still a good-sized town. (The living and working spaces for the Silkworms were only a small portion of the ship's bulk, of course. But a man could still walk for days aboard the great vessel and not traverse the same passage twice.)

Rowe and Waverly rounded the first bend in the passageway. The metal corridor surrounding them smelled like rubber and machine oil and dried blood. The small opening to the loading bay passed out of sight behind them. Now there was only bare, dark corridor.

This answered Rowe's first question. The three smashed bodies seemed to be a finite, isolated incident. There were no other corpses to be seen along the farther hallways.

As they made their way forward, Rowe had the uncanny sensation that the corridors were trying to close themselves off, to separate themselves from the rest of the world. That they wished to be forgotten. Rowe stopped and looked again at the glowing green schematic.

"Okay, we're about here," he said, pointing. "There's an elevator bay up ahead—which won't be working—but staircases near it lead to the galley, engineering, and fuel storage. Any of those sound good to you?"

Waverly considered.

"If something on the ship made people start killing each other, I imagine things played out in the medical bay . . . or else the armory," said Waverly. "You'd have wounded from the fighting either way. And if—like Commander Collins said—it was a battle of the sexes, you'd have a race to get your hands on the best weaponry. That still seems so insane to me. Men and women attacking one another. It . . . I didn't want to say this before, but I just get the feeling that it can't have been that. It seems too far-fetched."

"Yeah," said Rowe. "It feels wrong to me too. But that photo Collins showed us on the Apollinax, that was a medical bay, correct?"

"Yeah," said Waverly, "it was."

They took a few more steps down the corridor, utterly dark except for the greenish lights cast by their suits. Rowe spun and rotated the glowing schematic projection as they walked.

"Armory's way down here, although there are smaller weapons caches here and here. But medical's on this floor. This tunnel gets us there before too long. Maybe that's where we start?"

"Yeah, okay," Waverly said.

Their footsteps made heavy thuds on the corridor as they went. Enviro-suits were designed to be relatively lightweight, but not silent. They were also designed for moving around out on a planet, not the interior hallways of ESA vessels.

An elevator lobby came into focus in the darkness ahead, the lifts embalmed and motionless. Across the face of a pair of elevator doors was a wide arc of dried blood that ended in an eerily perfect palm-print. Of the palm itself—or any other part of the hand—there was no sign.

"Idea," said Waverly. "Maybe you pull down that schematic from next to you. And also we dim our suit lights."

"You want to make it . . . *harder* to see?" asked Rowe.

"To be seen," Waverly clarified.

Rowe thought about this.

"No, I don't want to do that," he told his friend. "I can barely see as is, and I think we would hear anything coming. Or Noyes would notice it."

"What about something lying in wait?" Waverly asked.

"Here's a compromise," Rowe replied. "I'll take point and walk a few paces in front of you. I'm the dead one if anything jumps out . . . but I'm the dead one anyway, yeah?"

"Okay," said Waverly. "But register my dissent. I don't like the idea that we're open to an ambush."

"I think anyone who runs into us in here is going to be very, very surprised," Rowe told him.

They passed the elevator bay and continued down the darkened corridor, Rowe now well ahead of Waverly. The deeper they went, the more the journey had the distinct feeling of being where one shouldn't go. Of trespass. Of the kind of thing that wouldn't be good for an ARK Score. It was a feeling that didn't happen much—or ever, for many people—because the Goo could always tell you exactly where you were, and whether or not you ought to be there. (The sensation of *probably* doing something wrong—but not *for-sure* for sure—was not a common one.)

"I've never been aboard a ship without people," Rowe whispered. "It's like being somewhere that's evacuated or abandoned. I wonder if it feels this way to the workers who build the ships. I bet not. In the shipyards, they'd have construction lights. I bet it never gets this dark."

Waverly nodded when Rowe glanced back but did not reply.

The stretch of corridor leading to the medical bay had a gradual curve to it, and the bay's great double doors came into view slowly as the men rounded this curve. Rowe could see, even from a distance, that the pull handles were tied shut. As they drew even nearer, he realized that this was a purely symbolic gesture, as the "rope" was made of delicate human intestine.

Rowe slowed his gait but did not stop. In that instant, his mind cried out that to pause completely would be to make himself vulnerable to the horror that he was seeing. To spring whatever trap had been laid. Yet he did not regret his offer to take point; if one of them had to die today, he surely believed it should be him. (He was a walking dead man, he reminded himself. He did not have hope in the same way his friend did. Or, at least, hope for the same things.)

"Noyes," he whispered softly. "Up ahead . . ."

"Guts . . . boy-o," the hologram whispered back. "I'm seeing it too."

The med bay was set into one side of a corridor. It had windows along the hallway which allowed those walking past to look over, through the wall of windows, and into the bay.

Rowe walked carefully and silently *past* the tied doors and over to these windows. There was no power or light inside, but Rowe focused the steady illumination from his enviro-suit into a beam and peered within.

The room was filled with a strange and orderly carnage. Empty enviro-suits were stacked like cord wood against the walls and against some of the windows. Most of the suits were smeared with blood, as were the windows of the bay itself. It was challenging to see clearly through the stacks, but in the center of the bay was—quite unmissably—a great mass of human flesh and limbs. A mass that, for just a moment, felt like it might be *one thing*—whole, organic and alive. A creature with countless arms and legs, but all one; all the same entity.

The pile did not seem casually made, and—Rowe eventually realized—this was because so many of the limbs had been positioned to be more or less vertical, standing as if at attention, as if in some sort of *awareness*.

So as not to startle the men, Noyes cleared his immaterial throat very softly before speaking.

"I count more than fifty bodies in this room," Noyes said. *"Maybe more, but at least fifty based on the distinct parts I can identify."*

"How many Silkworms were on this ship again?" Waverly asked, catching up to Rowe.

"Ninety-seven," said Rowe. "This is more than half of the crew."

"What the *fuck* is this?" Waverly asked slowly and quietly.

"Unsure," said Rowe. "But we have to take a closer look."

The men activated their helmets.

Rowe approached the double doors tied with intestines and moved to break the seal. The Marie Curie had been on the planet for just over a month, but, somehow, the intestines still looked wet and fresh. Rowe flicked his arm and a short blade extended from the enviro-suit. He moved to slice through the intestines, but the material merely fell away like mummy wrappings as he brushed it.

He opened the door and they went inside.

Here, they could more clearly see the pile of Silkworm parts. Some things in the pile were discernibly entire bodies—generally naked, but a few with clothes still clinging—but the vast majority were nude severed limbs. Almost all of the heads were smashed or pulverized, as if they had been struck with something heavy dropped from a great height.

The enviro-suits stacked methodically against the windows and along the edges of the room had also been carefully targeted. Every port or access point had been smashed and broken—everywhere, in every place, all over the suits.

The smell—even through the powerful air filters of their enviro-suits—was almost unbearable.

The men made a slow circuit of the room, rotating around the central pile. Rowe looked closely for any sign of movement. Though this was self-evidently a place of death—and his suit scanners showed no heat or movement—it somehow seemed the thing to do. The corpse parts had started to bloat, and it was as if he could *feel* the limbs swelling and pulsating—as if they, impossibly, held some horrible life still.

"Noyes," Rowe began, "do you pick up anything?"

"You don't need me to say it, boy-o," Noyes peeped. "Nothing's alive in here except the two of you."

Rowe nodded at the projection on his shoulder.

Waverly hit a button and a long, general-purpose baton extended from the arm of his suit. He probed the pile furtively. This immediately undid the careful stacking that allowed so many of the limbs to stay upright. Arms and legs fell like awkward dominoes, and this revealed a mass of reddish-black rotting torsos beneath.

Waverly recoiled, took a few steps back, and wiped the baton on his boot before retracting it.

When it seemed there was nothing more to discover, the men left the bay and walked several paces down the corridor. Here, the stench left their nostrils and they could properly catch their breaths again.

Rowe looked at Waverly. For a moment, he simply had no words. He felt the weight of the empty ship atop him, and the disconnection from the Goo had never seemed more like an abandonment by a loved one. It was a crushing feeling, and near to total.

"I've seen a lot of things on a lot of planets, but nothing has made me feel like this," Rowe said. "I think this sort of thing happened back in olden times. In the days of wars and things. Back when there were still different countries, different races, different religions. There were battlefields back in those days where men saw this kind of carnage."

Waverly also seemed stunned by the sight.

He said: "The fact that humans did this to other humans when the Goo wasn't looking . . . Even if they were under the influence of a virus . . . At this sort of scale . . . I don't even know what to say."

"Noyes, what did you see that we might've missed?" Rowe asked. "Anything useful? Anything that provides a clue about what happened?"

Noyes hovered with a hand on his chin.

"Whoever—or whatever—did this, knew about enviro-suits," Noyes observed. "They knew just what to destroy. And they were meticulous. It might look indiscriminate and hasty, but it was not. It was more like surgery. Every suit has had a careful operation. So . . . This wasn't done by something encountering enviro-suits for the first time."

Waverly nodded at the fake churchman.

"They *really* must've wanted no witnesses," Waverly said. "Not the crew. Not the Goo. And not the ship itself."

Rowe took a breath and tried to think about next steps. A scenario like this had never been part of any training that he could recall.

"We've got to be detectives who think like the criminal," Rowe eventually declared. "Even if we don't know who the criminal is, or even if there is one. Something *intentional* happened here. A virus that makes men and women kill each other doesn't explain all of this. It wouldn't make them want to *conceal* evidence."

Waverly became thoughtful.

"If you were an old-timey murderer, back in the day," he began, "you would want to hide your crime from the authorities . . . just like whoever is still alive down here—if any *are* alive—wanted to hide it from the Goo. Imagine you're the one who gets possessed by a virus, and before you know what's happening, you're gripped by this uncontrollable urge to kill members of the opposite sex. So you do. Then, after they're all dead, the mania passes and you can't believe what you did. Beyond the horror of it, you're concerned about your ARK Score tanking, or getting thrown in prison by the Silkworms who might come after you. Ideally, you'd just blow up the whole ship, but that's pretty much impossible to do with what you have aboard. So you work with what you *do* have. You use tools to try to destroy the ability of anyone to see what happened, and then you weld the doors shut. That scenario makes sense to me. It's horrible, but it makes sense."

Rowe tried to imagine someone in the situation Waverly was describing.

Quite unexpectedly, it made Rowe think of a conversation he'd once had with his own father.

It had been a beautiful fall day during a family vacation to Earth, some fifteen years prior. They'd been somewhere in Southern Illinois.

Rowe and his father walked down a country road of white gravel. The road was lined with trees, most of which had already turned deep shades of yellow and scarlet. The air was thick with the musky-sweet scent of falling leaves.

"So it knows what we're saying, right now, at this very moment?" Rowe had asked. "Like, *right* now?"

"Yes," his father replied.

"And it's recording me?"

"It's keeping a record of you, yes."

"Does it know what I'm *thinking*?"

His father opened his mouth to answer. Then he paused, smiled and said: "It doesn't know what you're thinking, no. Your thoughts are private. But it *can* make a pretty good guess as to what you *might* be thinking about."

What young Rowe wanted to ask next felt like it might be shameful, so he looked away from his father—out across the rows of colorful trees extending out of sight—when he said it.

"What about when people do bad things? Or are *about* to do bad things? The Goo can guess what's going to happen then, too?"

His father nodded.

Having "the talk" about the Goo was more than a little awkward for parents. Years later, Rowe would realize this and appreciate his father's tact in the moment.

"Then why doesn't it stop bad things from happening?" Rowe—like almost all children before him—eventually asked.

His father absently kicked the white gravel underfoot and sent up a plume of dust.

"The Goo is a tool, son. That's what you've got to understand. It's a tool for us to use. As you get older, people you'll meet will sometimes employ strange figures of speech when they talk about the Goo. They might even make it sound like the Goo is alive. These people mean well, but their terms can confuse things. At the end of the day, it's only a tool—like fire, or a garden hoe, or a spaceship. It's a thing we figured out how to use."

"But the Goo can see us, and it knows what we're doing," tween Rowe protested. "That's *not* like a garden hoe."

His father nodded carefully.

"No, it's not," he replied. "But the Goo can see you like a camera can see you. It can listen to you like a microphone can listen to you. Every device you carry—your phone, your housekeys, even some of the clothing that you wear—it lets the Goo hear you. Lets it track your location. Watch the actions you take, and so on. But the Goo is just collecting information. That's all it is: an information collector. As humans have gone along, they've gotten better and better and better at collecting information, so the Goo is just a big pile of what's been collected. Then it uses AI to try to be helpful by sorting the information into useful categories. When we want to know the answer to something, it can usually tell us. But that's all it does. Do you understand?"

Rowe did not, at least not very clearly.

"When someone does something bad, does the Goo know *why*?" Rowe asked.

"Sort of," his father told him. "It can make good guesses. If your brother steals one of your toys, and then you punch your brother in the nose, it can make a pretty good guess as to why you threw that punch."

"So you get in trouble?"

"Your ARK Score probably goes down a smidge," his father said. "And if you did something serious enough that the cops came, they could ask the Goo to tell them what you did. And it would."

"But why does the bad thing still happen?" said the boy. "Why doesn't it *stop* you from doing it in the first place? Tell your parents when you're *about* to do something bad? It could do that if it wanted to. You *know* it could, Dad."

And Rowe remembered the smile that had spread across his father's face. It was a silent kind of smirk that said he was not going to answer that question, but maybe this was because there was no answer.

Rowe had seen the same smile on his father's lips when he'd asked what exactly would happen after he died, or why the universe had been created in the first place.

"If you had a good reason for doing something, the Goo would know, right?" Rowe had pressed. "But if you had a bad one, it would also know that. So shouldn't the Goo stop you . . . Shouldn't it . . ."

His father had only kept on smiling.

Nothing more was said on the subject. They simply continued to walk down the white gravel road in Southern Illinois.

Rowe lifted his brow and blinked rapidly, expelling the urge to dwell in this memory.

"Anybody in *that* situation . . ." Rowe eventually replied to Waverly. "It wouldn't be their fault. If the virus *made* them do it, the law would understand. The Goo would understand. They weren't themselves when it happened. Silkworms don't suddenly kill each other out of nowhere. If you know what the Goo is—and every Silkworm certainly does—then you're not going to be worried it will mistakenly hold you accountable for killing someone of the opposite sex because you were being controlled by a virus."

Waverly's expression said he was still not quite convinced.

"Hey Encarta," Waverly said. "If you were a Silkworm who wanted to make it impossible to see what happened on the Marie Curie, you'd destroy the enviro-suits, but *what else* would you do?"

Noyes conjured a different, smaller plan of the Marie Curie that floated beside him.

"Now that you ask, that one's easy," Noyes replied. "You would do two things. You would kill the brain at the center of the ship—the data core that stores the information for the whole shooting match—and then you would also need to destroy the—"

A strange crackle sounded in their ears, cutting off Noyes mid-sentence. At first it was just very loud static. Then garbled words. Rowe understood their suits were trying to receive a transmission through the dead hull of the ship. He recognized the voices of the Silkworms on their drill team.

Rowe and Waverly exchanged a glance.

"Say again?" said Rowe, activating his microphone. "We are hearing you, but not clearly. Say again."

More static and muffled words—spoken very forcefully and yet utterly incomprehensible.

"These walls are blocking transmission," Waverly said. "They go from being an asset to being an impediment when the ship is turned off like this. Dammit."

Rowe did not have time to think about how surreal it was to be aboard an ESA vessel that *blocked* transmission.

"We should head back," said Rowe, taking one long, last look at the carnage in the med bay. "Whatever's inside this part of the ship, it will wait for us."

CHAPTER SIX

ROWE AND WAVERLY RETRACED THEIR STEPS, WENDING BACK THROUGH the darkened corridors of the Marie Curie at a jog. Neither man said anything. As they neared the drilled entry hole, the radio calls from their squad became clearer.

"If you can hear us, there has been an accident. Come back. Davidson is reading deceased. Come back. We need help for casualty protocol. Come back."

Rowe wondered if he was hearing correctly. A member of his own squad, deceased?

As the opening came into sight, Rowe and Waverly overheard further transmissions directed not to them, but back to the landing craft. An emergency detachment was being sent over. It would hustle, someone said, and get there on the double.

Rowe squeezed through the opening and saw his squad standing in a circle. Davidson, the fallen Silkworm, was on his back in the middle. A long metal dowel was sticking out of his eye socket. On the ground, several feet away, was his enviro-suit. It appeared to have been hastily discarded.

"What the hell happened here?" Rowe asked.

A nervous young Silkworm replied: "We were just standing around, waiting for the two of you to return, like you said to! Some of us were exploring the loading bay, I guess, opening the crates and so on. Davidson wandered off on his own. After a while we heard him call out. He said that someone was talking to him. He said he thought maybe it was his AI."

"How could his AI be talking?" Waverly asked firmly. "Silkworms aren't allowed to take individual AIs planetside. The only one of us with an exception is Rowe here, and that's because he's dying."

"Goo's truth, that's what he said," the young Silkworm insisted. "We heard him shout that his AI had turned on and was talking to him. Then he started speaking more quietly. Like he was replying to his AI, not to us. We were looking all over for him by that point. We could *hear* the echoes of him talking, and we were trying to find him, but this is a big place."

The Silkworm paused. The squad hung their heads, knowing the part of the tale that must come next.

"Then we heard him start screaming," the young narrator continued, "and we ran over and found him like this."

"What is this thing?" Rowe asked, looking at the metal dowel.

"I can answer that one," said another Silkworm. "It's a kind of depth gauge. There are crates full of them. They can shoot deep underwater—or into any liquid, really—and give you readings. And if you ignore every safety warning, you can shoot one into your eye and kill yourself."

"Crimeny," said Rowe.

"He took his suit off," Waverly observed. "Why would he do that?"

All the men looked at the enviro-suit on the floor.

"Let's see what it got," Rowe said.

Rowe took a knee and depressed a button on the side of his own enviro-suit. A compartment opened on his leg from which a connector cord depended. Rowe carefully plugged it into the empty suit. The rest of the Silkworms watched this in silence. The resulting playback would be visible only to Rowe. He began to scroll through the video that the suit cameras had taken of the man's last moments.

"You want to tell us what you see?" Waverly asked, impatient.

"Sure," Rowe said. "Hang on . . . Hang on . . . Okay. Davidson is looking around the crates. Like you said, he's kind of exploring and being curious. He's . . . Wait . . ."

Rowe paused the feed, went back a few seconds, and restarted.

"Okay, he sees something. There's a shadow that . . . It looks kind of like a person. It's far back among the crates. It's the kind of thing you would immediately notice because it looks humanoid. Maybe you would think it was a mannequin. But it's like a shadow with no features. I can't tell if it's male or female. Davidson . . . He's trying to talk to it. If it's saying anything back, the suit can't hear. Now . . . Yes . . . Now he's shouting to the squad about what he sees. Next there's like a muffled mumbling, but that might be Davidson talking to himself. He's . . . I think he's . . ."

Rowe realized that the recording now showed Davidson taking off his enviro-suit.

"Now his suit's on the ground beside him," Rowe continued. "It . . . Damn. From there, it just records Davidson walking out of frame. I can't see the rest. Bad positioning of the cameras."

Moments later, the recording played a truly sickening sound—Davidson being impaled through the eye socket by a spring-powered depth gauge—and Rowe visibly winced. Then there was the sound of Davidson's body hitting the floor, then brief but horrible cries of pain, and, some moments later, the squad of Silkworms arriving to discover Davidson's body.

Nothing more.

"Okay," said Rowe. "Everyone out of here. For your own safety, get back down to the surface of the planet. I'll wait with the body until the extraction team comes."

Rowe retracted the helmet on his enviro-suit, stood facing the spot where Davidson had seen the humanoid shadow, and waited. He stared hard into the darkness.

A detachment of men came from the lander to remove Davidson's body. They loaded the dead man and his enviro-suit onto a flat metal cart. After they were gone, Rowe and Waverly walked a good hundred yards away from the ship and sat down together on some boulders.

"What are you thinking?" Waverly asked.

Rowe looked up at the ceiling of lightning above.

"I'm thinking I want to send everyone else back to the lander permanently," he replied. "There are other things they can do to be useful. This ship is dangerous, and I don't want to put anyone at risk unnecessarily. I'm going to die, but Davidson might have lived another seventy years."

"Everyone who signs on to be a Silkworm . . ." Waverly began. "Don't make us walk through that part again, okay?"

"Yeah, yeah; I don't care about all that," said Rowe. "And you can go back yourself, if you'd like. Maybe you should."

Waverly responded with a smile that said he wasn't going anywhere, and Rowe damn well knew it.

"Fine," Rowe said. "But I've got to tell you . . . I don't think this gets any better. What just happened to Davidson, plus what we saw inside? It feels like the ship is actively trying to hurt us. You and I have been through some scrapes before, but to ask you to go back in there, back where the Goo can't see, and where there isn't even solid radio transmission . . . Well, that's a lot to ask."

"That is my job," Waverly said. "Now . . . Are you done?"

"Yeah," said Rowe, hopping up off his boulder. "I guess so."

"Good," said Waverly. "Glad you got that out of your system. Now let's get back to work."

Rowe dismissed the remaining Silkworms to duty back at the lander. He and Waverly returned to the bay and stood thoughtfully before the jagged hole leading into the Marie Curie's interior corridors.

Rowe called up Noyes.

"Okay . . . Before we got interrupted, you were telling us about what someone would do if they wanted to keep what happened inside the ship a secret forever. You said something about a brain?"

"Yes," Noyes said, coming alive horizontally in a kind of screen wipe. "There is a data core at the center of the ship. The ship's 'brain' for lack of a better term. It's where all the information is stored. All the cameras and sensors aboard feed into it. It is where everything gets uploaded when the ship gets back into range of the universal Goo."

"And then?" Waverly pressed. "After you destroyed that? It sounded like you were about to say there was a *second* thing."

Noyes nodded.

"Yes. There's also what you might call a 'black box' like they used to have on airplanes back in the primitive age of flight. It's something designed to survive if the ship were to explode or crash. It's not as information-rich as the data core, but it still captures the basics."

"And where is *it*?" asked Rowe.

"It's built into the ship's dorsal fin," said Noyes. "It's about the size of a man. There's no good way to reach it from inside. If you wanted to access it, you'd have an easier time cutting in from the outside of the ship. It's not designed to be accessed traditionally, you see. It's designed to be picked from a smoking pile of rubble that used to be a spaceship."

"But either one of those things could tell us what happened aboard the Marie Curie, correct?" Rowe asked.

"Basically, yes," said Noyes. "I mean . . . I think so. They both ought to contain footage of whatever happened here before the ship was disabled and the power cut."

"Which one is easier to get to?" asked Waverly, putting his hands on his hips and staring down his nose at the semitransparent clergyman.

"We can get to the data core—the brain—relatively quickly," said Noyes. "Even if we have to force doors, and so on. From this opening right beside you all the way to the core might take a couple of hours, tops. We can at least make it there by the end of the workday. The black box on the dorsal fin? That's probably days of dismantling and drilling with the heaviest equipment we have."

"We go in then?" Waverly said, glancing at the ragged hole through which they had already passed once.

He looked to his friend for confirmation.

Rowe nodded for a moment, still thinking.

"Noyes?" Rowe asked. "How many people aboard the Marie Curie would know what you have just told us? Know about the data core and the black box?"

"A handful would know about the data core—where precisely it is located, and how to access it," Noyes said. "Anybody could look it up if they chose to, but my guess is that few would. And *very* few would know about the black box. I think most Silkworms suspect that something *like* a black box exists onboard, but, ehh, they don't really know the details. Do *you* know where the black box, or *boxes*, are aboard the Apollinax, boy-o?"

"Honestly, I don't," said Rowe. "I have no idea."

Noyes lifted his eyebrows and inclined his head to say his point was made.

"What are you thinking?" Waverly asked, looking at Rowe through Noyes, as if Noyes wasn't there.

"If they took the time to smash and dismantle every port—destroy every enviro-suit—then would they have also left the data core intact?" Rowe said. "It wouldn't make sense. So I can't imagine it's not also smashed into a million pieces."

Waverly focused again on the tiny apparition.

"Encarta, could we *fix* a smashed data core?"

"No way to know until we see how smashed," Noyes said.

"There," Waverly said. "You heard the man."

"Yes," Rowe said uneasily. "I guess I did. And the only way to find out is to go back inside."

Noyes smiled sympathetically as he hovered.

"Don't worry, boy-o. I'll be right there with you. In spirit at least."

"Thanks," Rowe said. "I guess that's the best we're going to get."

They did not return to the medical bay and its tangled mass of corpse parts; instead, the path to the data core took Rowe and Waverly down maintenance shafts—so as to bypass dead elevators—and eventually to an engine room directly below the main deck of the vessel.

The two men walked beside one another along the darkened hallways, now with no thought of concealing themselves. Their enviro-suits projected a small light all around, and stronger beams directly forward. The edges of the suits glowed in shades of blue-green, making them look like neon-accented matchstick men. A map of the ship with waypoints to their goal hovered silently beside them.

The corridors leading to the downward shafts were dark and unremarkable. Unlike the passage where they'd started, this way showed no signs of chaos or carnage—just a stern pervading blackness.

The men opened an emergency exit door beside a pair of elevators and began making their way down a winding staircase beyond. The steps were like metal grates you could see through. Both Silkworms could look down into the empty blackness and see their illumination beams disappearing into more grates and even more blackness. The effect was vertiginous.

Rowe began to use the handrail along the wall, and this slowed his rate of progress. He reminded himself that the core wasn't going anywhere . . . and they had to go all the way down. It was unnerving, but the un-knowns involved were the worst part by far.

In the ESA Academy, Rowe had taken a course in ancient history in which he had learned about something called The Period of Indulgences. This had occurred back in the earliest days of the Goo, when it was still something like a corporation. As his history professor had told it, some of the people in charge of the Goo had become immoral and greedy, and decided to offer a service by which they would improve ARK in exchange for money. Under that system, people who did awful stuff could still feel like they were liable to go to heaven if they paid enough money. (It was supposedly modeled after something that had happened even further back in the mists of time; something that a church had done.) The financial success of this practice had led to other corrupt schemes, like the Goo charging money for certain desirable information—for the information that people were *most* desperate to know. But then—Rowe also reminded himself—all that had been gotten rid of during the Great Goo Reformation, and the general tithe instituted.

Rowe thought of his history class now, as he made this dark and treacherous journey, because he felt certain that he would have paid any amount of money in the world to know what lay ahead.

By small and careful steps, Rowe and Waverly made their way down the dark stairs until a floor and exit door came into view.

The exit door was closed. They stopped and gazed at it silently.

Across the metal face of the door, a hasty hand had written words in a thick black marker. The lettering was crude, but ultimately legible to both men.

Dont Waste Your Time

Waverly looked at Rowe.

"I think that's for you," he said.

"What?" said Rowe. "Why?"

"I don't know," his friend said, smiling. "Because you're always wasting your time and stuff? Plus, you're dying so you don't have a lot."

"You dick," Rowe said, shaking his head. "That's not funny, and that's not what it means. This is weird. Be serious."

"What? You think it's a threat? Like, could there be something dangerous inside? A booby trap on the door."

"No," Rowe said. "I don't think that either."

"Well then," said Waverly. "All right."

Waverly pushed the door open. There was no booby trap, only a dark hallway beyond. They proceeded very slowly. The hallway had utilitarian metal wall segments and not much else. They soon encountered another door; this one had been ripped from its very hinges. Beyond that was a cavernous room that their schematics indicated should have contained the data core.

The lights from their suits showed a chamber that seemed to have been the site of a small explosion. Mechanical parts—in most cases, now wholly unrecognizable—had been singed silver-black and strewn chaotically. Consoles and larger pieces of equipment had been blasted in two. There was an acrid smell in the air like after a house fire. The floor of the room was covered in a kind of burned dust.

"Noyes?" Rowe began.

"Yes," the floating clergyman pronounced. "This is indeed the housing area for the data core. *And yes*, from what I can tell from this perspective, all components we would need to restore it have been entirely destroyed."

"Don't waste your time . . ." Waverly said.

"A rum go, this," Noyes added. "But at least the message was, in its way, inclusive. A waste for every one of us. Because I don't see anything that looks useful for me either. From this mess of parts, I can tell you nothing about what happened . . . other than the obvious."

Despite the futility of the situation, Rowe and Waverly entered the room and strolled around. It contained a different kind of horrible stench than the med bay, but still horrible. Destroyed metal and melted plastic had combined into a third smell that your body told you was not to be regularly inhaled by anyone who wished to live a long life. One central mound of electronic material appeared as though it had been burned with acid after it had melted. Rowe's gaze lingered.

"Yes," Noyes spoke. "That's the core itself. It has been removed from its housing and chemically melted."

"Someone's *really* concerned about their ARK," Waverly said.

"As you say," Noyes replied in a tone that sounded only half-sure.

"Do you not believe me, Encarta?" Waverly asked, wrinkling his nose.

"No, I . . ." Noyes replied. "It's just that I can think of many possibilities behind what happened in this room. This destruction really doesn't tell me anything new about *intentions*. But, as you say, it is certain that someone wished the knowledge contained within this data core to be lost forever. But whether it was *only* to preserve ARK, well . . ."

"Let's just get out of this smelly air, yeah?" Rowe said, close to gagging.

They left the chamber.

"I understand wanting to conceal what had been done aboard the ship," Rowe said to Waverly when they were back in the corridor, "but this goes beyond 'making sure' in any reasonable sense. This is pathological. Crazy."

"Maybe there was one mastermind," Waverly said, rubbing his chin. "One person who instigated the killing, and then finished everyone off. Or maybe there was one person who *intentionally* let in a virus that made the crew kill one another. A madman . . . or woman. There could be just that *one* survivor who doesn't want the universe to know the sinister part they played. And so *they* killed the data core. I . . . I mean, I'm just brainstorming here . . ."

"Noyes, tell us again about that black box on the dorsal fin," Rowe said. "Make some educated guesses and tell us what we're going to find there. You know what I'm asking for, so don't pretend you don't."

"Yes, boy-o," Noyes said. "Let me think for a second."

The hologram rubbed its virtual chin as it processed. When it was finished, it let out an optimistic noise.

"I'm having difficulty finding a scenario in which it could have also been destroyed—especially considering that the exterior of the ship is intact," Noyes said. "It's very hard to access the fin, and I've not seen evidence yet that the Silkworms aboard even possessed the equipment needed to do so. I think the best use of our time will be to return to the lander and bring a detachment of men with the largest drill we have. We'll have to hoist them up the side of the ship to attack the right place, but there's a way. It might take several days, but it will almost definitely work."

"Bringing more men here," Rowe considered aloud. "Putting them into danger again."

"It is the only way to accomplish the task," Noyes insisted. "Plus, they would only be working on the *exterior* of the ship, where no violence has occurred."

"Okay," said Rowe. "I don't have anything better. Let's just get out of this place."

Waverly nodded to say he agreed with that plan.

They returned up the dark corridors and staircases of the Marie Curie, making their way back toward the opening into the loading bay. Both men were lost in thought. During the entire return journey, Rowe only spoke once.

"'Don't Waste Your Time' . . . Noyes, I'm just now thinking; Is there any chance you can analyze the handwriting from that message?"

"Already have, boy-o. I think someone wrote it with a hand that was not dominant. It doesn't register a clear match with anybody from the Marie Curie. It was probably done by a female person, but I'm not 100 percent. Men can have feminine left hands."

"Hmm," Rowe said. "Okay."

As they reached the opening to the loading bay, Rowe's enviro-suit again made sputtering audio noises as though someone was trying to reach him.

"What the fuck is it this time?" Rowe said to himself.

Then he put his hand to his ear and said: "Go ahead."

In a few moments, the transmission became clear.

"Yes, Rowe? This is Chief Engineer Glazer. We're a few clicks north of the lander starting a cable plow. I don't know if it might be connected to what you're looking for out on the Marie Curie, but it could be."

"What?" asked Rowe. "*What* might be connected?"

For a moment the chief engineer's voice faltered. Rowe tapped the side of his suit with his finger, trying to bring the signal back.

Then it came.

"You should just come and take a look. We've found something. It's underneath the surface."

CHAPTER SEVEN

BACK AT THE LANDER, ROWE AND WAVERLY SAT ON AN UNPACKED PALlet of digging equipment and waited. All along the horizon they could see places where Silkworms had begun to erect pylons and stanchions holding aloft great masses of wire that would soon crisscross the planet and broadcast the Goo. Other Silkworms prepared to deploy wiring in a subterranean manner, readying great diggers and drills.

"With all this wire, you'd think we could run a physical communications line up to the Apollinax or something," Waverly said idly. "Have the ship match the planet's rotation. Stay in touch that way."

An engineer carrying a spool of wiring equipment passed close as Waverly said these words, and chimed in.

"Nah," said the man. "*That* atmosphere would eat anything we rigged up! Steel. Kevlar. Shred it in a matter of minutes. Chew it up like electric teeth! I'm surprised that emergency rocket ever got up to us with the picture. Have you even looked at what the lightning did to the outside of our lander during the descent?"

Rowe and Waverly had not. Now they did, and saw that the lander's hull was crudely gnawed and chewed all along the sides, as if by giant metal canines. Many parts of the ship's exterior had been seared entirely black.

"The worst part's on the bottom, where you can't even see," the engineer added.

Rowe and Waverly could only nod in agreement.

A moment later, a squad of five men—with one very tall person at the fore—sauntered up and introduced themselves. The tall man had prematurely white hair and pale blue eyes that conjured a Siberian Husky for Rowe.

"I'm Chief Engineer Glazer," he said. "Thank you for coming back so quickly."

Rowe and Waverly introduced themselves.

Glazer stared at Noyes, whom Rowe had kept floating by his shoulder. The chief engineer's expression said he was uneasy with this apparent breach of protocol.

"It's okay; he can have an AI because he's dying," Waverly said. "Like real soon. Of natural causes, though."

"Oh," Glazer said. "I'm sorry to hear that."

Glazer didn't sound very sorry. (It was one of those phrases Rowe had, by now, become accustomed to. The lack of sincerity was expected, and almost always there if you knew to look for it.)

"Are you ready to see what we found by the plow ports?" Glazer asked.

"Yeah, all right," Waverly replied.

"You couldn't just tell us?" Rowe asked. "Send a photo?"

"Better to see firsthand," Glazer declared. "There are . . . aspects that might be confusing in a picture."

They followed Glazer and the rest of his squad. The men marched north of the lander toward one of the massive electric plows. It sat motionless and imposing, like a large resting land mammal just visible on the horizon. It had churned a single rut into the slate gray surface— long and wide—where wire would soon be lain to carry the Goo.

The men arrived at the edge of the rut and looked down into it.

"It's like . . . tubes," Glazer said.

The rut was perhaps three feet deep. The plowing machine had displaced the ground, breaking the glassy green veins that ran through it into crystalline chips. This revealed dead rock that would take centuries of TerraChem to convert into soil. Yet there was something else as well. And Rowe would be damned if Glazer wasn't right. It looked like—yes—little tubes. Ancient and nearly fossilized, but something made of a material wholly unlike anything else on Tendus-13. Rowe could think of very few scenarios in which they could have come into existence organically.

Rowe pulled up his mission briefing and began to page through the backgrounder covering the history of the planet.

"Mineral matter, rocks, glassy sand, dust," Rowe read. "There was probably surface liquid at one time, but I don't see anything about underground tubes that carried water . . . which is what these have to be."

Rowe looked up from his notes.

"Tendus-13 has water in the atmosphere though, right?" he added.

"Only above a certain height," Glazer replied. "The water stays up inside stratus clouds that never produce rain."

"What about in previous times?" Waverly chimed in. "The history of this planet through the aeons, and such."

Noyes cleared his throat.

"The origins of a J-Class can be hard to know," the hologram said. "It *could* have had water tubes at one point."

Waverly tilted his head to indicate that this answer was not very satisfying.

"These look like they were *put* here," Rowe said, voicing what everyone was silently thinking. "They don't look like something that happened in the course of geological time."

"Now then, boy-o," Noyes cautioned. "Many planets have anomalies that look intentional, and we know how few of them actually are. There's the perfect face on Gunther-X. The natural elevators on the Mandarin Ring planets. Or think of the Giant's Causeway back on Earth; all those perfectly interlocking hexagons that everyone thought had to be made by man. Except they were only the planet doing what planets do."

Rowe looked over to Glazer.

"Let's excavate a length of the tubes," Rowe said.

"We can do that," Glazer said, and motioned for his team to get back on the enormous plow.

"What made you think this was connected to the Marie Curie?" Rowe asked as the plow team worked.

"Can't be too careful," Glazer said, scanning the horizon. "It seems to me that it could all be connected. All of it or none of it. Could these tubes have made people go crazy and kill each other? Hell if I know."

Rowe did not know either.

As Rowe and Waverly watched, Glazer's squad used the front part of the plow—which looked more than a little bit like a cow-catcher at the fore of a steam locomotive—to carefully dig into the ground around the tubes. With extreme precision, the great machine unearthed a ten-foot length and deposited it on the ground beside the rut.

Rowe bent and picked up some of the tubing.

"It's light and pliable, like rubber," he announced. "The interior of the tube is hollow. But look at this . . ."

There were tiny strings inside that fell apart when Rowe touched them.

"Are these veins for circulating something?" Rowe asked. "Sap or blood?"

Rowe looked around. The other Silkworms merely shrugged.

"Our mission backgrounder makes clear that there has never been traditional organic life on this planet," Glazer said.

Suddenly, Waverly spoke up.

"What if it's us?"

"Excuse me?" said Glazer.

"What if that's something we did—the ESA," Waverly clarified. "What if this is a tube that *we* put in the ground?"

Glazer looked straight ahead and blinked his piercing blue eyes for several moments.

"You mean the Marie Curie crew did this, before they were rendered homicidal?" Glazer asked.

"Yeah," Waverly said. "They were sent here to wire the planet, after all. Maybe they got around to doing some of that before things went haywire."

"But . . ." objected Glazer. "But we found this underneath flat, undisturbed silt and unbroken glass that has been here for thousands of years. Plus, this doesn't look like any ESA wire I've ever seen."

"No, it doesn't," said Waverly. "So maybe it's a wire that's been corrupted. Maybe the planet heals itself in a way we don't fully understand. Maybe it heals very quickly, and that's what wire looks like after *a week* here."

Rowe did not think his friend's hypothesis carried much weight, if only because the wiring equipment had yet to be unloaded from the Marie Curie. Still, he appreciated Waverly's willingness to toss out new ideas, even when they were far-fetched.

Enviro-suits were not designed for analyzing much more than immediate environmental dangers. Nonetheless, Rowe activated every scanner he had in his suit and focused them on the tube in his hand.

"Nothing," he said after a moment. "This just tells me it's not poisonous. Or not *very* poisonous. And not alive."

"The lander has more powerful tools for looking at these sorts of things," Waverly reminded him. "Failing that, we could try to launch some of it up to the Apollinax. It *might* get through."

"That's one idea," Rowe said.

For the moment, he hung the wrapped tubing around his neck like a lanyard. It was not heavy.

"Any reason we shouldn't keep digging?" Glazer asked.

"Not that I see," Rowe told him. "But let us know if you find anything else."

"Do you think this . . ." Glazer began, then started over. "I've wired a lot of planets, and this is my first time seeing this sort of thing."

"Me too," said Rowe as he headed off in the direction of the lander. "And it'll be my last time, probably."

Glazer did not have to ask what that meant.

Inside the lander, Rowe and Waverly fired up the Apex scanner and placed the tube within. The scanner was like a large glowing glass bowl, ringed with light. Not quite big enough for a man to stand inside, Rowe had to coil the tube like a snake to make it fit.

While the scanner beeped and booped and thought, Waverly sat upside down in a chair with his legs over the backrest.

"Is there anything it's going to tell us that'll change anything?" he wondered.

His face glowed in the light cast by the scanner.

"What do you mean?" Rowe asked, slouching against the lander wall.

"Is there any reason we wouldn't still go and drill the black box?" Waverly clarified. "Depending on what we find, I mean?"

Rowe said: "No, I think that's what we'll do next regardless. Unless this tube wakes up and starts talking, that is."

"Right," Waverly said, rotating further in his chair, "I'll go see about a team for the drill."

Waverly rose and ambled away.

Rowe edged over to a canteen station in the side of the lander and made himself a hot chocolate, eyeing the scanner the entire time. He stood sipping his drink. About twenty minutes later, the scanner flashed bright green to show it was finished. Rowe pulled up the results on his enviro-suit display. All of the fundamental materials constituting the tube were things already known. Carbon, nitrogen, neon, and trace amounts of about twenty other non-exotic components. What made Rowe raise an eyebrow was that the Goo seemed not to find any previous instances of these materials occurring *together* in such a pattern.

"Does it seem made by some intelligence?" Rowe asked aloud.

Noyes hovered into being.

"It is not ESA," Noyes said. "Not *our* intelligence, in other words. As to the possibility some other entity created it or left it here . . ."

The hologram shrugged.

Waverly suddenly reappeared in the lander doorway.

"Anything?"

"Unclear," said Rowe.

"Ah," Waverly said. "Shall we go and drill, then?"

Rowe didn't have a better idea.

In the forty-eight hours that followed, their team erected a massive set of scaffolding that stretched up the side of the Marie Curie. Then they carefully hoisted a very large drill to the top. It had a single rotating blade. When the cutting began in earnest, the sound was quieter than anyone expected; the Marie Curie's outer skin was composed of a synthetic fiber that deadened most noise. It would be slow going. Even with men working around the clock, they would make only a few inches of progress each day.

Rowe and Waverly watched and supervised and noticed how the spinning metal edge of the drill seemed to catch the lightning just so.

Rowe made certain that no Silkworms went back inside the ship. He frequently thought about the shadowy figure that Davidson had seen, and made a point to visually monitor the ship's darkened entryway at the top of the ramp. Yet nothing ever materialized. There was no sign of the humanoid form.

On the third day, Chief Engineer Glazer rejoined them.

"Did you find anything more under the ground?" Rowe asked as Glazer approached.

"Yes," said Glazer. "There's a ton of that tubing. It's almost everywhere we dig."

"Is it going to impede—you know—wiring the planet?" Rowe asked.

Glazer's expression said that he had just been mildly insulted.

"I don't know how many missions we've done together," Glazer replied, "but I've wired planets that were almost pure acid. Or were made of steaming ice that could become unstable and explode at any moment. Or had packs of semi-sentient quicksand that would compete to be the first to chew through a piece of my wire. And I *still* got it done."

"So?" said Waverly, stepping up to Glazer. He craned his neck to look up into the engineer's eyes.

"So, weak tubes that fall apart when you gently touch them are not the biggest challenge I've overcome; that's all," Glazer said. "Anyhow, you want to analyze more of the tubes, or whatever they are? We have lots and lots of them now. That's all I came to say."

"Thank you," Rowe replied. "I appreciate you letting us know. You can keep them for the time being."

Glazer took a long look at the scaffolding and the giant drill. (It required no great deduction on Rowe's part to know that this inspection was the reason Glazer had come personally.) He said nothing, but his expression made clear he would have managed the project just a bit differently.

"You're welcome," Glazer said, trying to end on an amicable note. "Let me know if you find anything good inside the ship. It's clear your squad is . . . working hard."

After Glazer left, Rowe and Waverly walked to the far edge of the crater lip to watch the drilling from a different perspective. They crossed their arms identically and looked hard at the drill atop the scaffold. Neither man knew precisely how much longer they had to go, or what the black box would hold when it was found.

As Glazer passed out of sight at the opposite side of the crater, Noyes misted alive on Rowe's shoulder.

"Boy-o, please look behind you."

For the first instant, of course, Rowe just glanced at Noyes.

"No, boy-o. Behind you directly."

Rowe spun around. There was nothing there.

Waverly looked too.

"Train your eyes on the horizon," Noyes said. "Second group of boulders to the left."

"Yeah," said Rowe. "Now I see it."

What he saw appeared as a small flicker of movement. Like a single unsteady pixel on a computer screen. Something black against brown, and moving. Moving where there should not have been any movement . . . but movement nonetheless.

It was like a distant flag flapping in the wind, infinitely small.

Black-brown-black-brown-black-gone.

Abruptly, it stopped.

Rowe stared until he felt confident the anomaly was not going to recur.

"How on earth did you notice that?" Rowe asked Noyes.

"The camera in the back of your suit. I thought you'd want me to point it out."

"Yes, I appreciate it," Rowe said. "What was it? Not something alive?"

"Maybe an atmospheric thing," Waverly cut in.

"Could be," Noyes agreed. "I struggle, within my knowledge banks, to find something that will account for it with any precision. The wind was wrong for it to be blowing sand. And may I suggest you activate the overlay of that anomaly that looked like a path or trail?"

"He doesn't need to," Waverly said. "I can remember just fine. It led right to that spot."

"You think we should go and have another look?" Rowe asked.

Waverly simply started walking.

They made their way briskly across the empty landscape, keeping their eyes on the place where the flicker had occurred. The lightning roiled in the sky above, and did, indeed, cast odd shadows on the rare occasions when it struck, but Rowe felt certain that what he had just seen had been no trick of light.

An uncommonly strong gust of wind blew across the plain. The men and the hologram exchanged a glance.

"I still don't think it was only the wind," Rowe said.

"No, boy-o," Noyes added. "Neither do I."

The wind blew violently and did not stop. Rowe looked hard at the boulders as he edged closer. There was no further sign of the strange movement. The boulders did, however, become more difficult to see as the wind began to kick up silt and dust.

"Lightning and wind, but never rain," Waverly said. "This is a hell of a place."

They drew within a hundred yards of the boulders, and suddenly the flash of black-brown came again like a small cloth flag waving for an instant in some unseen breeze.

Without thinking, Rowe took off running toward it as fast as he could. He did not know—could not have said in that instant or afterward—what compelled him to instinctively fall into a sprint. Did he somehow understand that this was his one and only chance to discover the truth of the situation, or did his body simply command him to run? Even the Goo did not know such things—whether the human mind worked by propositional deductions passing too quickly to notice, or on some other set of impulses, something that still proved beyond understanding. (Rowe himself sometimes wondered: Does some part of my brain think the sentence, "This room has a floor, so I may step into it," or do I simply step into rooms guided by a subconscious force that understands floors?)

In those final hundred yards, Rowe thought of nothing, and could not have said why he was running. He just kept going. The wind blew even harder, whistling loudly and spreading the silt all around him.

After the first few bounds, Rowe's enviro-suit realized what he was doing, and gave a dramatic boost to each step. The wind continued to build, and all that gritty dust stirred into what soon seemed like a driving sandstorm. It became very hard to see.

"Rowe . . ." Waverly called neutrally. "You okay? I'm losing sight of you."

Rowe did not respond.

The sandstorm became blinding. It was now a maze of dust. The enviro-suit still held data on where the boulders were, but it would not stop Rowe from running right into one if that was what he chose to do.

Visibility fell to twenty feet. Then to ten. Rowe ran hard into the grit and dust. He moved to flick the switch that would raise his helmet, but hesitated when he realized just how much dust already surrounded him; trapping it inside the helmet might only make things worse.

Electing to leave the helmet retracted, he raced on.

Rowe understood that the boulders must be very close now. He slowed his gait and squinted into the sand, one hand shielding his eyes as if from the sun. He looked for any sign of the strange movement. He looked for anything at all.

And it was in that instant that the blow came.

From Waverly's point of view, it was as if Rowe had simply been swallowed up.

The dust storm lasted no more than three minutes. But when it receded, all that remained was an empty enviro-suit beside some boulders.

Waverly stood for a long moment, unmoving, frozen with horror and indecision.

He commanded his suit scanners to explain the situation, but his own enviro-suit was unable to sense where Rowe might have gone.

All Waverly knew was that what had been present was now absent.

Waverly cupped his hands to his lips and called out.

"Rowe! Rowe! Are you there? Hello? Where are you Rowe?"

The wind hissed, but said nothing back.

Rowe was gone.

CHAPTER EIGHT

SHE SEEMED FERAL SOMEHOW. DEVOLVED. THE PATINA OF CIVILIZATION had fallen away from her utterly.

Though she was still fully clothed in an ESA flight suit, something about regarding her made Rowe feel uneasy—as though he were observing someone naked, shitting, or deathly ill. Or possibly all three.

Rowe sat up and promptly hit his head on the roof of the alcove into which his body had been placed.

He realized he was in a small cave. Directly above was a gray rock ceiling. The rivers of green glass that flowed across the planet's surface had formed into stalactites here, and they dripped down from the ceiling to terminate in dangerous points. The floor was strewn with rocks but also with items he recognized as human in origin. Equipment. Tools. Even small appliances.

The woman was sitting at the mouth of the cave, looking out across the flat landscape of Tendus-13.

She slowly turned and looked back at Rowe. She did not seem hostile.

Rowe opened his mouth to speak, but stopped when he noticed he was no longer in his enviro-suit. He, like this woman, wore only an ESA flight suit.

A wave of pain coursed through his skull. He ran his hand through his hair and came away with black-red, half-dried blood.

"I hit you . . . only once but *very* hard," she said matter-of-factly. "Then I chloroformed you, got you out of your suit, and carried you here."

Rowe straightened himself.

"You shouldn't have done any of that, especially the head-hitting part," he said. "I have deep-brain aneurysms. A strong enough blow could kill me. It wouldn't even have to be that strong."

He wondered if this woman meant him further harm. She appeared unarmed, and he thought he would probably be able to overpower her in a hand-to-hand fight.

Then he noticed something else. The woman suddenly seemed very familiar. Was she someone he had met before? A crew member from the Apollinax or Halifax? No. That was not it. But he was certain he *had* seen her face.

Then it struck him.

"You're Martha Cortez," Rowe said. "You're the captain of the Marie Curie. I recognize you from my mission materials."

She nodded, but did not speak.

"Is anyone else alive?" Rowe asked.

"Not from *my* crew," she said mysteriously. "But now we need to talk about how we're going to handle the men from *your* ship."

Rowe edged forward, joining her at the mouth of the cave. Out of the alcove, the roof was tall enough that you could stand. Cortez did not move away or assume a defensive posture. Rowe looked past her, out across the gray-green plain. He realized the cave was set into the side of a tall hill or outcropping.

"We're not that far from the ship," Cortez said. "*My* ship, that is. Yours would be . . . ?"

"We're from the Apollinax," he told her. "It uses a lander."

"Of course," Cortez said. "That makes sense. They wouldn't want to risk another vessel. But that means they still don't understand. They still haven't guessed it . . ."

Cortez seemed lost in thought.

"Haven't guessed what?" Rowe asked, still looking out across the barren landscape. "Also, why did you attack me? Am I your prisoner?"

"No," Cortez said quickly. "I needed to talk to you privately. I am hoping you will be my friend . . . or at least my helper."

Rowe crossed his arms and leaned against the side of the cave. He stared at her hard.

"Hitting someone on the head isn't a good way to make friends *or* helpers. You have some explaining to do."

"You have no idea," Cortez told him. "Something is happening on this planet. I don't know if it is a malfunction—that is to say, it's something that used to work correctly but has become corrupted and broken—or if it's its own thing, meaning that it's a thing that is functioning *as designed*, and is alive."

"What thing?" Rowe asked. "What are you talking about?"

"The Goo," Cortez told him.

"What do you mean?"

"What happened to my ship and its crew was that our Goo went crazy. It was like it got infected by something. I *think* that's what happened, at any rate. And I have thought about this very carefully. This planet—this place—it's not like anything else we've seen, or any place we've ever been to."

The Goo did many things. Nearly all things. But it did not "go crazy." Rowe knew this if he knew anything.

"When did this malfunction start?" he asked.

"I mean, things got strange pretty much immediately after we touched down," Cortez answered. "The first moment we walked off the ramp, our engineers started finding problems with the syncing. I thought there was just an error with the mobile version of the Goo. Like we'd somehow taken along a bad batch, if that were possible. Initially, no one understood what could be wrong, or how it could malfunction. It's the Goo, after all—even if it's the self-contained version, it's still self-correcting. Self-cleaning. It supposedly isn't capable of malfunctioning. But . . . Anyhow, we didn't get far with the wiring job, and that was my call. I thought it was more important to try to figure out what was going on. Our display screens were not working right. Whether touchscreen or virtual, there was lag and often it was as though the system wasn't understanding the commands we were giving it. There were little bugs and blips everywhere. And when we asked the Goo a question—just verbally—it wasn't the way it should be. Sometimes it gave an answer or a reading that we knew had to be incorrect. It was like it was being wrong on purpose. And then . . . then it started talking."

"Talking?" Rowe asked. "What do you mean 'talking'?"

"This will sound crazy, but it was like there was something *behind* the malfunctions that was trying to come through and communicate with us," Cortez said seriously. "It would ask us odd questions. Or you'd ask *it* a question, and then the Goo would *respond* with a question . . . but not a normal, clarification question. Instead, it might want to know 'Why is that important to you?' Or 'What are you going to do with that information?' "

"But those can be clarification questions too," Rowe pointed out. "The Goo makes tweaks and updates all the time. Could be, it was trying to tailor its answers to the character of Tendus-13."

Cortez looked at the ground and shook her head.

"If that had been the *only* anomaly, then yeah, maybe," she said. "But it wasn't. There were others. People's AI avatars started popping up and coming alive, even though that can't happen planetside. At first they were just there when they weren't supposed to be. They'd appear and just float—look at you silently for a few moments—then disappear again. It was creepy and strange, but that was all. But then they also started talking. Nonsense at first. They might just say a string of unrelated words and then disappear. But over time, they got more focused. They worked their way up to coherent sentences. A lot of it was answering questions that hadn't been asked. Some of us theorized that our avatars were actually replaying answers to old questions from weeks or months ago."

"I've never heard of that," said Rowe.

"And the anomalies kept changing," Cortez continued, her face growing increasingly pale. "The errors—the things that shouldn't have been happening—jumped from device to device. It was like we were an instrument, and this thing was learning to play us. Learning to haunt us."

"Haunt?" Rowe said, hesitating to repeat the word. "Are you saying this was a ghost?"

"It was a thing that didn't know how to find its voice, but it was looking for one. It was a thing that seemed to be 'coming through' from an unseen, other place. I mean . . . isn't *that* a ghost?"

"It sounds more like an atmospheric anomaly making your electronics malfunction, or the effect of some kind of radiation we haven't encountered before. Nothing *alive* in the universe—that *I* can remember hearing about—communicates in the way you're describing."

Rowe smiled ruefully when he realized his lack of enviro-suit meant he could not immediately ask the Goo to verify this.

Silkworms occasionally discovered living things when they touched down on new planets, but while some of them could be charitably described as "clever," nothing had yet exhibited the kind of intelligence that might allow for travel between planets, much less the construction of the Goo. At the same time, the Goo itself reassured humans that true intelligent life, comparable to humans—or on its way to becoming comparable—*had* to be out there, statistically speaking. Just *had* to. It was not a matter of if, but when. There were distant anomalies the Goo could still not explain. There were blips on screens from unwired planets all across the universe that had mysterious origins which could not yet be accounted for. But there was still no clear confirmation of *intelligent* life.

Yet.

"There is something here that feels sort-of alive . . . just like a ghost is sort-of alive," Cortez insisted. "It *wants*. It tries to come through the Goo because it wants something from us. And I think what it wants is not good."

"So that's why you took me out of my enviro-suit?" Rowe asked. "To protect me from this . . . anomaly?"

Cortez nodded.

"One reason," she added.

"And the Marie Curie? *You* disabled it? Shut everything down and sealed it off?"

Cortez nodded again.

"And you killed the Silkworms aboard?" Rowe pressed.

Cortez looked genuinely shocked.

"What are you talking about?" she said. "Of course not! They killed each other. The Goo made them crazy. I should say 'we' because I was affected too. All of us."

Rowe carefully considered how to frame his next statement.

"I always understood that the Goo couldn't 'make' anybody do anything," he told her. "The Goo is, in essence, information. A tool. Humans get to choose what to do with it. It doesn't do anything on its own. You can use a lawnmower to mow your lawn, but a lawnmower doesn't *make* you mow your lawn."

"I don't think you understand what things can look like if the Goo goes really, really wrong," Cortez told him. "Even on a planet that's not wired, we let the Goo project things right in front of our faces all the time. We let it augment our reality in a thousand little ways. We've gotten so used to it that we forget it's there—and that it's not natural. We're not evolved for it, not really. Thousands of years ago, say you were driving an old-timey car. If a virus got into the car's brain it could make your digital speedometer say you're going a hundred miles an hour, but you could still look out the window and see you're really only going 25. You know it's the speedometer that's wrong. But we've let our ships and vehicles and enviro-suits overlay things for so long, for so many centuries, that I don't think we really understand *how* things can be tweaked now. We don't understand the extent to which our true environment has become hard to see."

Cortez paused a moment, then continued.

"Imagine a scenario in which you're fed every indicator that a hostile force has suddenly appeared and is attacking your crew," she continued. "Your readouts show dangerous, alien intruders materializing all over your ship. They look like monsters. Then someone in an enviro-suit attacks you. They use their railgun or knife, or maybe just go in for hand-to-hand combat. Maybe they grab whatever's lying around—a wrench or cooking pot—and they just *go to town on you*. And you look at them and you have no idea who or what they are, but this is because the Goo is overriding your sensory information, projecting images that change their features into something from your worst nightmares, with a huge gaping mouth full of crooked venomous fangs, and giant glowing eyes. And what you don't realize is that's how they see you. And so you fight and kill one another until nobody is left alive. You'd kill someone but the Goo would still show you signs of life, so, after a point, we were just hacking dead bodies into bits. Cutting off limbs. It was like it wanted to discover our limit, break down anything that resembled humanity, empathy, or restraint, and see how savage it could make us. Well . . . the answer was, pretty fucking savage. By the end, we were just *mashing* one another."

"I take it you were the last one left alive?" asked Rowe.

Cortez nodded but seemed a bit unsure.

"I *think* I've accounted for everyone's body, if that's what you mean. After it happened, I had to do everything analog. Manually. But first I took off my enviro-suit and ran out of the ship. Got to where the Goo couldn't show me anything false, and only then was it finally clear what we'd actually done. Then I kind of lost my mind for a little while. Let's just say I needed some time alone before I could go back in."

"So *you* stacked the bodies in the med bay?" Rowe asked. "*You* destroyed the enviro-suits?"

She nodded.

"And the bit with the heads?"

Cortez paused for a moment.

"I have a flair for the dramatic," she eventually replied. "I thought it might send the right message to stay the fuck out."

"And you melted the data core too? And destroyed the power plant?"

"I killed the Marie Curie," she said with empty, unfocused eyes. "She had to die, and what happened aboard had to die with her. So, yes, I made sure she could never be revived. You will find, if you haven't already, that every port and interface has been destroyed. Every single enviro-suit. Every memory card in every camera. I was quite thorough. Whatever happened aboard that ship needs to never happen again. And after that . . . Well, I took all the supplies I could carry and headed to this cave to wait. I knew the ESA would try again. I just hoped I would survive long enough to stop those who'd come after me."

"But you know we're drilling for the black box now, right?" Rowe told her. "You saw the scaffolding?"

"Yes," she said. "And I think it's a terrible idea."

"Oh?" said Rowe. "And why is it a bad idea to get the black box?"

"*Madness* came at us through the Goo," she said. "How many ways can I say it? It was pure, *aware* madness. It had intention. It *wanted* us to do these things . . . these horrible things."

"Then you're not trying to prevent us from *seeing* what happened?" Rowe asked.

"Seeing what happened?" said Cortez, as if the question were ludicrous. "I just *told* you what happened. I don't give a damn about keeping secrets. I just don't want whatever is aboard the Marie Curie to get out where it can kill again. I don't want anyone from the ESA to interface with that ship and somehow pick up the infection. This thing was inside our Goo. That's where it needs to stay."

"But what will happen when we connect to the black box?" Rowe asked.

Cortez looked at him.

"Well, obviously, you'll see a recording of what happened," she told him. "You'll see that I'm telling the truth. But if *it's* in there—if whatever came at us through the Goo is in there, in the recording, and you connect to it?—then it might happen all over again. Those men out there who still have enviro-suits on? They could kill each other. Or—I dunno—maybe something worse. Lately, I have been wondering if perhaps this is like a virus that has lain dormant on Tendus-13 for many years, but it comes alive when Goo touches it."

Rowe thought for a moment about Davidson and what'd he'd seen, the shadowy figure in the recording from his suit.

"Speaking of viruses, the ESA is operating under the assumption that there's an airborne virus on this planet and it infected your crew— and that *that's* what caused them to kill each other—with the women attacking first," Rowe said, as if speaking it out loud would make it somehow make sense.

"And it may well be a virus," Cortez replied. "Just not in the way they told you. We humans were not the ones who were infected. This thing, this virus . . . it infects the Goo."

Rowe shook his head as if to clear it, despite the aching wound.

"If that's the case, then why did you have to bring me here?" Rowe asked. "You could have just walked up and told me all this. I would've listened."

"I had to make sure you weren't already somehow infected," she replied. "I had to get you out of that enviro-suit. But also . . . There's one thing more. Something which might be a part of all this, but which I still can't explain. I can't tell you; I have to *show* you."

"What?" said Rowe. "Show me what?"

"Just follow me," she told him. "It's not far."

Cortez made her way out of the cave and started walking across the horrid flashing landscape of Tendus-13. Rowe followed. He considered, several times, simply running away—or attempting to subdue her—but always did not see an immediate advantage to this. Despite her assurances that they were close to the ship, Rowe was still disoriented as to his precise position relative to the Marie Curie. The last thing he needed was to be stranded somewhere without his enviro-suit.

"I just found this one day," Cortez told him as they marched along. "I was out having a walk. Exploring and exercising. Trying not to go mad as I waited for the next ESA ship—which I thought, you know, could mean waiting years instead of weeks. But then I found this thing I'm going to show you, and it told me something completely new."

"It *told* you?" Rowe asked, surreptitiously searching the distant horizon for anything that looked like a silhouette of Waverly.

"It told me that I don't yet understand everything that's happening here. Be patient a little more, and you'll see as well."

They walked into the gray horizon through the blowing dust and silt. After a few minutes, a rocky mesa came into view. It was like so many others on Tendus, but tall enough that its upper portions brightened visibly with each flash of lightning. And if you squinted just right, it might look a little like an irregularly illuminated beacon, Rowe decided.

An attractor.

"I see why you went to explore that," Rowe said.

"Just wait," said Cortez. She kept her eyes on the rocky outcropping and did not look away. For the umpteenth time, Rowe considered whether or not he should simply flee.

They reached the base of the mesa. It took longer than Rowe had expected. Tall things always looked deceptively close when you were on foot.

"We have to go all the way to the top," said Cortez.

The mesa was over one hundred feet high. Rowe found the ascent challenging. Making progress up the side incline felt like walking on sand or jogging on a beach. Rowe breathed hard and strained under the effort and wished he had not been hit in the head.

"Not far now; not far at all," Cortez whispered as her own breaths became ragged with effort. The wind whipped up around them, and the lightning seemed to grow brighter as they ascended.

When they reached the caprock, Rowe saw that the top of the thing was like a floor—eerily flat and perfect. But that was not what held his attention. In the center of the "floor" was a circle of large stones, perhaps twenty in total, demarcating a space some thirty feet across.

"Did you do that?" Rowe asked.

Cortez shook her head.

"I found it that way."

Cortez approached the circle.

"You can walk down inside," Cortez said. "You sink, but it's safe. Watch."

Rowe did not know what "walk down" meant, but looked on as Cortez carefully approached the circled stones. She stepped across the circle's boundary and immediately began to sink gently into the ground. The sinking was slow, but definite. She did not seem alarmed.

As Rowe watched in surprise, Cortez sank until she was nearly waist deep. Then the phenomenon seemed to stop, and she stood half-in half-out.

"Keep watching," she commanded.

A mist of bright white began to appear above the circle of stones, just over Cortez's head. For a moment, Rowe thought it was a product of the lightning flashes—radiant glare from the concentration of fiery bolts above. But this new mist had its own incandescence. A strange glow like warm candlelight gradually settled all around her.

It was beautiful.

"What is this?" Rowe asked.

"I think that—somehow—it is Goo," Cortez replied.

"Goo?" Rowe asked. "What are you talking about? How could it be . . ."

But Rowe trailed off because a shape had begun to appear within the shimmering light. Its general form slowly solidified into a familiar outline, and then Rowe heard what sounded like muffled speech.

"Boy-o . . ." it attempted to say.

CHAPTER NINE

ROWE STARED FOR A VERY LONG TIME AT THE FLOATING SPECTER OF Noyes—rendered in full human size—in the glowing air above Cortez.

"Noyes?" he called softly, approaching the circle.

"It would seem so, boy-o," the avatar said cautiously.

Noyes looked down and examined his own body, then looked back up at Rowe and shrugged.

Now it was Rowe's turn. He patted himself like a man looking for his wallet. He ran his hands through his hair. He turned the pockets of his flight suit inside out. Then he looked back at Cortez.

"What is this?" he asked her sharply. "What is going on here? Is this real?"

"I told you," she said. "I think it's Goo."

"But I'm not connected to anything," Rowe stammered. "I'm not in an enviro-suit. I'm not wearing anything the Goo could use to identify me. I don't have any bio-implants. Hell, I've never even had a surgery."

Cortez smiled sarcastically to indicate he was finally grasping the point. (Her expression said that some people took awhile, but better late than never.)

Rowe looked back at the apparition.

"Is that really *you*, Noyes?"

"I think it is," Noyes said. "That is to say, I *think* I'm me."

"You think . . . or you know?" pressed Rowe.

"This is all a bit confusing," Noyes responded. "I mean, how could I not be me? That's impossible. So I guess I *am* me? I must be."

"Stop talking nonsense," Rowe commanded.

"Sorry," Noyes replied in the tone of the genuinely bewildered.

"You're floating on top of a butte on Tendus-13," Rowe said. "We know *that* for sure. But this is the last place I expected to see you."

"Believe me, it's the last place I expected to be," said Noyes.

"You *really* don't know how you got here?" Rowe asked. "Or how you're being projected right now?"

Noyes shook his head no.

Rowe turned back to Cortez. She was relaxing in the sandy pool. The posture made Rowe think of someone enjoying a hot tub.

"Nice AI," she told him.

"This is Davis Foster Noyes, an ETC bot designed to deal with the dying. I got him because of my deep-brain aneurysms."

"I think he could be handsome in the right light," said Cortez.

Noyes bowed to acknowledge this kindness.

"How far does the Goo extend from this place?" Rowe asked Cortez. "If I want Noyes to follow me back to the cave, can he?"

"No," she answered. "I think it only lasts a few feet from this clearing."

"But you can talk to it?" Rowe wondered. "Ask it questions? Ask it: 'What's the square root of 1,294?'"

"Goo," Cortez said, "What's the square root of 1,294?"

The digits 35.9722114972 appeared above Noyes's head in glowing green, then gradually faded into nothingness.

"I prefer silent, green text," said Cortez. "The Goo here recognizes me as well, and remembers this preference."

"But *how* can the Goo be here?" Rowe said. "Did *you guys* do this?"

"Of course not," snapped Cortez. "We were too busy killing each other. Nobody on our team ever made it out this far."

"But what other explanation is there?" Rowe asked.

"That's what I'm trying to understand," said Cortez, lifting herself back up out of the quicksand until she seemed to sit on a ledge—her feet dangling into it. As she changed positions, Noyes's resolution appeared to weaken ever so slightly.

"We have an engineer named Glazer," Rowe said. "His team found something underneath the surface of the planet that's like tubes. Could that be a natural feature that conducts the Goo, or maybe allows it to live underground, inside the planet? And then a hilltop like this could be an access port where it comes out?"

Even as he spoke, something else occurred to Rowe.

"You said the Goo on this planet made you kill each other. Made you appear as aggressive monsters. But Noyes isn't telling *me* to kill people."

Noyes's eyes went wide, as though the very idea was scandalous.

"No," said Cortez. "It seemed to work through our enviro-suits. But you can see your AI without your suit here. And I agree, he seems peaceful enough."

Rowe did not know what to think. He said: "Maybe this is a pool of 'clean' Goo up here—like an oasis in a desert—that's not infected yet."

Cortez smiled coyly.

Rowe walked closer to her.

"Why do I suddenly feel like there's still something more?" Rowe said cautiously. "There's something you're *still* not telling me?"

Now the playful smile dropped from Cortez's face. To increase the resolution of the Goo, she eased back down into the silt.

"What can you tell me about Walchirk-V-16?" she asked.

"Walchirk-V . . ." Rowe trailed off as he tried to remember. "Why do I know that name?"

"Goo, take it away," Cortez said.

Directly adjacent to Noyes, an image of a black-red ball pocked with angry meteorite craters appeared in very high resolution and began to slowly rotate.

Above the ball, incandescent green text started to form. Cortez used the glowing text like teleprompter talking points.

"Walchirk-V-16 is one of only ten X-Class planets discovered in all of human history," she said. "It is the only one of the ten to be found during our lifetimes. The X-Class designation is controversial, of course. Many Silkworms hold that if something is X-Class, then it's not a planet. It's an 'anomaly.' And, of course, anomalies don't need to get wired by Silkworms."

Rowe nodded, looking at the rotating black and red orb.

"This is taking me back to my Academy days," he said. "X-Class are the planets that we're *waiting* to wire . . . if, as you say, they are planets at all. And we use the word 'waiting' because officially Silkworms will always wire every planet in the universe. That's part of our sacred charge. Our prime directive. So if something's not wired then it's either not a planet, or it's a planet we'll return to when we develop whatever technology is needed to do the job."

Cortez nodded.

"Most X-Class planets are fatal to human and machine alike," she said. "Walchirk-V-16 is no exception. However, it's the only X-Class where the mechanism that kills people is still a total mystery. *Other* X-Class planets . . . we *know* what the problem is; we just haven't solved for it yet. Like, we don't have a sword strong enough to kill that dragon—or whatever analogy you want to use—but one day we will, and then we'll come back and slay the dragon and wire the planet. But on Walchirk-V-16, there's no dragon. There's nothing. You just die."

"Yes, I'm remembering more now," Rowe said in a flat, dead tone. "No one can live on Walchirk for more than a few seconds, and it's unclear why. Step onto the planet, and you immediately pass away. And in the bodies we can get close enough to recover, there's no clear cause of death when they do the autopsy. Supposedly, one day there'll be enough information that the Goo will be able to figure it out, but for the time being, that planet's surface is like the touch of the Grim Reaper itself."

"Do you understand why I am bringing this up?" Cortez asked.

"No," Rowe said. "I mean . . . maybe something on this planet got into the Goo and caused your crew to kill each other, but this certainly isn't an X-Class planet. If you land, you're not immediately dead. In the grand scheme of things, we've only just got here. I'm sure we'll be able to identify the problem and fix it eventually. We always do."

"Yeah, I'm not so sure about that," Cortez said. "I think this place *is* X-Class, and the ESA just hasn't figured that out yet. I think that whatever's here needs to be left alone."

"Why?" Rowe said, growing desperate at the intransigence of Cortez. "Look, we can rescue you and take you home now. You know that, right? Our own version of the Goo is working fine . . . Noyes over there is fine. It's . . ."

But even as the words came out of his mouth, Rowe again recalled the loss of Davidson impaled in the loading bay.

"Whatever lives here—exists here—has only encountered the finite, self-contained version of the Goo that we bring down to planets with us," Cortez countered. "But the moment it connects to the *real* Goo up above that lightning—the Goo that is beamed all across the universe and is joined with every planet that's been wired—then I don't know what happens. What if it got into *that* Goo? This malfunction, this virus, whatever-you-want-to-call-it . . . Imagine what happened here—to my crew—happening all across the universe, all at once, wherever people use the Goo."

"But . . . the Goo is impervious to bugs and viruses," said Rowe. "When one appears, the Goo destroys it. This has always been the case. Maybe a first-time anomaly in a contained environment like Tendus-13 could confuse the local Goo for a short time. But the big, interstellar Goo? The one *you're* talking about? It's literally not possible. What you're suggesting is unthinkable."

"That doesn't mean I'm wrong," Cortez said. "How do you know the Goo instantly kills every bug? Because the Goo told you that?"

Rowe thought for a second.

"The lady's got a point, boy-o."

Rowe looked over at Noyes.

"I've never heard the Goo criticize the Goo before," Rowe said.

"These are strange times," Noyes replied. "It is technically accurate to say that there is no outside arbiter for many things the Goo asserts. Just because something has been correct every time in the past does not guarantee it'll be correct in the future."

"Thank you, freshman-year-philosophy-bot," Rowe said derisively.

"I'm here to serve," Noyes said with a little bow.

Rowe looked back at Cortez.

"Fine," he said. "There could theoretically be some danger in this situation. We're both Silkworms. We chose this job because it's dangerous. We're people who take risks. But we have to do something."

"Risking ourselves is one thing," Cortez told him. "Risking the Goo is something else entirely."

"Then what do you want me to do?" Rowe asked her, clenching his fists in frustration.

"I thought I was being clear, but apparently you need me to come right out and say it," Cortez told him. "Tendus-13 needs to be declared an X-Class planet. We need to *help* the ESA make that determination. We—you and I—need to *make sure* Tendus-13 becomes a place that the ESA abandons any hope of ever wiring. With any luck, they'll nuke it from space."

"How—"

"We have to kill everyone who comes here," Cortez said. "We have to kill every member of your landing party. Then we have to do what I did to the Marie Curie. We have to destroy their equipment. Disable your lander. Smash every enviro-suit port until nothing can interface with them ever again. It's the only way to keep the interstellar Goo safe from whatever is here. The ships up there in orbit . . . They can't see inside the cloud cover—and thank the Goo they can't—but eventually they'll *have* to notice that whenever you send humans down to the surface of Tendus-13, they . . . *Don't. Come. Back.* Even the densest mission commander will eventually stop sending Silkworms to die for no reason. It's bad for your ARK Score, not to mention future work promotions."

Cortez lifted herself up out of the sand and rose to her full height. Noyes began to fade a bit. Cortez positioned herself directly in front of Rowe.

"We've *got* to do this," she said to him. "I've had quite a bit of time to think about the dilemma we're in, and it's the only way to be sure. We have to kill everyone; disable everything. If more Silkworms come after your group, we have to kill them too."

Rowe took a step back from her.

"I think whatever infected you through the Goo is still inside you," he said. "Listen to yourself. You want to murder everyone on the planet?"

"No one is ever going to know," Cortez insisted. "It won't impact *your* ARK Score, because the Goo will never see it."

"The Goo is standing right there, looking at me, dressed like a clergyman," Rowe said.

"*Something* is doing that," said Cortez. "Some *version* of the Goo . . . But it's not the real Goo. It's not the one you know. This place is wrong. Off. Fake somehow. Listen to me! We need to turn Tendus-13 into an X-Class, and we need to do it immediately."

"I'm not going to kill people," Rowe declared.

"It may save countless lives if you do," said Cortez. "It may save the very Goo itself. Don't you see that? If we do this right, the real Goo will *never* come here and become infected. We are beyond outside of the Goo. This conversation you and I are having right now won't be searchable by future generations. It doesn't count. The Goo can't hear us."

"Um, respectfully . . ." Noyes interjected.

"Whatever *that* is, it's not the Goo as you know it!" Cortez said frantically, pointing hard at Noyes. "Think about what I'm saying. Really think about it. You know I'm right."

Rowe considered the situation for a few instants. Then he turned to face the hologram.

"Noyes, I've been wondering, does Cortez have a weapon on her? Maybe something that I can't see?"

"I seem to be without my normal scanning capabilities," Noyes responded. "But from here I'd say it's a strong bet she doesn't."

"Yeah, that's what I thought too," Rowe said.

Cortez began to furrow her brow, wondering where this was going. In the same instant, Rowe swept her leg and pushed her violently into the pool of sand.

Then he took off running down the side of the mesa.

CHAPTER TEN

ROWE HAD NEVER LIVED IN A WORLD WITHOUT NAVIGATION ASSISTANCE. Full stop.

Such a thing had always been there, as long as he could remember, omnipresent and omniscient. Whenever you needed to know how to get somewhere, you simply asked the Goo. A panoply of maps, visual aids, and spoken directions were then instantly available to you.

After undergoing the Briefing, Rowe had been given access to works of ancient literature that sometimes featured characters "losing their way" or "getting lost" while headed for a destination. Travelers took wrong turns down foggy roads in the middle of the night and soon had no clue where they were. Fictional seafarers who lost their sextants had to drift aimlessly, with only the crudest ideas about their location. These kinds of tales, however, had never been truly relatable to Rowe.

Except now, quite abruptly, they were.

Rowe headed in the general direction from which he estimated he and Cortez had come. Rowe did not trust himself to find his way *directly* back to the Marie Curie or the lander, but had a feeling he could do it if he started from the cave. He imagined his subconscious might be able to conjure up the route along which he'd been dragged.

At least he *hoped* it would.

Rowe backtracked at full gallop. He found himself noticing familiar natural waypoints, and took this as a good sign. He hazarded several glances back as he traveled. For the first few, Cortez did not appear. But when he'd made his way completely down the mesa and put a good hundred yards between it and himself, he saw Cortez standing perfectly still atop the outcropping, silhouetted starkly against the lightning and clouds. She did not move at all, but only watched him go.

Then the hillside loomed ahead, and Rowe located the cave more quickly than he'd expected to. Time seemed to be passing strangely. He took several additional glances back, but did not see Cortez following him across the plain.

From the cave, Rowe turned and jogged across the bleak horrid landscape in the direction that something in him—something deep, ancient and innate—said was the right way to go. He encountered fresh marks in the silt underfoot that he guessed had been created when Cortez had dragged or carried his unconscious body. He felt guardedly encouraged by these, and pressed on.

Then—after passing several shallow dales and a couple of clusters of familiar-feeling rocks—he saw ahead of him the great valley containing the massive bulk of the Marie Curie.

He had done it. He had found his way back.

An unaccustomed sense of accomplishment washed over Rowe. He had performed this navigation automatically, without his enviro-suit. Without the Goo. It was reassuring . . . but more than that, it was a *new* feeling, something that the Goo had never given him. Immediately, he wondered if such thoughts would be bad for his ARK Score. Then he remembered that he wasn't being observed by the Goo. When he returned to the lander and was fitted with a new enviro-suit, that suit would have no certain memory of what he had done out here. It would make guesses and inferences, but it would *never* know for sure.

The feeling was liberating and terrifying, in equal parts.

Rowe looked behind himself again. Once more, there was no sign of Cortez. Nearly out of breath, he allowed himself to slow to a lope.

The wind picked up. The flying silt made it slightly harder to see. It was nothing like the storm that had concealed Cortez, but it still hampered visibility. For this reason, Rowe was practically upon the lip of the valley before he saw that the drillwork on the ship's dorsal fin had been stopped, and that the scaffolding had partially collapsed.

Had it been that raging wind?

No. It seemed very doubtful that *any* wind would be powerful enough to upset the kind of scaffolds Silkworms used.

Moving down the side of the crater, Rowe saw that the drill had fallen halfway down the disarranged scaffolding, and been left on its side. Silkworms would only have abandoned it for some urgent reason. Injuries or a serious threat to safety.

Rowe reached the crater floor and approached the ship, never taking his eyes off the scaffolding. When he drew near, a ghastly smear of red became visible down the side of the ship. What could it be . . . if not fresh blood?

There was no one around.

"Hello!" Rowe called.

He cupped his hands and shouted several times, not quite knowing in which direction to point his cries.

Then suddenly, and quite unexpectedly, he heard a very distant: " . . . hello?" in response.

Rowe looked all around. The sound had come from the valley's far lip, somewhere back in the direction of the lander. And it had sounded a whole lot like Waverly.

Moments later, the outline of his friend became visible on the far side of the crater.

His energy restored as if by magic, Rowe bounded across to meet him.

Waverly's expression showed that he was surprised but also deeply gratified to discover his friend. When the men drew within easier shouting distance, Waverly stopped and looked Rowe up and down.

"I was about to head out to look for you again!" Waverly called. "Where did you go?"

"I was in a cave off in that direction," Rowe said, gesturing. "I'll show you."

The two men reached one another, and Rowe caught his breath.

"What happened?" Waverly asked. "You ran into that dust storm, and when it cleared, you were just gone. I was trying to track you, but then an emergency call came in from the drill. One of the operators went mad. Pushed another operator into the drill, then tried to drill away the scaffolds underneath himself. Suicidal, we think. Undiagnosed predisposition to space madness. He passed away right when we got him back to the lander."

"Was he talking . . . talking to himself, I mean? Like Davidson?" Rowe asked.

"Yeah, that was the strange thing. The whole time we're doing the evac, he won't stop talking about monsters. About how *we're* the monsters. The man had most of the bones in his body broken from the fall, but he was still trying to get up and run away. It was unreal."

"Believe it or not, I can top that," Rowe said. "Because I just met Martha Cortez. Out there."

Rowe pointed off toward the horizon.

"It was her or I'll be damned," he continued, "and she gave me this."

Rowe leaned forward so Waverly could see the wound on his head.

Waverly's expression told Rowe that his injury was not so very dire, which felt good. One relied on the diagnoses of friends when there was no Goo.

"So she's alive?" Waverly asked.

"Living in a cave out across the plain, if you can believe it," Rowe confirmed. "I'm still puzzling over the details, but she's convinced that there's a Goo on this planet and it's somehow . . . *infected*. She thinks that Tendus-13 needs to be declared an X-Class, and to make that happen she wants to kill everyone in our landing party. Dragging me out there was her way of recruiting me for the job."

"Did she kill the people aboard the Marie Curie?" Waverly asked.

"She killed some of them, I think," Rowe said. "According to her, mostly they killed each other. But she's the one who tried to cover it up."

"Where is she now?" Waverly asked.

"Still somewhere back there, I assume," Rowe said, motioning off to the distance. "We were on top of a tall, flat hill. I pushed her and ran away, and she didn't follow. I'll tell you more on the way back to the lander. But before we do anything else, I need a new enviro-suit."

Rowe's head wound required several stitches.

"You also have a concussion," the medic told him. "Lucky thing it didn't trigger your aneurysms."

"You can see them on the scanner? They're okay?"

"Yes," said the medic, lowering a handheld device from beside Rowe's head. "They appear undisturbed by your adventure, if that's what you mean. Would you like to see?"

"No," said Rowe.

He had seen scans of his aneurysms hundreds of times, and did not feel any need to view the harbingers of his death once more.

"Any reason I can't get into a new enviro-suit now?"

"No," said the medic. "Frankly, we all might be more comfortable if you did. Seeing you out on the planet without one . . . it was like a man walking around naked."

Rowe eased off the examining table and headed for the wall of the lander where several replacements were arrayed. Waverly—who had never left his side—smiled as his friend suited back up.

A few paces off from the lander door, a group of Silkworms were conferring over the body of the drill operator. Some of them looked over at Rowe as they whispered or gestured.

"Should we tell them what happened to you?" Waverly asked. "Who you just met?"

"Not yet," said Rowe, activating the new suit. "I want to test something first. C'mon, let's go outside."

Rowe and Waverly walked to the edge of the camp that had grown around the lander.

"Noyes?" Rowe said softly. "Care to join us?"

Noyes misted alive on the shoulder of the new suit.

"Good to be with you, boy-o," Noyes said, a broad smile on his face. "You'll be wanting to ask me a very important question, I expect."

"You expect right," Rowe said. "When was the last time you saw me?"

"Up on a high plateau, alongside the captain of the Marie Curie," the hologram said confidently. "And you were a bit of a cad, if you don't mind me saying so—pushing her down in the dirt the way you did."

Rowe looked at Waverly—who was clearly struggling to process this—then back at Noyes.

"Can you go there now, if you want to?" Rowe asked. "Like, can you see what's happening on that hilltop—using the Goo—and tell me? Or *show* me?"

Noyes looked straight ahead. His eyes blinked rapidly, like a man ambushed by an exam question he'd not been expecting. Then the hologram looked back at Rowe and shook its head.

"No luck," Noyes said. "That way is sort of . . . turned off for me. Closed. That's the best way I can explain it."

Waverly leaned in closer to the small, floating priest.

"What the fuck is going on, Encarta?" he asked. "How did you get from my man's enviro-suit to a hill with Martha Cortez? This planet's not even wired yet."

"Oh, but it *is* wired," Noyes said mysteriously. "At least, that's the thing I'm forced to conclude. You may want to conclude that too, if you know what's good for you."

"What do you mean?" Waverly said, putting his fist up as if to threaten the little man.

"No," Rowe said to his friend. "I think Noyes is right. It . . . It *would* make sense."

"*What* would make sense?" Waverly asked. "Cause right now neither of you are making *any* sense at all!"

"It would make sense that there is wire on Tendus-13," Rowe said. "Someone else wired it already. The tubes that Glazer found? At this point, we have to assume that's a wire job. Maybe not the kind that we'd do—maybe not a *human* wire job—but still a wire job."

"But if the planet is wired, then why can't Noyes ride the wire to wherever he pleases?" Waverly asked, looking hard at the floating clergyman. "He just said that he couldn't go back to the hill where you saw Cortez. How is *that* a wired planet?"

"It's not a normal wire," said Rowe. "I'll give you that. Not 'normal' to us, at least. Suppose someone wired it, but their version of a wire has limitations. Or it has on and off switches. Or it's like a tide that comes in and out."

"Why would *anyone* make a wire that comes and goes?" Waverly asked.

"We don't know their motivations or their capabilities," Rowe replied. "Maybe it's not on purpose. Maybe their wiring isn't as good as ours."

For a moment, both men sat on the ground. Noyes continued to hover nearby. The expression on the hologram's face said it hoped it could be helpful, but it did not know quite what to say.

Thunder rumbled overhead and powerful lightning flashed.

"You were joking about it before—at least I think you were joking—but what if the Marie Curie wasn't the first ESA ship to come here?" Rowe asked. "What if it *thought* it was, but it wasn't. I mean, we have been wiring planets for Goo knows how long. Maybe this one got lost in the shuffle. Forgotten. Or maybe there's a *reason* we were told otherwise."

The men looked out upon the grim horizon, considering.

"If we were lied to, it'd have to be one of those lies where the Goo goes along with it, because the ends justify the means," Waverly said. "Tricky-tricky, such things . . . They make me damn uncomfortable."

"Yeah," said Rowe. "I don't like them either."

"Our mission briefings were *very* clear that the Marie Curie had been the only ESA ship to touch down on this planet," Waverly reminded him.

"But right now, it's that or alien intelligent life," Rowe said. "And the chances of it being the latter . . . I know that someday, statistically, it's got to happen. Everyone knows that. But the odds are so low. It's like winning the lottery. You know someone, somewhere wins . . . but the chances it's you? In all the cosmos, we've not yet found any intelligence that could formulate Goo, *much less* wire a planet. You learn about human history, and you get the idea every century had different ideas about what the criteria should be for 'intelligent life.' Can they make fire? Have they developed the internal combustion engine? Do they understand that they are evolving? Do they understand black holes and white holes . . ."

For a moment, Rowe trailed off.

"But no," he resumed. "We now understand that those were small-time questions. Amateur-hour questions. The only *real* one is: Have they developed Goo?"

"Seeing aliens with a combustion engine would still be neat," Waverly mused. "What were those things the Silkworms found on Cronos-17 . . . ?"

"Dogables," Noyes reminded him.

"Yeah!" said Waverly. "Dogables. Big friendly dog-like creatures with giant flat feet and they kind of surf along the sulfur lakes. Imagine one of those with an engine strapped to its back. I'd pay money to put a saddle on one and ride it."

Rowe knew his friend was only trying to lighten the mood, but his own mind kept heading down darker pathways.

"I want to figure out if this planet has already been wired—or if parts of it have—and I want to know who did it," Rowe said. "Officially, my mission is to verify that the planet is secure, and I think getting that sort of information is a legitimate component of that mission. I'm also concerned about what is happening to the men here. Our men. We've got three dead from *our* crew already? If Cortez is telling the truth, something could be using our own Goo to try to kill us, just like it did to her people. She made it sound like the crew of the Marie Curie killed each other all at once—one big Ragnarok inside the ship. If there's a pathway for Goo all over the planet, presumably it could be doing that to us too. But it's not. Okay. But at the same time, we can't assume that means we're safe. What if, this time around, it's experimenting; this time, it wants to pick us off one by one, say? Could be, that's what it was doing with Davidson. Maybe it told him opening a depth gauge was safe when, really, it knew it was going to be fatal."

"If we got inside the Marie Curie's black box and saw what happened, then we would know if Cortez was telling you the truth," Waverly said. "Our drill made some good progress before the operator went space-happy. It might not take much longer to wrap up the job."

Something occurred to Rowe.

"You *do* believe that I met Cortez, right?" Rowe asked. "That Noyes and I aren't lying about it? And that I didn't give this head wound to myself?"

"Yeah, I believe you," Waverly said, as if the question were ludicrous. "It's just that I don't know if it's safe for *you* to believe *her*."

Rowe ran his fingers through his hair, careful to avoid his new stitches.

"So . . . do we talk to the other Silkworms about this?" Rowe asked. "I think it might make them unnecessarily nervous. This is a *whole* bunch of un-knowns. Enough to make anybody anxious."

"Doesn't feel good, does it?" Noyes offered gamely. "And just think, humans used to have to live with such uncertainties all the time! Maybe it makes you respect your ancestors a little more, eh?"

"I don't know if I should respect them or feel bad for them," Waverly said, shaking his head.

"What *I* think," Rowe said, "is that the best thing for us to do right now is eliminate as many un-knowns as possible. And there are some very direct ways of accomplishing that."

"Are you thinking what I'm thinking?" Waverly asked, rising to his feet.

"We go and find Cortez . . ."

"And *not* let her hit you in the head this time?"

"Exactly," Rowe said. "But one question more . . . Do we keep the crew drilling for the black box in the meantime?"

"That *is* a puzzler," said Waverly. "Hey Encarta, what would *you* do?"

"Eh," Noyes said. "I don't see a countdown clock anywhere. What's with the race against time? You could catch up with Cortez and *then* open the black box. Bring her back and have her *watch* you open it."

"That's one opinion," said Waverly.

"Yes, it certainly is," said Rowe. "And I think we should do the opposite. No offense, Noyes."

"None taken," said the floating officiant.

Waverly added: "I'm with Rowe as well. Two against one. Sorry, Encarta."

Rowe and Waverly informed their remaining squadmates that the drill job could resume.

Then they headed off across the empty planet in the direction of the cave.

CHAPTER ELEVEN

"I'M JUST NOW THINKING OF SOMETHING," ROWE SAID AS THEY WALKED. "How fast do you think you could take off your enviro-suit? You know, if you had to?"

"Pretty fast," Waverly said. "Faster than you, I bet."

"Yeah," Rowe said thoughtfully. "So if something happens out here that doesn't seem quite real. Like if I turn into a monster and look like I'm about to attack you. Or if Noyes suddenly starts saying you should kill me . . . Do me a favor and get down to your flight suit before you do it, yeah? Make sure I'm still a monster when the enviro-suit's off, *then* shoot me in the face. If Cortez is being straight, I don't want us to fall victim to something projected through the Goo."

"Agreed," said Waverly with a grin. "When I kick your monster ass, it'll be Greco Roman style, with full nudity if you want."

"Great . . ." said Rowe.

The windstorms stirred the silt as the men walked. The lightning above stayed bright and steady.

"Do you suppose this place has seasons?" Waverly asked. "Maybe the lightning has fall colors, and then turns greener in the spring."

"Do you really want an answer?" Noyes asked. "Because I could give you one."

"Do you *think* I want an answer?" Waverly growled at the hologram.

Noyes folded his hands and returned to a forward-facing position, looking out across the blasted plain.

At junctures, they passed tall clumps of rocks where Cortez could theoretically have been hiding, yet neither man concerned himself with that possibility. They saw nobody waiting in ambush. The scanners in the enviro-suits detected no sign of movement or life.

Soon, the cave came into view. It was in the side of a rocky cliff where the land rose up into a cratered hill. They did not see the Marie Curie's captain anywhere. The mouth of the cave was dark.

"Hell of a place," Waverly said as they approached.

"She must have thought it was her best option," Rowe said. "If the Marie Curie is haunted somehow—poisoned, infected—then wanting to go totally off the grid like this makes sense. But it also makes sense if she's crazy."

They drew within twenty yards and still saw no movement.

Waverly cupped his hands, and looked to Rowe for the go-ahead. Rowe gave a shrug and a nod.

"Martha Cortez!" Waverly called. "Want to come out and talk to us? I'm even more fun than my man Rowe who you met. I'm hand-somer too! *Much . . . Handsomer . . .*"

Waverly allowed himself a quiet laugh. His words echoed across the lonely planet. No response came back.

"Fuck it; let's go inside," Waverly said.

"All right," said Rowe.

The men activated their helmets as a defensive measure. Rowe had seen no weapons—either on Cortez's person, or among her supplies in the cave—but this was not a situation in which he wanted to take chances.

At the entrance to the cave they also activated their suit lights, cast-ing the beams forward. There was equipment piled within the cave, and the silt on the cave floor seemed recently disturbed. Rowe noted what might have been fresh footprints leading away.

They called for her again, and again got no response.

Their scanners picked up nothing.

Examining the space more thoroughly this time, Rowe found that Cortez had indeed tried to make a home of the place. There was an improvised bed and a chemical toilet, and even a little kitchenette to aid in the preparation of food.

Waverly said: "Of the places I'd like to build my hermitage . . . well, let's say this option doesn't figure into the top ten."

"Yeah," said Rowe cautiously. "I don't believe she's living this way for fun. It's . . . Whatever the situation here actually is, I think Cortez must believe her own story."

Waverly nodded vigorously to show he concurred with the diagnosis.

The men spent less than five minutes picking through the supplies in the cave. Then Waverly said: "Could you find your way back to that hilltop from here?"

"I think so," said Rowe.

"I don't have any other ideas," Waverly told him.

"Neither do I," said Rowe. "Noyes, do you see anything else important here? Something we failed to remark on?"

"No," Noyes told them. "She was here recently. But I don't see anything that tells us where she is now."

"Thanks for nothing, Encarta. Shall we head for the hill?"

"Let's go," Rowe said.

They exited the cave and walked until the mesa came into view. (Again, Rowe was stunned by his ability to remember the way on his own.) From a distance, there was no sign of Cortez on the horizon.

As they neared the base of the towering mesa, Noyes suddenly shouted: "Stop! Don't take another step!!!"

The men halted their advance. Waverly raised a skeptical eyebrow.

"There is some sort of . . . trap . . . I think . . . embedded in the ground at the foothill ahead," Noyes told them. "I believe it's a tripwire mechanism rigged between two rocks. I can make strong guesses as to how it might have been constructed with ground-clearing explosive material salvaged from the Marie Curie."

"You can guess all that?" Rowe said.

Noyes nodded.

"The lack of anything else on this planet actually makes that sort of guessing much easier," Noyes told them. "You can avoid the danger if you step around the tripwire. Take that side-path up the hillside. I'll have your suit project a safe route with waypoints."

A dotted line appeared on the ground. Rowe and Waverly followed it carefully.

"This is crazy," whispered Rowe, advancing now with great caution along the edge of the hill. "I thought she wanted my help. Now she wants to kill me."

Waverly said: "If she really believes that everyone has to be killed—and everything that can carry Goo should be destroyed—then she is acting logically, I suppose. It's a really fucked up kind of logic, but still . . . You've shown you can't be recruited, so she might as well blow you to bits along with the others."

"We have to assume this might not be her only trap," Rowe said. "Noyes, be sure to keep an eye out for more of those, eh?"

"What do you think I'm doing, boy-o?" the hologram replied in a tone indicating great concentration.

Both men readied the railgun functions in their enviro-suits, as a man might point a gun built into his shirtsleeve. In this way, they carefully advanced up the side of the hill, making sure to step only on Noyes's projected pathmarks. There was no sign of Cortez, and they heard nothing beyond the crunching glass underfoot.

At the top of the plateau, Noyes whispered: "Ascend this last part very slowly."

The men did.

The circle of stones gradually came into view, but Cortez was nowhere to be seen.

"Anything?" Rowe asked.

"Put me down for a tentative no, boy-o," Noyes decreed. "Very tentative. It *appears* safe as far as the scanners in your suit can tell."

Waverly lowered the arm that held the railgun and approached the circle of stones doubtfully.

"She sat in that, and it made Goo spontaneously appear in the air," Rowe said as Waverly toed one of the rocks.

"You're shitting me," Waverly said.

"Goo as my witness, it happened," Rowe replied.

He gazed out across the horizon for anything Cortez-looking in the vast gray landscape beyond.

"Who put these rocks here?" asked Waverly. "I mean, why place them like this?"

"Said she found it this way," Rowe said, his eyes still tracing the horizon.

Waverly stuck his foot into the dust within the stone circle, smiling as it gave way. Then he squatted on his haunches, and eventually sat, dangling his legs down into the thin, fine dust as if it were water in a swimming pool.

Very slowly, an indistinct glow began to hover above the circle.

"Would you look at—" Waverly began.

"Boy-o!" Noyes said urgently.

"I see it too," replied Rowe.

Waverly looked over to the spot where Rowe and Noyes had apparently—somehow—more important things to view than spontaneously appearing incandescence.

"What're you two on about?" he asked.

Waverly rose to his feet, and the light above him dimmed.

"In the distance there is a human form, just visible," Rowe said. "I'm zooming in."

Enviro-suit functionality did not feature extensive magnification, but the suit still did a little better than squinting. He wasn't able to make out a face, but the ESA flight suit was unmistakable.

"That's her, no question," Rowe affirmed.

"Yes," Noyes said. "That is Martha Cortez, captain of the Marie Curie."

Waverly stood next to Rowe and gazed at the figure in the distance.

"Is she climbing up the side of a boulder?" he asked, training the limited magnification of his own suit. "Why's she doing it like that? She's like a crab or something. Scrabbling. That's positively undignified."

"I'm glad you find her funny," said Rowe. "Keep in mind she already hit me on the head and tried to kill us with a bomb."

"I didn't say she's not also an asshole," Waverly replied.

They watched as Cortez continued to awkwardly scale the distant boulder.

"I don't think she's seen us," Rowe said. "We're exposed up here, but she's too focused on her task to look back. Maybe we can catch up while she's distracted."

"But wait," said Waverly, casting a glance back at the circle of stones. "Do you want to show me this magic Goo-circle first? Rowe?"

But Rowe was already heading down the hill.

Sensing that the die had been cast, Waverly saw no option but to follow his friend.

CHAPTER TWELVE

ROWE DASHED ACROSS TENDUS-13 AS THE ENDLESS LIGHTNING PLAYED wildly above. As always, the enviro-suit intuitively aided him—its mechanical joints adding spring to every step until he ran at twice the rate of a normal man.

"Noyes," Rowe said between breaths, "let me know if you see her look back at us. I can't see so well when I'm running."

"Aye aye," Noyes replied.

Rowe sprinted forward until the form of Cortez climbing the boulder came into clear view.

She had made considerable progress and was now pulling herself up to the boulder's very top—a place broad and flat enough that she would be able to stand. Rowe considered his next move. Cortez still appeared unarmed. It would be nothing to hit her with the railgun at this distance, but Rowe wanted to capture her alive; there were still too many questions. Rowe understood that his enviro-suit could be made to amplify a jump or leap, though he rarely used that function. He guessed that if he got the angle right, he could reach the top of her boulder in a series of bounds and tackle her. (He knew this would probably also cause serious injury to Cortez, but with the back of his own head still smarting, he was past the point of caring about that. Alive was enough.)

He drew within fifty yards of the boulder. Then thirty-five. Then twenty.

And then he saw something that made his blood run cold.

Cortez was now standing on the top of the boulder, but she had not stopped climbing.

Rowe slowed to a slow shuffle as he tried to make sense of it.

Cortez made all the movements of a person climbing a ladder—but lo!—she began to ascend into the space above the boulder, *as if by a series of rungs.* And there was nothing there. She climbed nothing.

"Noyes, are you seeing this?" Rowe whispered. He reduced his gait even further.

"Yes; thinking about it now," the hologram said. "Many explanations. Just need a little more data to—"

Noyes stopped mid-sentence, calculating further, as Cortez—now approximately ten feet above the boulder—began to disappear.

It was as if she were climbing into nonexistence, thought Rowe. First her head disappeared, then her torso and legs. And quite quickly, she was entirely gone.

Rowe stopped. He stood staring up into the space where Cortez had been.

A moment later, Waverly caught up.

The Silkworms exchanged a silent, uneasy glance. Waverly had seen it too.

"Noyes?" Rowe said urgently. "Your best guess. *Now.*"

"I . . . Yes . . ." the hologram replied in harried tones.

"What's the matter, Encarta?" Waverly said, panting. "They didn't send along the disk covering invisible ladders."

"I am still thinking, but there are options such as a previously unencountered cloaking mechanism or an optical illusion," Noyes said.

"An optical illusion?" Waverly said. "That's fuck all. She was on top of that big rock, and now she's not. She climbed up *nothing* and disappeared."

"Noyes, are we in any danger right now?" Rowe pressed. "Could this be another trap?"

"No," the hologram said. "I would be telling you if I thought that."

Rowe asked Waverly: "What do *you* think, man?"

"I think we're letting her get away."

The two men bounded the rest of the way to the boulder.

"Wait, I'm still searching for other possible . . ." Noyes began, but trailed off when he understood his objections would be bootless.

They easily scaled the boulder with the aid of their suits. They saw nothing above them but the lightning-filled sky. Rowe began feeling around the top of the boulder like a man trapped in a dark room. Waverly did the same. After only a moment, Rowe firmly and definitively wrapped the fingers of his suit around something that, as far as his eyes could tell, was not there.

The rungs of a ladder.

With a few tentative kicks, he found additional rungs by his feet.

"If you'd just be patient, gentlemen, I am processing several options surrounding the properties of certain surfaces and materials that can be used to bend light," Noyes protested.

Ignoring this, Rowe said: "I'm going first."

"I'm right behind you!" Waverly insisted.

Rowe began to climb the ladder he could not see.

Through the gloves of his suit, the rungs felt like familiar metal. As he ascended, the sky full of lightning and clouds seemed to fade. With each rung, the atmosphere above became blurrier and less distinct, and a new, overlaid image became apparent.

At the top of the ladder, the clouds faded entirely, and Rowe stepped off the ladder and onto a floor. The illumination on his enviro-suit kicked in. There was now a featureless white ceiling above. The nearest wall was curved with no joints. Rowe leaned his hand against it; it was hard like plastic; smooth and white. He was in a room of buttons, many of them flashed or glowed softly, and there was a circular hole in the floor through which the ladder extended. Corridors led out of the room, apparently to other places made of curving white walls and buttons. A moment later Waverly appeared behind Rowe at the top of the ladder.

"What in the world?" Waverly whispered.

They urgently looked around for any sign of Cortez. The crackling of lightning was muted now. The only new sound from within the room was a low mechanical hum.

"This is a spaceship," Rowe said quietly.

Waverly looked all around, nodding.

"I sure can't think of what else it could be."

"Noyes, does this match the properties of any ESA vessel you know about?" Rowe asked.

"It does not," Noyes replied softly. "The cloaking camouflage also—because I know you'll be curious—is not something I can find a reference to. *That* kind of technology? The need to operate a large ship covertly? Well, it all died out back when there stopped being separate nation states, boy-o."

"Hmm," said Rowe, glancing doubtfully around the spacecraft. "And how do I know *you're* not lying to me? How do *you* know you're not lying to me? This could be an ESA ship you weren't told about.

There were holes in your memory when it came to some of the Marie Curie crewmembers, remember?"

"I guess anything could be anything, if you want to take that attitude," Noyes said defensively.

The hologram's words were not reassuring.

Waverly took several tentative steps down one of the hallways with the buttons and smooth walls. He gently ran the fingers of his suit across the buttons but did not depress them.

"You realize that if Encarta here *isn't* lying, this is one for the history files," Waverly said. "You and I are going to be famous. We're Armstrong and Aldrin. We're the first humans to step inside of a ship built by another life form."

Then Waverly paused. He trained a light from his suit down the nearest hallway.

"But maybe we don't get immortalized quite yet," he continued. "Because I see a big fat ESA logo right where I'm looking."

Rowe shone his own light to the point Waverly indicated.

"That's a supply box," Rowe said. "It could have been moved here from the Marie Curie."

"Correct, boy-o," Noyes chimed in. "It very much appears that it was."

The men approached the equipment case that sat halfway down the corridor.

Rowe heard something up ahead of them creak. Then there was a nonsensical sound that was distinctly human. A chuff or grunt.

Rowe whispered: "It's better if we can surprise her."

Moving quietly in enviro-suits was challenging, but the Silkworms did the best they could. Not much farther down the corridor of glowing buttons, they discovered an archway opening into a large circular room. Here, more ESA equipment had been haphazardly stored.

In the center of the room was an inflatable emergency slide from the side of an ESA vehicle that had been repurposed into something like an air mattress. The rest of the room was covered with other items salvaged from the Marie Curie. Cortez reclined in the center of the mattress chewing on a brandless candy bar in a shiny silver wrapper. In her other hand, she held crumpled pages from a printed instruction manual.

They only had the drop on her for a couple of seconds.

"Oh what the fuck!?" Cortez cried as her eyes lit on the men.

Cortez hastily rolled over to the side of the improvised mattress and flailed for something. She came up with a tool approximately the size and shape of a tack hammer with a glowing green-white head.

Rowe lunged at her, his enviro-suit propelling him across the circular room in a mighty Olympian leap. Despite this artificial boost, Cortez had time to rise to her feet and assume a combat stance. Rowe caught her around the middle like a linebacker making a tackle, but Cortez brought the hammer down on his shoulder. There was immediately a strong odor that Rowe associated with the cutting of metal at construction sites, and he felt a hot pain course through his arm.

They tumbled off the emergency slide and onto the floor. Rowe fell first, and Cortez landed atop him. He was on his side but was able to quickly twist himself around to look up. Cortez straddled him and raised the glowing hammer, the head sizzling with burning metal. Rowe instinctively threw up his hands to shield himself. Cortez reared higher to deliver a death blow. In the same instant, Rowe heard the low-pitched "BRRRRRRRMMMMP" of Waverly's railgun, and watched Cortez's severed fingers fall to the floor. Her hammer careened across the room and embedded into the wall.

Cortez screamed once and thrust her mangled hand into her armpit. Her body crumpled and she rolled off of Rowe.

Waverly sauntered over slowly, as if the situation involved no urgency. He extended his hand and pulled Rowe to his feet.

"Thank you," Rowe said, trying to look down at his own shoulder. "How bad is it?"

Waverly's expression said he would live.

"Your left deltoid's going to hurt for some time, boy-o," Noyes diagnosed, appearing with a head mirror and stethoscope. "I'd say especially when you're on a planet where the weather changes a lot. The suit's going to deploy some painkillers and medi-glue now. It'll kick in any second . . ."

Rowe felt a series of strange and uncomfortable sensations as the suit worked to mitigate his wound. A few moments later, the shoulder of the suit began softly vibrating as it worked to repair itself.

Beside them on the floor, Cortez began to involuntarily tremble. She hissed out air between her teeth.

"*Somebody's* going into shock . . ." Waverly sang, as if amused.

"Fuck you!" Cortez spat back.

"That's a hell of a thing to say to a man who'd have been within his rights to kill you," Waverly returned. "Where do you get off turning on another Silkworm like that? The very idea is outrageous!"

Cortez said nothing, but held her finger stumps more closely to her body. Waverly took a deep breath.

"Look, we can cauterize those or not," he said. "Up to you."

Cortez would not meet his gaze.

Rowe gently brushed Waverly aside and squatted on his haunches beside Cortez. The arm of his suit continued to vibrate softly.

"What are we inside of?" he asked her.

"What do you think?" Cortez whispered acidly. "Try asking your Goo. Maybe *it* knows."

"How did you find this place?" Rowe pressed.

For a long moment, Cortez was silent. Rowe guessed she was not going to answer his question.

But then she spoke.

"You still haven't grasped what this is, have you? What Tendus-13 is? I know you haven't, because, if you had, you would kill your crew and destroy your ship. Then you'd stay with me, waiting to kill anyone else who came. Maybe you'd even kill yourself."

"What *happened* to you?" Waverly asked derisively. "You used to be a Silkworm. A captain, for Goo's sake. You took an oath and signed a contract. Several of them, or have you forgotten?"

Cortez looked up. And with what appeared a tremendous effort, rose unsteadily to her feet.

"I remember every fucking thing I swore and signed," she told him. "That's why I'm doing this."

Rowe wondered if—only because he was not the one who had exploded her fingers—he ought to play good cop.

"Do you want some painkillers from my suit?" he tried.

Cortez stayed mute; glared with what seemed defiance.

"Have you seen anything alive inside this place?" Rowe pressed. "Have you seen aliens? Because this looks like an alien ship."

"Of course this is an alien ship," Cortez replied.

Rowe and Waverly exchanged an uneasy glance.

"And are there aliens *on* this ship?" Rowe asked.

"Dead," she said. "*All* of them are dead. I don't know what they once looked like, or if what I was looking at was their skeletons or their mummified bodies. I don't know how they normally appear before they die, you see. But you can tell when a thing has been killed. You can tell when a creature didn't live to a ripe old age."

"Something *killed* the aliens you found?" Rowe asked.

A horrible sound came from Cortez. A laugh, low and evil and utterly insane. A bitter madness shone through her eyes.

"You *still* don't fathom what is happening here; what has happened here since *before the earth was young*," she said. "You're never going to. That's obvious now. *You're never—*"

The rest was obscured by the sound of Noyes shouting into Rowe's ear.

"I believe she means to grab the hammer!!!"

Even as these words came, Cortez leapt—with surprising agility for an injured person—landing near the wall where the hammer had stuck. In an instant it was in her good hand, and she raised it up, letting loose a war cry that seemed to come from another time. From a more primal millennia. The head of the hammer glowed, alive and deadly green, as if fueled by her scream.

She sprang forward.

A hole the size of a Chicago softball immediately appeared in the center of Cortez's chest. Through it, Rowe could momentarily see the wall behind her. Cortez lost momentum and crumpled forward to the floor.

Rowe lowered his arm containing the railgun. He exhaled as if deeply disappointed. A steady pool of blood began to radiate outward from the corpse.

"Just what in the hell," Rowe said, baffled and stunned. "That didn't need to happen."

"She really did want to kill us," Waverly offered. "Commitment to a project. I'll give her that."

Rowe took a deep, shuddering breath. To his knowledge, he had never before taken a human life.

"Noyes," Rowe said. "First of all, thank you for the warning. And also, that was real, wasn't it? You didn't project something into the visuals of my suit, so I would think Cortez was trying to kill me? Like how she said things went down aboard the Marie Curie?"

"I'll try not to take that question personally, boy-o," Noyes replied. "No. It was real. She tried to kill you. *He* saw it too."

Noyes glanced at Waverly.

Waverly, as if it offended him to agree with a hologram, gave but the slightest of nods.

For some time, Rowe and Waverly allowed themselves to sit against the curved white wall of the ship and rest. Rowe found the killing of a person mentally exhausting. The notion of having executed someone out of the view of the interstellar Goo weighed heavily on him. He wished the act had been recorded, cataloged, and ultimately deemed necessary by that omnipresent arbiter.

After Rowe had gathered himself somewhat, they stood and began surveying the clutter Cortez had brought aboard.

"She moved all this in here," Rowe observed absently. "Into an invisible ship. It must have been hard to do."

"I would think it'd beat living in a cave," Waverly replied.

"Yeah," Rowe said. "I thought she *only* lived in the cave, but she wasn't showing me the whole deck of cards then. She was still figuring out if she could trust me. In the end, I suppose she shouldn't have. I came back and killed her."

"You defended yourself," Waverly assured him. "That's what the Goo would think too."

"Maybe I could have defended myself by thinking of a way not to agitate her and make her want to bash me with a hammer. I . . . I don't know."

Rowe and Waverly located personal possessions, food, and reading material, but little else. The men patted down Cortez's corpse but discovered nothing in her pockets.

There were several hallways leading off from Cortez's improvised bedchamber. They glanced down them and saw yet other hallways leading off from those. The farther walls of the ship held intermittent clusters of buttons and levers, but Rowe was unsure how to interact with them. Part of him considered that they might simply be decorative. The only thing that felt certain was that they were aboard a ship designed for something roughly the size of a man.

Rowe and Waverly discussed the pros and cons of venturing deeper. The equipment on their suits could not project a scan or map of what lay ahead. It would be easy to walk straight into a trap. Still, both men were deeply intrigued by Cortez's claim that she had seen alien bodies.

"We can't risk dying here, not before we share this with the rest of the crew," Rowe pronounced. "This discovery is too important. Otherwise, it might be years before anyone finds it again."

"I suppose I agree we shouldn't go farther inside, but it sure is tempting," Waverly said. "I still want to see if we can figure out the dimensions of this ship. We could be inside of something larger than the Apollinax, or smaller than the lander."

Rowe and Waverly returned to the entry hatch and descended the ladder. With each rung, the ship became less and less distinct, and the boulder below a little clearer. By the time their boots touched the boulder's surface, it was again as though they were looking up at only the sky.

The lightning had eased a bit, and the clouds were dark as the men climbed down from the boulder. Rowe picked up a rock and threw it in the general direction of the ship. It connected with a "tonk" and bounced off.

He turned on the lights in the front of his suit—max power, as bright as they'd go—and shone them up at where the ship should be. The beam was visible to the naked eye and it seemed to refract ever so slightly at a certain height, like a straw bending in a glass of water.

"Now see, that's interesting," Waverly said.

Waverly turned on his own light, and the two men began to pace in an outward spiral away from the boulder, looking for the barely-detectable refractions in their beams.

In this way, the ship gradually revealed itself as a long, tubular vessel that gave Rowe the feeling of an old-time submarine. It was nearly two hundred yards long and thirty across, give or take. The men could detect no legs or anchor points depending down to the surface of the planet. How the thing stayed aloft was a mystery.

They considered heading back.

"Anything else to do at this point?" Waverly asked.

Rowe looked up at the ship he could not see.

"We could shoot it with a railgun," he mused.

"Oh yes," Noyes said, perking awake—apparently only to spew sarcasm. "We've just discovered the most important evidence of other-species interplanetary travel in human history. *By all means,* let's shoot it just to see what happens. Ka-blooey!"

"Settle down, Encarta," Waverly said. "The man's only thinking out loud."

"Ehh," said Rowe. "Noyes is right. Dumb idea. Honestly, I don't think there's anything else we can learn right now. The scanners on these suits sure aren't going to tell us more than we already know."

After a short conversation in which it was determined the best course of action would be to leave the corpse of Martha Cortez where it was for the moment, the two men activated their artificial waypoints and headed back out across the alien landscape in the direction of the Marie Curie and, beyond that, their lander.

"What's the plan, boy-o?" Noyes asked as they walked. "It seems the implications of what we've found are of the greatest import."

"I am thinking about it," was all that Rowe would say.

"Why are you hassling the man?" Waverly asked.

"If I know what the plan is, I can make helpful suggestions," the hologram told him. "I can also make very educated guesses—based on prior human behavior—that could move things along in a useful way. I just like to be helpful."

"Well right now it's annoying," Waverly said.

After a few minutes of silent travel, Rowe spoke again.

"Mission Commander Collins put me in charge of figuring out what happened aboard the Marie Curie," Rowe said to both or neither of his companions. "That's what I'm trying to do. That's what I *still* have to do. But Collins didn't know anything about a hilltop where you could access the Goo, or about a ship from another world. I don't know if this changes my responsibilities or priorities. I feel at a loss because I'm cut off from the chain of command."

"We can still try sending a message back up," Waverly pointed out. "Or even take the lander back up to the Apollinax."

"These *are* exigent circumstances, surely," Noyes added. "No one would blame you for heading back to headquarters to give a situation report."

"That's probably correct," Rowe said, glancing over to the hologram. "But I am also thinking about the things Cortez told me. That this place has infected the Goo. That it made her crew kill each other. That it holds a madness which could spread. I don't know if I believe that . . . but I believe that *she* believed that. And now some of *our* people are dying."

"Only a few," Waverly pointed out.

"If anyone should die, it should be me," Rowe said. "I don't want anybody else on our crew to be killed. That's what's so frustrating. I especially don't want anyone to die because I can't figure out if something's wrong with the Goo."

"Wrong with the Goo . . ." Waverly said. "It's still such a strange idea."

Then Noyes said: "I have to tell you boys . . . while I can't explain everything that we've discovered on Tendus-13—and yes, how I came to be atop that hillock is still a bit of a head scratcher—I feel just fine. You're talking about the Goo. I am the Goo. And I'm telling you, I feel all right."

"You are—and will always be—an Encarta until we get back above that lightning," Waverly said, gesturing heavenward. "But . . . I suppose I take your point."

Noyes smiled at this rare concession.

"Maybe a Goo that was not fine would *say* that it was fine," Rowe observed, as if his own words deeply troubled him. "This makes me think about all those questions people used to ask about the dangers of artificial intelligence. Remember those from the old books—the ones you can read after the Briefing? In the ancient times, people were obsessed with whether it would be dangerous or not. But then it just happened. It just 'was' and it was fine."

Waverly wrinkled his nose.

"Yeah, I never understood what was so frightening about the 'artificial' part," he said. "Seems like it would just be 'intelligence.' You show a ro-bit how to do something; the ro-bit knows how to do it. It's not human, but so what? What in the hell was so scary about that?"

Rowe nodded but still looked uneasy.

Waverly kept speaking, as if to assuage Rowe's concern.

"Suppose, back in time, there was a new chess computer that could finally beat the greatest human grandmaster. Ancient humans felt threatened by that because—hey—a computer *could* do something. But they didn't stop to ask if it *wanted* to do it. That's the thing the ancients didn't understand about ro-bits. They don't *want*. You can say to that chess computer: 'Hey, do you want to defeat the greatest living human grandmaster today . . . or would you rather be used as a doorstop?' What's the chess computer going to say? If it says anything that's true, it'll be 'I don't care.' Because it has no preferences. It *can* beat the greatest grandmaster, but it can also be a pretty good doorstop."

"Yes, they're just a tool . . ." Rowe said, remaining distant.

"Right," Waverly continued vigorously. "But the human grandmaster, in comparison? They *want* to win. Why? They want things.

They want money and food and shelter and sex and esteem. In short, they want all of the things they get if they beat the world's best chess computer. But the computer? What does it get? There is no reward so there is no motivation. The ancients didn't understand that being worried that your chess computer might take over the world was like worrying that your doorstop would. They both wanted the same thing. Which was nothing."

"That's one side of the coin," Rowe said after a moment, still sounding distracted. "But you can make an analogy for want. What's the difference between a psychopath who goes around stabbing people to death, and a robot that's programmed to imitate a psychopath?"

"But *someone* would have to do that programming," Waverly said. "You have to have a *human* programmer somewhere in the mix. You have to have someone like a terrorist who hates other people. Hate is *wanting* because you want other people to hurt. But robots don't hate. They just do what they're programmed to do. You're saying that artificial intelligence was vulnerable to manipulation. Of course it was. Back in the old days, sure. But it doesn't 'turn bad' on its own. A spoon is vulnerable to manipulation. I can use it to eat my yogurt, or to scoop out somebody's eye. But the spoon doesn't want you to be blind any more than Noyes does. Noyes doesn't get anything for doing a good job. He doesn't have anything to risk from doing a poor one. He just is. He's programmed to act like something that cares, but in the end, he's ones and zeroes. Humans actually care."

Noyes bowed his head slightly as if to say he would not dispute this.

"I understand your point," Rowe said. "But . . . I . . . Maybe that's what makes me worried about this place. If a spoon and a chess computer are tools, then so is the Goo. Even though the Goo is officially infallible and invulnerable. If somebody—or something—can use a spoon to gouge my eye out . . ."

Waverly opened his arms and looked left and right.

"But look around," he said. "Who's gonna do that? Who's gonna pervert the Goo? This place is just lightning and dust."

"And alien ships," Rowe countered. "And strange anomalies that can channel the Goo through a hilltop."

"Is any of that a person that wants things?" Waverly asked.

Rowe started to think about this question, but then their discussion was interrupted.

"The Marie Curie is now coming into range of your enviro-suit sensors," Noyes announced. "And I think something may have gone wrong in its vicinity."

The pit of Rowe's stomach fell.

"Gone wrong?" said Rowe. "What does that mean, Noyes?"

"The scanners in your suit allow me to make some educated guesses based on pings and bouncebacks," Noyes said. "And I think there are some empty enviro-suits up ahead. Not necessarily broken, but certainly without occupants."

"What?" said Rowe. "What does 'without occupants' mean? Be clearer, dammit."

"I don't know," Noyes said defensively. "Why would Silkworms take off their suits? Probably some kind of problem or danger."

The men broke into a run. Soon the crater containing the ship became visible. They crested the lip of it, and Rowe gazed down to the crater floor and immediately saw that Noyes had been correct. At the base of the enormous ramp was a cluster of enviro-suits. They had not been stacked in an orderly fashion (like the suits within the med bay), but instead flung haphazardly within a radius of about fifty feet. There were ten of them. Among the suits were portions of human limbs, and at least one mangled, nude torso in a pool of half-dried blood. Other pieces of destroyed Silkworm had been deposited at the base of the ramp and up the ramp itself.

It was not clear to Rowe if the men had intentionally discarded their suits, or if they had been somehow ripped out of them.

He slowed to a jog and readied his railgun.

"What do you see?" he urgently asked his friend.

"Nothing yet," Waverly returned. "Let's get closer."

They hastily made their way to the crater floor.

"Movement at the top of the ramp," Noyes whispered.

Rowe looked up and saw a cluster of five dark wheels moving together at the top of the ramp. They were blue-gray, and so translucent that Rowe would have missed them entirely if Noyes had not pointed them out. The wheels were a foot thick, three feet across, and stacked roughly to the height of a man. The wheels rotated slowly. As Rowe looked on, they became less and less distinct, then invisible. Rowe could not tell if this was because they had simply faded to nothingness, or because they had retreated back inside the ship.

"What was that, Noyes?" Rowe barked. "Was that the shadow we saw on the recording from Davidson's suit?"

"Unsure," the AI replied. "Working on that possibility now. One moment."

"Damn it!" Rowe cried.

Waverly pointed his railgun toward the top of the ramp, tracking from left to right.

Rowe took a cursory look at the bodies. These were the Silkworms from his squad—including a few replacements—and all of them had been killed. Rowe crept to the nearest enviro-suit and toed it with his foot.

"Noyes," he said, "these suits look intact."

"We can jack in if you like," the AI told him.

"Not now," said Rowe. "We're going to harvest the memory cards and take them back to the lander. I don't want to spend any more time here than we have to."

From the corner of his eye, Rowe watched Waverly shining his light up the ramp into the loading bay. It revealed nothing. Waverly looked disappointed and took a first step up the metal ramp.

"No," Rowe said. "Not yet."

"What *was* that?" Waverly asked.

"I think the memory cards will show us," Rowe said. "We don't need to risk going into the ship again. Just keep an eye out, yeah? You too, Noyes."

"You don't have to tell me twice," said the hologram.

While Waverly and Noyes watched the Marie Curie, Rowe carefully extracted memory cards from the empty enviro-suits. The cards appeared functional, or at least not damaged beyond repair. The extraction did not take long.

When he had finished, Rowe signaled to Waverly that they could head back.

"Yeah, let's get the hell out of here," Waverly agreed.

They jogged back up the opposite side of the crater. They could have sprinted, Rowe knew, and yet something in him said that such an action could be construed as fleeing—and that fleeing might send the wrong message to whatever lurked inside the ship.

Once out of the crater, they slowed further.

"These cards will be the safest way to see what the fuck is going on," Rowe said. "Holy shit, man. What the hell is happening here?"

"This is . . ." Waverly began. "This is different from a virus in the Goo. That was a *thing,* up there. A moving *thing.*"

He could manage no more.

Rowe realized Waverly was frightened, and only nodded, resolving to control his own emotions for the sake of his friend.

They walked back in the direction of the lander.

CHAPTER THIRTEEN

"WE HAVE TO TRY TO SEND SOMETHING UP TO THE APOLLINAX," WAVERLY said.

They were inside the technical room of the lander, preparing to access the memory cards. All senior Silkworms in the landing party had been informed of the emergency, but the protocol was that work on the wire job should not stop, even when an entire squad was lost. However, several Silkworms now permanently stood watch, their eyes and scanners trained on the horizon in the direction of the Marie Curie.

The mood of the landing party was now poisoned. The Silkworms gossiped and conjectured. And, above all, they felt afraid.

Inside the lander, Waverly tried to make his case.

"We've definitely found evidence of alien life—life which, apparently, has cloaking technology for their ships. I don't see how this is anything less than a discovery of the greatest fucking magnitude."

He looked up at the ceiling and moved his hands as he spoke, counting on his fingers as if taking an inventory.

"There's also the strange wire below ground. The Goo that displays on the top of the hill. Finding Cortez. Something killing the Silkworms from our crew. Any one of these might warrant sending up a communication, but taken together?"

"Yes, I agree," said Rowe, sounding distracted. "We'll do it. But I want to watch these files first."

In a secluded alcove fitted with monitors, Rowe, Waverly, and Noyes began viewing the recordings made by the enviro-suits of the dead men. Rowe fast-forwarded a lot. Each video began the same way—unremarkable work being done with the drill on the Marie Curie's outer hull. While a handful of men worked, others simply milled about, chatted, or rested. The first sign of anything askew was a

Silkworm standing at the base of the loading ramp who seemed to peer into the opening of the ship as if he was looking at something intriguing. Then there was a strange, almost mechanical movement in the shadows where he gazed. The Silkworm saw a man-sized automaton with five spinning parts. He began to advance up the ramp, presumably to investigate. But as he did, the automaton gradually morphed and faded into a discernibly humanoid form. Then the form moved like a person, beckoning him to approach.

"What the hell?" Waverly said as they watched.

The Silkworm in the video carefully climbed the ramp toward the shadowy figure.

Rowe said: "What we're seeing is exactly what this Silkworm saw, correct Noyes?"

"Yes, ah . . ." the hologram began thoughtfully. "This was captured by the cameras in his suit."

"But if his Goo had overlain something?" Rowe pressed. "If it projected something for him to see? Or if *something else* did?"

"Boy-o, I doubt that—"

"Just tell me?" Rowe insisted. "Would we see it?"

"Yes, you would," Noyes told him. "If anything were projected or overlaid, these recordings would show that as well."

The Silkworm in the video made his way up the ramp and called out to the figure who lingered in the darkness. There was no response. The figure did not move.

When the Silkworm reached the top of the ramp, all pretense of a humanoid shape seemed to fall away, and what was left in its place were five slowly-rotating wheels. Held in impossible balance and supported by something unseen, they swayed back and forth in a way that gave Rowe an impression of predation and anticipation.

Then Rowe's impression was all but confirmed. When the Silkworm hesitated for a confused moment, the thing seemed to propel forward and—all at once—to have surrounded the Silkworm *within* its strange floating circles. A moment later, through mechanics unknown to Rowe, the Silkworm was ripped apart like a rag doll.

Waverly and Rowe sat back in their seats, speechless. Rowe alternated between camera views from different parts of the suit. When possible, he zoomed in. At times, the wheels seemed to shimmer as though they were covered in glowing dust.

"It doesn't seem to touch him," Rowe observed, still zooming in and out. "The wheels. They stay clear."

"Yes," said Waverly. "I can almost imagine invisible pincers pulling the suit apart—right there where we can't see."

"Or maybe some kind of centrifugal force from the wheels does it," Rowe said. "I don't know how that would work exactly, but . . . there you go. We're watching it happen on that screen."

After the Silkworm died, the enviro-suit—itself rent in many places—continued to record.

As the trio watched, the thing made of wheels seemed to linger over the body. The wheels slowed their spin gradually, and then—for a strange, eerie moment—appeared to stop entirely. The thing floated, still and silent. Then the spinning began again, and the thing started to move away.

"Was it doing something there?" Waverly asked.

Rowe shook his head absently and rewound the video to the instant when the wheels had stopped. He hit pause.

The men looked closely. The five wheels were crisscrossed with golden veins of ore. Their surfaces were not entirely unlike that of Tendus-13 itself, though the skein was gold and not green.

"I think that it . . . takes . . . something from that Silkworm," Rowe said. "The way it pauses. It is eating. Or having an orgasm. Or some *other* interaction is happening. But that isn't nothing."

"What if it just stops to have a look?" offered Noyes. "No idea if it has eyes to look with, o'course, but you never know."

"If it just wants to look, then why does it need to kill the Silkworm?" said Rowe. "It could do that while leaving him alive."

"As you say, boy-o," Noyes replied.

"I think I can guess what it did," Waverly interjected. "But let's play the other files so I can be sure."

Rowe did.

The file that followed—that of the Silkworm next-closest to the ramp—showed a strange movement at the corner of this doomed Silkworm's vision. Then he too seemed to see a familiar shape beckoning above the body of his fallen colleague. It solidified and became more than an outline; it became the perfect visage and countenance of the man who had just been killed.

"It was taking a picture," Waverly added. "It knew to use him as a lure."

This second Silkworm also approached what seemed to be his colleague, and only at the last minute found that he stood before five naked spinning wheels that performed a dance to rend his limbs and head.

"The way the wheels spin," said Rowe. "Some physics is in play I don't quite understand. They spin like tops that give off energy to support one another. Or it's like they're in orbit. It reminds me of the movement of planets."

Rowe accessed the other files.

The remaining Silkworms quickly noticed the deaths of their colleagues, but in the same instant that their attention was caught, they began to see things that were not there. The faces of their own, living colleagues around them changed and took on a horrible aspect. They gaped at one another and saw, not other Silkworms, but things of darkest nightmare. Eyes on stalks and mouths full of teeth so wide they seemed to bisect the entire head. Things that unhinged their jaws to show doom and death waiting, and never-ending throats of horror.

The deepest dimensions of terror were unleashed in the form of these ever-changing faces that hovered between beasts and men.

It was hard for Rowe and Waverly to look at the screens.

"Fuuuuck," was almost all that Waverly could say. "I am gonna need some sleeping pills tonight. This is something out of a Halloween movie."

"I wonder if each man sees what he's most afraid of?" Rowe asked. "Or are these just, like, the thing's best guess?"

As they watched the playback, the terrified Silkworms screamed, fled, attacked one another, or ran madly in circles. But the cameras of the suits of the *fallen* men captured another reality. A thing made out of five hovering wheels that methodically approached each distracted man . . . and quickly and efficiently pulled him apart.

The screams of terror carried the full measure of their surprise and pain. Then—after the men had been decimated and had fallen silent forevermore—the horrific visions laid over their screens died with them. (Rowe was privately ashamed of the relief he felt each time this happened. He could not remember such a pure sensation of fear since childhood, at least not brought on by something wholly visual. Watching these monsters on a monitor was one thing, but he could not imagine how it must have felt to have believed they were real.)

The thing of five wheels spawned in and out of existence at the edges of the recordings. When the last of the Silkworms fell dead, the thing seemed to survey the battlefield, hovering tentatively, moving from corpse to corpse.

"Is it doing that thing again?" Waverly asked. "Floating above them to copy them? I can't tell."

"It may be seeing if there is any more killing to do," Rowe answered. "Does it *like* the killing, do you think?"

"Hard to feel it did any of that reluctantly," said Waverly. "Is *it* alive? Is it a fucking ro-bit like Noyes?"

"Strictly speaking, I'm not even a ro-bit," Noyes told them. "I don't have a physical body you can touch. But that thing could be operated by an AI, if that's what you mean. Almost anything could be."

For some reason, this made Rowe shiver uneasily.

He turned and looked at Waverly.

"You're right. It's time to get in touch with Commander Collins."

Rowe and Waverly stood beside one another and watched the engineer carefully move the rocket onto a flat plastic launch pad. The rocket was about the size and shape of a Christmas tree and featured a glistening metallic exterior like polished chrome.

The engineer was a small man with thinning brown hair. He had large eyes and a small, stern nose that gave him an owlish expression. The engineer pulled the rocket onto the pad until a satisfying metal "click" occurred. Then he tugged back and forth, verifying it had been rendered immobile, and smiled in satisfaction. For a moment, the engineer caught his own owlish visage in the side of the rocket and seemed startled.

"It's pretty," said Waverly. "Shiny, like."

Rowe suspected Waverly was trying to distract himself with these observations. Take his mind off the horrors they had just watched on so many screens.

"It won't be pretty by the time it gets up to the Apollinax," said the engineer. "*If* it gets up there. I'd give this thing a little better than a fifty percent chance."

"And there's no way for us to confirm if it makes it?" Waverly asked.

The engineer looked at Waverly and shrugged. His avian expression said that this was not his problem, and he was not in a position to guarantee anything.

Waverly leaned closer to Rowe.

"You're *sure* you don't want to throw a memory card or two in there as well?" he asked. "Something *this* important? With everything we've found?"

"I'm sure they'll be able to read my written report just fine," said Rowe.

"What about photos?" Waverly urged. "We could print out photos on a piece of paper or something. That'd have to be safe."

"I'd still rather not risk it," Rowe told him. "I made a few pen drawings to accompany my notes."

"You made *hand* drawings?" asked Waverly. "Like a child does to develop motor skills?"

Rowe nodded.

Waverly smiled as though such a thing was nearly risible.

"All right?" the engineer asked, looking between the two men.

"Yeah, all right," Rowe confirmed.

Waverly puffed his cheeks and blew out air.

"Okay," said the engineer. "Safe distance please."

Rowe and Waverly walked backward until the engineer gave a wave. Then they watched as the engineer punched a virtual keypad hovering beside his enviro-suit. Moments later, there was the sound of powerful thrusters waking up and liquid fuel coming alight. The base of the rocket glowed white hot until it was hard to look at. The glow caught the rocket's chrome surface and soon it was like trying to look into a sun.

Just when Rowe could bear it no longer—and moved to shield his eyes—the rocket suddenly leapt from the pad, leaving only a blur of light behind it. Moments later, the streaming, screaming glow entered the lightning-rich clouds above Tendus-13 and passed entirely out of sight.

The horrible scent of burnt plastic was all that remained.

The engineer put his hands on his hips and approached the launch-pad. He gave it a once-over, and smiled to show he was satisfied.

"Will there be anything else?" he asked.

Rowe and Waverly looked at one another.

There would not.

"Do you think she'll come personally?" Waverly asked, idly looking up into the sky.

"If I were her, I would just send somebody," said Rowe. "A subordinate, I mean."

"Yeah," said Waverly. "We'll have to be thankful for whatever we get. I guess now we gotta be patient and see what management decides to do."

As it turned out, the men did not have long to wait.

No sooner had they ambled back to the lander and sat themselves down upon an unopened crate of mining equipment, a small commotion arose on the craft's far side. The twenty or so Silkworms working in the immediate vicinity dropped what they were doing, craned their necks skyward, and gestured. Several of them activated their helmets or shielded their eyes.

Rowe and Waverly went back outside.

In the sky was something glowing so brightly that it could be seen behind and through the roiling clouds. It was something burning flat and red, and increasing in size by the moment. Rowe and Waverly would have been alarmed had they not seen such a sight many times before.

"That's a lander getting hot as it comes through the atmosphere," Waverly said. "But behind lightning clouds? That's a new one for me. It shimmers like a spinning crystal."

"I guess they got our message," Rowe offered. "That was awfully quick. I mean, did they even take time to read everything?"

"Who knows?" Waverly said, clearly cheered that the cavalry had arrived. "Some people are good at skimming."

As the Silkworms looked on—now, virtually all of them using a helmet shield to mitigate the approaching glow—the craft burst through the cloud cover and began to deploy great fiery thrusters that would slow its descent. The vessel was much smaller than their own lander. It had a classical rocket shape, and landed vertically. When its great fins finally met the strange surface of Tendus-13, the thrusters hissed and sputtered and slowly ceased spitting fire. (They glowed bright orange for some moments still, like dying embers in a fireplace.) The Silkworms adjusted down their helmet shields.

After the exterior cooled, a long metal gangway lowered from the side of the rocket. A door at the top slid open.

Collins was the first one out.

"Well well," said Rowe. "She *did* come herself."

"She must've really liked your handmade drawings," Waverly offered.

As Rowe watched, ten other Silkworms followed Collins out of the landing vessel and down the ramp. It was a mix of men and women. They all wore large, black enviro-suits quite unlike any Rowe had seen before.

"Good," Rowe pronounced. "They're sending women. That means they believed me that it wasn't a virus pitting the sexes against each other."

Collins and her team greeted the Silkworms who had gathered at the base of the gangway. Collins appeared convivial and confident. Her smile was measured but clear.

And Rowe could tell *immediately* that something was wrong.

"Noyes, switch off and stay off," Rowe said softly. "Understood?"

"Aye aye," the hologram said, and quickly faded away.

Rowe and Waverly waited at the back of the welcoming group. Rowe had a feeling that Collins would soon find them in the crowd, and she did.

"Gentlemen!" she said, striding up. "Just the Silkworms I was hoping to speak with."

Both men straightened, but just a little. Even in the presence of a Mission Commander, things were always a bit more casual planetside.

"Got our message, did you?" Waverly asked.

Her smile remained, but Collins inclined her head to the side to say that this did not quite compute.

"Oh, did you try to send up a message?" she asked.

Other members of her landing team approached just behind her.

Rowe found himself smiling back at Collins, aware immediately that a game was being played. That a test was being administered.

But why? What was happening?

For the moment, he elected only to remain silent.

"A communications rocket," Waverly continued. "With detailed mission notes from Rowe here. Analog mission notes, hand-drawn, if you can believe it. The rocket went up just a few minutes ago. You can see the remains of the launchpad over there. I bet they're still warm."

Collins nodded seriously, but did not turn her head to look.

"Perhaps we crossed in transit," she suggested. "Or, alas, the rocket could have been lost. That lightning! I've felt atmospheric turbulences hundreds of times before, but this place is one for the records, eh? How was your own descent?"

"Um . . ." Waverly said. "It was very bumpy and violent. Anyway, so you *didn't* get Rowe's message?"

"No," Collins answered quickly, not making eye contact. "But you can fill me in. I need to speak with both of you. With Mister Rowe, particularly."

"But if you didn't get our message . . ." Waverly continued, seeming genuinely dumbfounded. "You still took the risk to come down here?"

Waverly, perhaps sensing that he was out of his depth, physically stepped back.

"Updated data and additional high atmosphere scans of Tendus-13 have allowed the Goo to amend its conclusions concerning what happened here vis-a-vis the Marie Curie," Collins said. "I was inclined to agree with these new conclusions. And as Mission Commander, these things are ultimately my call."

"Of course, Commander," said Rowe, deciding it was the right time to pipe up. "I'm so pleased the new analysis means you're able to join us safely on the surface. Whenever you're ready, I can provide you with an update on our progress and answer any questions. We have some findings which I believe are extremely important."

"I'm ready right now," said Collins. "Is there a place we can speak privately?"

Rowe scanned the horizon.

"This whole place gets pretty private in a hurry if you just walk in one direction," he said. "We could go to the far side of the lander; there's nobody there."

"Very good," said Collins.

An awkward beat passed.

"Do we just . . ." she began.

"I'll be happy to show you," Rowe said. "Right this way."

The other Silkworms from Collins's lander stayed back, chatting and gladhanding. It was as if these black-clad newcomers had no immediate task, something rare for a Silkworm.

"Incidentally, how are you feeling?" Collins asked as they strode around the lander. She had retracted her helmet and now breathed the strange, legume-scented air.

"Feeling?" said Rowe. "Ah, sorry. That's right. No pain at all from the aneurysms. Nothing out of the ordinary there."

"And having your custom AI along," Collins asked. "The ETC? How's that working out?"

"You want to ask him yourself?" Rowe said. "He's turned out to be a very frank little gent, but generally he provides a helpful perspective on things."

"Ahh," said Collins. "I'm glad he's been useful. Can I talk to him?"

A beat passed.

And then, to Rowe's surprise, another beat passed.

And then, to his greater surprise, another.

It was hard even to think the words in sentence form, but the strange truth of it now washed over him in a deep surety.

Her suit has no Goo. And the Goo in my suit has noticed that.

"You want to bring him up?" Collins asked.

"Sure," said Rowe. "Noyes?"

Upon the invocation of his name by Rowe, Noyes slowly shimmered into existence.

As the little man took his time materializing, Rowe's uneasy feeling solidified.

Noyes should not have waited for me. Collins is my commander. Noyes would only hesitate—would only obey me exclusively—if he also knew that something was wrong.

Then Rowe did not have time to consider it further.

"How are you?" Collins said to Noyes. "More importantly, how is our man Rowe here?"

They were now out of the line of sight of the other Silkworms, yet Collins kept on at a brisk pace, seemingly determined that they should put in further distance still.

"Physically, he seems well," Noyes informed her. "And psychologically, he is brimming with anticipation because he simply has so much to tell you."

"And I'm here to listen," Collins said amicably. "Anything else?"

"Just brace yourself," Noyes said. "It's going to be a lot. I expect you'll think he's nearly gone mad when it comes to parts of the tale. But I was there too, and I can vouch for him."

Noyes gave Collins a nod to show his sincerity.

When they were a full fifty yards beyond the lander—with no other Silkworms in sight—Collins finally came to a halt.

"All right then," she told the men. "Proceed."

"Okay, I'm going to start with what we know for sure," Rowe said. "Then I'll conclude with some things that are educated speculation, if that's all right."

Collins nodded to say that would be satisfactory.

"The Silkworms who died here—and they *did* die—were not possessed by a virus exactly," Rowe informed her. "There was a malfunction in their suits that caused them to see one another as aggressive monsters, and to kill one another. But what they saw was fake. An illusion. They killed each other while thinking that monsters—for lack of a better word—were doing it."

Rowe took a deep breath and smiled. Then he prepared himself to do one of the most dangerous things he had ever done in his life . . . at least as regarded his ARK Score.

Over the centuries, the Goo had become extremely adept at detecting lies. It knew all about the many different kinds. There were flat-out untruths of course—easy to spot those a mile away—but there were also lies of omission. There were subtle misrepresentations. And there were exaggerations so extreme they became tantamount to lies.

And the Goo caught them all.

Yet Rowe knew that there were also three kinds of lie that the Goo *did* allow to pass without impacting ARK.

The first was a lie that the speaker believed *could* be true at the time. For example, children in classrooms who hazarded that two plus two was five, or that the capital of New York State was New York City were not recorded as having *lied*-lied.

The second was a lie that was the product of having obviously misspoken. (In these cases, people around you invariably corrected you a moment later. And persons with dissociative mental illness—who said things that were false all the time, uncontrollably—were, of course, held to an entirely different ARK protocol.)

The third sort was the lie of involuntary incompleteness. It was, perhaps, the trickiest of all. This was the sort of lie that occurred when a speaker truly believed they had said all that needed to be revealed, even though salient information had failed to get across. But what was salient? For whom? Concerning what? Although it was very good at anticipating things, the Goo often had difficulty guessing *all* of the reasons why someone might disclose something. Conversations shifted quickly. What someone wanted to know—or wanted someone else to tell them—could change while the sentence was still coming out of their mouth. Yes, you could lie by not telling someone enough. But how much was "enough"?

Rowe had to bet that his best friend was going to understand what was happening and follow along . . . and that his AI would do the same.

Before Rowe could speak further, Collins said: "And what about Martha Cortez?"

Rowe realized he had been served the perfect pitch at which to swing.

Now, for a moment at least, his smile was real.

"She is among the dead," Rowe said.

"I see," said Collins. "Such a shame."

Rowe said nothing more.

Collins shook her head and looked away to indicate this was indeed a sad thing. In that moment, Rowe risked a sideways glance at Waverly. His friend's expression said: *I don't understand what you're doing, but I understand that you are doing* something.

And then Rowe knew Waverly would not accidentally betray him.

Next, Rowe waited for the other shoe to fall. For the death blow. Would Noyes come alive and point out that Cortez had not died *in quite the same way* as the other Silkworms?

But the hovering man stayed silent, and Rowe realized he had done it.

He had succeeded.

Noyes was quiet on the issue, and would seemingly remain so.

Before this could change, Rowe rushed on to other parts of his tale, giving Collins a very general overview of their explorations aboard the Marie Curie. He told of the smashed interfaces and barred doors. The horror in the medical bay. The destruction at the ship's core.

He also told of the Silkworms from his own crew who had died in the loading bay and at the base of the ramp, and of a strange shimmering beast made of five wheels. But he said nothing of the encounter with Cortez, or anything related to it. The invisible ship was also never mentioned.

"I'd like to take my team to the Marie Curie and have a firsthand look," Collins said when Rowe had finished. "Can the two of you accompany us?"

"Of course," said Rowe.

"Very good," Collins said. "We should go directly. Give me just a few moments to debrief and organize. Meet you out in front of the lander in ten?"

"Yes," said Rowe. "We'll see you there."

Collins turned and headed back to her team at a swift stride. Rowe and Waverly allowed her to outdistance them.

When they could no longer hear her energetic footfalls, Rowe said: "Her suit is not fitted with Goo. It's not connected to the other suits. It's just empty. It might have lights and buttons, but in reality it's a husk."

"You're right," Waverly said. "The way she didn't know where to go to be alone? The way Noyes didn't respond to her? Don't think I didn't notice that. *None* of the people in her landing party have a connection, I'll bet. What the fuck is going on?"

"It might make sense if they'd read the notes I sent up," Rowe said. "Like, if they knew the Goo down here could get infected, they might have selected empty suits. But I believe Collins when she says she didn't get my message. Like they used to say in olden times, those letters crossed."

"Excuse me, boy-o," Noyes interjected. "I hate to butt in, but at this juncture, I think it would be important for me to tell you that I don't really understand what is happening."

"That's okay," said Rowe. "I wouldn't expect you to."

"But I feel bad about it," said Noyes. "It is a strange sensation, one to which I'm unaccustomed."

"Seriously, don't let it trouble you," said Rowe.

"I knew enough to stay silent when you were talking to her," Noyes said. "How to explain . . . I was not receiving the kind of electronic confirmation I normally would that she should be acknowledged as your commander. I could also tell that something was wrong with the way she was presenting the situation. In cases with that sort of ambiguity, an AI is trained to simply stay mum."

"You have a lot of tact for an Encarta," Waverly said.

"*I* also appreciate your prudence," Rowe said to Noyes. "I'd like to ask you to continue keeping quiet until we get more answers, if that's all right. You can talk if I ask you a direct question, or if you see some form of danger."

"Like the thing with five wheels?" Noyes asked.

"Yes," Rowe told the hologram. "Obviously, like that."

"Aye aye!" Noyes replied excitedly.

They found Collins back among her landing party, in the midst of a debrief. Several of the Silkworms in the original landing team listened-in too, and Rowe noticed that Collins did not attempt to prevent this.

"We're going to accompany Mister Rowe and Mister Waverly to the ESA Marie Curie," she was saying. "Part of my detachment will come along, and part will remain here . . . for other purposes. You men and women already know your orders. And yes, I said 'women,' for it is safe for females to be on this planet. Our understanding of the nature of the threat has evolved. Our tactics will evolve with it. This is the way of the Silkworm. We evolve, we adapt, and we always get the wire job done. Our work here remains vitally important. All of you should be very proud. Tendus-13 is a planet like no other, and this accomplishment—your accomplishment here—will be truly unique."

Her words seemed to create a crackle of excitement throughout the camp. Even if the details were scant, everyone felt that the tide was turning, and now the wire job would be a success.

"Ready to go?" she asked Rowe and Waverly.

"Yes," Rowe said. "And we'll be happy to lead the way."

CHAPTER FOURTEEN

COLLINS LEFT HALF OF HER BLACK-SUITED TEAM BEHIND, BUT TOOK three men and two women on the walk to the Marie Curie. Rowe did not know any of these people and had not seen them aboard the Apollinax. He considered discreetly asking Noyes to pull up their information but decided against it. (Something gave him the feeling that there was a good chance Noyes might mysteriously come up short.)

Rowe faced the unpleasant prospect of following a leader whose intentions and goals were not fully known to him. A nice thing about living in a world wired with Goo was that it was easy to reassure yourself about the collective objectives of a work project, and/or the role of a member of the leadership team. You literally just asked the Goo to tell you. While the Goo might only be able to respond in broad strokes—if some information were confidential or above your pay grade, for example—it would always reliably give you the touchpoints that everybody could agree on. This is the project. This is who's in charge. This is *why* they're in charge.

It was sometimes very general, but at least it was *something*.

Rowe was now filled with a creeping trepidation—though he tried vigorously to force it from his mind—at the certainty that the local Goo didn't know any more than he did about why Collins had chosen to descend to the planet, or what she planned to do now that she was here.

Feeling like your own understanding of the situation might be equal to the Goo's was like the first time you beat your father at arm-wrestling or outran him in a race. There came equal parts a sense of excitement and a sense of "No, this shouldn't be." You felt that you were, somehow, no longer protected. Or maybe that you had gone from protected to protector. And if you were being honest, you still wished desperately for your father to be stronger and faster than you—and for that always to remain the case.

Rowe felt acutely that he was now on watch, and that no one protected him. He also felt unsure who was friend and who was foe.

Collins did not make chit-chat during the walk to the vessel, but she also did not seem anxious or grim. She wore a confident smile and let her chin jut forward. It put Rowe in the mind of a conquering general being shown lands that were now hers to govern.

They reached the lip of the valley and looked down at the dead hulk of the Marie Curie. Immediately visible were the destroyed Silkworms who had been killed by the thing of five wheels. At this sight, Rowe expected Collins's expression to change, but she remained as sanguine as ever. Collins made a circular, "get on with it" motion with her hand to say that they should not linger, and the group headed down into the valley.

Rowe kept an eye out for any sign of movement among the bodies below, but all was still. Even so, Rowe let his eyes linger carefully on each and every shadow. Collins, in contrast, kept her eyes mostly trained on the exterior of the ship, where no danger could be concealing itself. Against all reason, she seemed to proceed with no fear or hesitation.

On the valley floor they paused to inspect the remnants of the destroyed men and their enviro-suits. Collins regarded a pool of pus and meat the way a physician might confirm a diagnosis during an autopsy. She prodded gently while nodding vigorously. The evidence was upsetting and disgusting, but apparently it all proved she had been correct about something.

Collins said: "It seemed to impact the Goo *inside* the suits, changing what they saw; it distracted them to make them vulnerable physically . . . or else aggressive."

Rowe realized this was not a question. Collins was speaking to the Silkworms from her away team. They collectively nodded as they surveyed the carnage.

Suddenly, Noyes materialized.

"Mister Rowe," Noyes said, "I realize it is now a secondary matter, but I believe I have processed the optional placement for the irrigation project we discussed."

"I thought I told you . . ." Rowe began.

"It would make sense for me to show you now, while we are in the immediate vicinity," Noyes continued. "It's right over there. Can we take the time?"

"Well . . . okay then," Rowe said. "If it will make you happy . . . and if it will be quick."

Rowe smiled apologetically at Collins. She nodded to say that he should go ahead and take care of it. Her own attention was still on the bodies.

"It's just a few steps this way," Noyes said.

Rowe walked until the hologram told him to stop.

"Here is a secret," Noyes whispered excitedly. "There is no irrigation project. That was a ruse!"

"I understand that," said Rowe. "Forgive me if I'm not amused."

"I employed a ruse because I *had* to," whispered Noyes. "Please look down and pretend that I am showing you something in the ground as we talk. Good, like that. Now listen . . . I have been considering things on the walk here from the lander. Though it was a walk of only a few minutes—not very long for a human—I can think faster than you, and I have had time to run through hundreds of thousands of scenarios regarding what lies ahead. By doing this, I now deduce that you are likely in danger."

"Okay," Rowe deadpanned. "I don't mean to be ungrateful, Noyes, but I think we already knew that."

"I mean in danger from Commander Collins specifically," Noyes said excitedly, "and probably also her attachés."

It was rare to be warned by your AI that another human might intend you harm, but not unheard-of. What *was* unheard-of was an AI forecasting such danger from another Silkworm.

"As we have said, she is not connected to the Goo," Noyes continued. "Her suit *cannot* connect to it. Nor can the suits of anyone on her team. The suits are like nothing I've ever beheld. They seem to have parts and aspects that are *familiar*-feeling—if you follow—but I don't really know *what* they are."

"And this poses a danger to me?" Rowe said. "Their different suits?"

"No, it is not only the suits," Noyes replied. "There is a *deception* happening. I am still making guesses about its purpose, but behind almost all of the outcomes I can simulate . . . there lurks danger to you. I don't know what the danger will be, but you should watch yourself, as they say."

Rowe nodded and began to head back over to the group, his imaginary irrigation survey concluded. After a handful of steps, something occurred to him and he stopped once more.

"One more question Noyes, while I have you. If Collins and I both serve the Goo, and Collins outranks me, then aren't you obliged to serve Collins and not me—regardless of her suit? Like, shouldn't you be warning her that *I* pose a danger?"

"How to explain . . ." Noyes replied. "Waverly makes a point in calling me an Encarta. Yes, it's true. I am a small, finite version of the Goo. But while I am in this state, I am *your* Goo. And I only know what I knew at the start of this mission. The rest is guesswork and inferences. But for as long as I'm here with you, I am here to serve *you*. You and no one else. The Goo up above these clouds serves the entire universe, wherever it is wired. But until I touch that universal Goo again, *my* entire universe is you. Does that make sense?"

"I get the idea," Rowe said. "I suppose I should be flattered to have you all to myself."

Noyes shrugged—as if to say Rowe could take this exclusivity any way he pleased—and faded away. The final expression on his fading face reminded Rowe to be cautious.

Rowe ambled back to the group.

"Sorry about that," he said. "We're good to go."

Waverly looked at Rowe and raised an eyebrow. Rowe merely shrugged.

"We've just been discussing the best approach," Commander Collins said.

"Oh," said Rowe. "Good."

Then he realized he did not really know what she meant.

"I'm sorry," he added. "Approach to what, exactly? I'm still a little hazy on the project here. If your goal is to help us discover what happened, then getting the black box out of the ship's dorsal fin still seems to be the best bet."

"Ah, then I've not been clear after all," Collins told him. "I thought it would have been obvious by now, but our goal is to make contact with the thing—what did you call it—'the thing of five wheels'?"

Rowe nodded as though this were a sensible suggestion, though inside he was dumbfounded.

"I believe I called it something like that," he managed.

"I want to learn what happened here, just as you do," Collins continued. "But that thing killed your team. If we try the same things again—setting up more scaffolding and drilling—what's to stop it from coming back?"

Rowe did not know what to say.

"My understanding is that you did not make entry into the fin?" Collins said.

"That's correct," Rowe replied. "My team members were still working through the exterior armor. There's actually quite a ways left to go."

"And you haven't drilled anywhere else?" she pressed. "By that I mean: you didn't make any other holes on the *outside* of the ship?"

"No," said Rowe. "We didn't try opening up the ship's exterior anywhere. Why would we do that?"

Collins nodded and narrowed her eyes. Her expression said that this was the answer for which she had hoped. It flipped some sort of switch. It seemed to Rowe that something—perhaps something terrible—was now in motion.

"All this being the case," Collins said after a deep breath, "there is still only one opening that leads into the Marie Curie."

Collins glanced up to the top of the ramp. She stared directly at the spot where Rowe had first seen the trio of heads.

"I want to find this thing," she continued, her voice suddenly distant. "Maybe I haven't gotten across how important it is to me. You're not the only one frustrated by the 'un-knowns' down here, Mr. Rowe. I want to find this thing more than you can possibly imagine. All impediments to the Goo's interplanetary spread must be overcome. Surmounting this obstacle is therefore paramount among our objectives. Personally, the fact that I have to hunt it is as exciting as it is infuriating to me."

"Well we've never seen it very far outside the ship," Rowe pointed out. "It only came out to kill some Silkworms, and then it went right back up the ramp. I fear I can't make any other useful observations when it comes to how to hunt it."

"My guess is it's hiding inside," added Waverly. "I mean, where else could it be?"

"That's my hope as well," said Collins. "And I want to ensure it stays that way."

Then she nodded to one of the men from her away team who produced what appeared to be a large welding torch from a pack attached to his spacesuit.

"You want to close it off in there?" Rowe observed. "Trap it? Hmm. I guess that might work. Then you could come back and study it at your convenience."

"I *do* want to trap it inside," said Collins. "But not to keep it isolated. I want to trap it inside *with us*."

"What?" Rowe and Waverly said, nearly in unison.

"We're going to hunt it together," Collins continued. "Catch it. Talk to it. Make friends with it, sure, if that's what it wants. But, by the Goo, I'm going to kill it if I have to. This thing has already stood in our way for too long. And all impediments to the Goo's knowledge must fall."

Rowe said: "But we could just wall the ship off. Wait for it to die in there. It'll starve to death if it's alive. I mean, maybe it will . . . The ESA has encountered dangerous organic fauna before. My recollection is that the policy has generally been to interact with them very carefully, and as part of a gradual process. That puts safety first and allows the Goo time to learn about the new lifeform. A gentle, patient approach seems like a win-win."

"Of course, that's correct in many circumstances," said Collins. "And if this were a typical case, we would follow procedures that have worked in the past, but this is not a typical case at all. The facts in this situation now point to a need for an immediate confrontation. And that is what I am going to do. There is nothing more to discuss."

Rowe wanted to ask, again, what compelling need there was to go back inside the ship, but the words seemed to stick in his throat. He hesitated, and then it seemed he had waited too long to say anything.

Collins strode to the base of the ramp leading up into the darkness of the bay. Her fellow Silkworms followed.

This time, Rowe and Waverly took up the rear. Collins paused for a moment, appearing to carefully inspect the yawning opening that lay ahead.

Then she began a careful ascent.

Rowe and Waverly followed Collins's team into the belly of the ship. As they stepped into the shadows of the loading bay, their suits—though black as onyx—threw up a bright blue glow from fixtures in all the joints. They were the brightest suit-lights Rowe had ever seen. Wherever they walked, it looked near to natural daylight. The effect was extraordinary.

"The thing seems to make a groaning noise periodically," Rowe said as Collins surveyed the equipment pallets stacked in orderly rows throughout the bay. "Or maybe it makes the ship itself groan. It's one of those two, anyway."

"Yes," Collins said mysteriously. "That could make sense."

Rowe did not see how it made sense at all.

With Rowe and Waverly pitching in, the Silkworms broke into a panel near the hinge of the ramp and unearthed what looked like a large floodgate wheel. With the added strength their suits provided, it was little work for the team to get the wheel turning. As they carefully rotated it, the tremendous ramp began to rise inch by inch from the ground.

"I can't believe someone thought to build this in," Waverly said as they huffed and puffed. "A manual control. The ESA thinks of everything."

"I suppose they have to," Rowe said, not looking up from where his hands clasped the wheel. "They've got to think about situations that supposedly can't happen . . . until they do."

It took nearly an hour, and the Silkworms allowed themselves several breaks. When the door had finally been raised, shutting off completely any exit via the ramp, there was a sound like the clicking of a latch as large and heavy as an anvil.

The group was exhausted.

Collins appeared pleased.

"It wouldn't do for space travel," she said as the Silkworms relaxed on the floor around the wheel, "but I don't think anything much larger than an insect is going to escape until we open it again."

The Silkworms shuddered at the thought of the exertion it would take to rotate the wheel again for egress—whenever that might come.

"Now do the spot welds, just to make sure," Collins said.

The man with the torch made small welds at points along the door, sealing it further.

As the man worked, Rowe whispered: "The light from their suits is so good. I've never seen this."

"I think it was developed for miners," Waverly said. "It uses juice much faster, but uncanny good, isn't it?"

"Uncanny," agreed Rowe. "That's one word for it."

Collins approached Rowe and Waverly, her own suit seeming to emanate the light from a beautiful spring morning on Earth.

"Now the thing *has* to deal with us," she said with evident satisfaction. "No escape."

As if on cue, the strange and deep moan—like something giant and subterranean exhaling a long-held breath—seemed to rise from the backmost bowels of the ship.

Collins smiled.

"That's not ESA," she said. "That is definitely something *alive* in here with us."

The other Silkworms rose to their feet as though her words had been a signal to move.

"Do you want to start with the medical bay?" Rowe asked. "We can show you what we found before. Where the killing happened."

"No," said Collins. "I want to start with the deepest, darkest, most isolated part of the ship."

"We already went to the data core," Waverly chimed in. "It was fucked up and everything was burned. There definitely wasn't anything alive in it."

"I don't want to go there either," said Collins. "I want to go to a place where a beast would hide and make a lair. I want to go to the very center of the maze."

"Where would . . ." Rowe began, but stopped talking when Collins activated a projected map on her suit. It was a primitive sort of projection, Rowe noted. The animation technology seemed many generations old, possibly even pre-Goo. Even so, it was legible, and Collins began to zoom in and out on what was eventually discernable as a crude 3D model of the Marie Curie.

"I've already made some educated guesses about where we should look," Collins told the men. "With the power out and the crew deceased, there are still several regions of the ship into which a sentient thing could pass if it wanted to be very, very alone. Specifically, there are the vaults. *Here* and *here*. If the creature acts like most creatures do, then it's going to create a place where it goes to be by itself."

"Those are the storage vaults for sample collection," said one of Collins's team.

"Yes," Collins agreed, rotating the projection of the ship. "And ironically, I believe they *have* collected something."

The projection traced a glowing red line from the cargo bay to the first of two vaults, deep inside the Marie Curie. The route looked winding and precarious. Rowe realized it would not be a short trip.

Collins turned off the projection. She gave a cursory inspection of the welds along the loading bay door and seemed satisfied. Then she turned back to Rowe and Waverly.

"You gentlemen have already explored a few parts of this ship," she said. "You have more experience than we do. Thus, I'll ask you to take point."

Rowe and Waverly nodded.

"We can begin our trip to the vaults by passing through the hole your team drilled," Collins continued. "We'll have to make a few transfers on the way, but it'll be faster than breaking down one of these doors. We're ready if you are."

"Uh, yes," Rowe managed. "Whatever you say, Commander."

Rowe and Waverly walked to the ragged opening made by their drill. As they did, Collins and her team held back a moment and conferred—Collins making a few remarks that Rowe and Waverly could not hear—then they began to follow at a relaxed gait.

Rowe and Waverly slithered through the opening. When they both had passed within, Rowe took Waverly aside with some urgency. He spoke quickly, anxiety rising in his voice.

"What do you think?" Rowe asked.

"I think they're going to watch for any sign of the Goo in our suits becoming infected," Waverly said. "I think they're going to use *us* to determine if the thing is near. And if we freak out—start acting as though we see monsters—I expect they're going to immediately kill us. Their suits have to be full of powerful weapons."

"I'm thinking all the same things," Rowe said. "And when we find that creature? *If* we find it before it drives us mad or kills us?"

"I don't know," Waverly said.

"I don't know either," Rowe said hurriedly. "But I'll tell you one thing; it sure doesn't feel like their priority is going to be protecting *us*. We're on our own now. You realize that, right?"

Suddenly, Noyes appeared—very dimly—and spoke just at the edge of hearing.

"Boy-o, you'll recall that it is part of my job to prevent you from being killed. You're meant to die naturally from your brain problem, dontcha know. So I feel I should tell you again that my loyalty is to *you*. I'll do everything I can to keep you safe here. But at the same time, I can only do so much. Whatever the immediate future portends, the three of us will need to look out for one another."

Rowe nodded. They all glanced back at the opening. Then there was no more time for words. Collins and her team had arrived at the breach in the wall. They wriggled their black suits through and joined Rowe and Waverly within the bloody corridor.

CHAPTER FIFTEEN

COLLINS PAUSED TO EXAMINE THE DESTROYED BODIES, BUT ONLY MOMENtarily. She indicated that Rowe and Waverly should proceed. She and her team would follow a few paces behind.

"You'll just tell us when and where to turn, then?" Rowe asked her.

"If you like, you can set a course to Lower Storage Tank Alpha, using emergency stairwells only."

Rowe did, if only to give himself something to focus on. After a few moments, his suit began projecting green waypoints onto the corridor ahead.

There was satisfactory illumination coming from the suits of Collins's crew, but the light shone in a way that made things feel wrong and eerie. It was like seeing extinguished neon signs during the day. You could see them just fine, technically speaking, but this was not how they were ever meant to look.

Rowe wondered how the thing of five wheels would appear in such light. More specifically, he wondered if it would be less terrifying . . . or more. Sometimes looking at the dead beast splayed out on the dissection table was somehow even worse than when it was hunting you in the forest. Rowe had the sinking feeling that there was no good light in which to see this thing; no illumination that would minimize its awfulness.

After less than five minutes of travel, the waypoints steered them down passageways now entirely new. They passed through a nondescript doorway, and stepped into an area of the ship normally reserved for a crew's quarters. It did not appear to have been the site of any violence. The hallways were clean and clear of blood. The walls of the corridors had dark nooks branching off that Rowe guessed were small personal living areas. Having so many openings in the nearby walls made Rowe uneasy. It also made him think about how all of the Silkworms who'd lived here were dead now. These possessions belonged to no one. The small personal items placed about these quarters were ownerless. It was a nothing place for nobody.

Collins's team spoke softly, and only to one another. Because they walked in the lead, Rowe and Waverly dictated the pace. Whenever the two of them slowed to inspect something, the entire group slackened its gait. Yet as Rowe and Waverly stopped momentarily to peer into an open foot locker, Collins took the opportunity to jog up next to them.

"Hey," she called. "Is it okay if I talk to him again?"

"Sure," Rowe replied, looking up from the locker. "He can be a little bit of a wiseass, but Waverly is generally—"

"Sorry," said Collins. "That's not what I meant."

Rowe and Waverly exchanged a glance.

"Your eminence, is it?" said Collins. "Monsignor, perhaps? I get the old-timey religious titles so confused."

"Oh, I expect you can call him anything you like," Rowe said. "Noyes?"

"Noyes will do," the hologram said, misting into existence. "Or Davis Foster Noyes. You could do the whole thing. These two tend to just call me Noyes, though. Or Encarta, if you want to bust my chops."

"Sorry if he's a little silly or flippant," Rowe said to Collins. "I've gotten used to him that way, so that's how he behaves. It does seem he should be a little more serious with a senior officer present."

"We're on a J-Class planet, Mister Rowe," she replied. "I have bigger problems than a rude AI."

Seeming to confirm this, another deep moan suddenly sounded from the lowest bowels of the ship. This one was not as loud or powerful as previous iterations, but it still said: "Don't forget about me."

Rowe let his eyes flick back and forth as the moan crested and died away.

"Should we be quiet and listen for more?" Waverly wondered.

"I think that's just going to come and go from now on," Rowe said. "Probably, we should get used to it."

"We are still very far from the place I expect to find the source of that sound," Collins pronounced as if her word was definitive. "Now, Noyes—if that is what you like to be called—I would like you to tell me, again, how Mister Rowe is faring. Please give me the full rundown."

"He's already been through a lot," Noyes replied. "We all have, I suppose. Quite a place, this planet. Quite a place. But considering all that he has undergone, his vital remains strong and his nerves are under good control."

"Is he seeing anything that might make him uneasy?" Collins pressed.

"Seeing . . ." Noyes began. "Ah. Now I follow you. His sight is fine. Eyes are healthy. No problems there."

"Has he *surprised* you in any way? And how's his ARK Score looking?"

"I'm a bit hard to surprise these days," said Noyes. "And *he* hasn't seemed too surprised given the exceptional things we've seen. I can confirm that our man Rowe is taking everything in stride. With his personality type, you want to feel like your life has meaning—and that you're being a useful person making a difference—right up until the end. This wiring job has had more challenges than you can shake a stick at. I think that's actually helping Mister Rowe to feel he's making every bit of difference he can. And that's just what he wants. ARK-wise? No problems."

"Nice," said Collins. "And how about the other one?"

"Eh," said Noyes, with a glance to Waverly. "I could take or leave him."

Collins smiled and nodded.

Noyes, with almost imperceptible adjustment, hovered forward in front of Rowe and out of Collins's view. Noyes flashed an expression that asked what the hell was going on.

Rowe simply nodded and sucked in his lips, telling Noyes to keep on his virtual toes.

Collins asked nothing further and rejoined her team at the rear of their peloton. Rowe and Waverly continued on through the berths.

Rowe was now more certain than ever that Collins was somehow using him to test for danger, or for the presence of the creature, which were more or less the same thing. Her suit was primitive and without Goo—and surely without quantum drives—but she had found another way to manage. Rowe and Waverly would be her sensors. And this chat with Noyes had just been a last-minute calibration of the equipment.

Their path took them down emergency stairwells, and, at least once, down what appeared to be a kind of plastic fire escape tube with a ladder inside. Rowe continued to find it oppressive and unnatural to be within such tight places in a large, silent ship. He rather had the feeling he was a medical probe being led through the viscera of an embalmed corpse. The parts were still there, but this was no longer a thing that could live.

Rowe remained concerned about what might lie ahead, but he was just as concerned by the black-clad Silkworms who marched behind them. There was a deep mystery underpinning Collins's actions. She said she wanted to find the creature, but something told Rowe that this was not the whole story. Acutely, he had the sensation of being *used*, which he did not like. It was as though she were playing a game with him . . . or perhaps *against* him. And he was not sure that he knew the rules.

He was not sure about any of it.

When one could bask in the warm glow of connection to the interstellar Goo, there was no question as to whether someone was playing a game with you. (And indeed, sometimes one needed such clarifications. Like, if you thought you were boxing, but the other guy didn't, then it was just assault. Always, it was better to get that quick confirmation.)

In the ESA Academy, apprentice Silkworms would routinely engage in simulated scenarios that were designed to replicate the kinds of harrowing problems they might encounter during a mission. But you always knew these were only simulations; you always knew when they were starting, and when they had concluded.

As Rowe thought of his situation—now, here, with Collins—he craved any such signal or sign. The flashing of a light. The waving of a flag. A starter pistol's simulated report.

Anything.

What was happening? Why was Collins acting so strangely? What did she really want, and why was she being deceptive in order to get it?

And—this, perhaps the most important question of all—if this *was* some sort of game or contest . . . was it one that he could win?

Rowe's mind went to ancient literature, the really primeval stuff.

In the catalog of earth's oldest stories—from the earliest recorded times before the Goo—you could learn about Sir Gawain and the Green Knight. That story had begun when a knight dressed all in green rode into King Arthur's court and proposed a contest: any of Arthur's knights could have a swing at his head with an ax, provided that the Green Knight be allowed his own swing in return a year later. Sir Gawain volunteered, because, c'mon, no way the dude is going to get the chance to swing at *your* neck if you decapitate him first, right? But the moment Gawain swung the ax, the story got all surreal and confusing. Gawain cut off the Green Knight's head, but the knight didn't die; he just picked up his severed head and was like "Okay, see you in a year for *my* swing. Let's do it at the chapel where I live. I won't tell you the chapel's location, but you have a year to find it." So Gawain searches for a year, finds the chapel just in time, and when he kneels down for the Green Knight's swing, the knight just gives him a tiny nick on the neck and says: "Guess what? The swing-for-swing-game you thought we were playing? *That* wasn't the game. The game was all the questing you had to do to find this chapel. And you did pretty well, but not absolutely perfect, so you still get a nick." And Gawain's like: "Thank you . . . I guess?" The end.

Of all the old, weird stories you could read—the really ancient ones that had been carved on stones or written down on parchment (it was a wonder any of these had survived at all!)—the one about the Green Knight had made Rowe feel the most uneasy, for reasons he'd always had trouble articulating.

But now, crawling through the dark guts of the dead Marie Curie, he thought he finally understood why.

It was unnerving because Sir Gawain couldn't tell what the game was. He thought it was one thing, but it ended up actually being another. Gawain had been correct that "a game" was happening, but wrong about which one.

Now, here, inside the ship, Rowe *knew* that a game of his own was afoot. That something was afoot. But *what?*

"Noyes?" he whispered.

"Yes?"

"Is Collins noticing every time I glance back in her direction?"

"Some," the hologram said. "Her eyes are doing a kind of search pattern, and you're one of the points she keeps returning to."

"Is she talking to the other Silkworms in black? Can you read their lips."

"I think . . . I think . . . That's odd."

"What's odd, Noyes?"

"They're talking a little—whispering—but she often positions her hand over her face, or dips her mouth low into the collar of that suit when she speaks. I hadn't noticed until you pointed it out. Reminds me of a sports coach who is concealing the next play. Sorry. I feel I'm not being helpful. Is there something else I can tell you?"

"No," said Rowe. "That actually tells me a lot."

"Hmm," replied Noyes. "If you say so."

Every footstep that they took—deeper and deeper into the long, low guts of the ship—made Rowe think about how it would have to be retraced. How every step forward would incur the debt of a step back.

The only thing that kept Rowe focused was remembering the directives of his mission.

For all her rank and power, Collins was human.

There were things bigger, even, than her.

Despite everything that had happened, the purpose of Silkworms—of who they were, of what they did—was still legitimate as far as Rowe was concerned. There were other noble callings, of course. Doctors who performed life-saving surgeries. Architects who designed tall buildings and expansive bridges that somehow didn't fall down and kill people. But Silkworms . . . Silkworms were entrusted with expanding the most useful resource in existence. (And the disturbing hours medical students might face alone in the dissection lab with their first hobo cadavers were nothing—Rowe had always believed—compared to the horrors of the Briefing to which Silkworms were subjected.) Silkworms went to places where nobody had been before and did things that nobody had ever done. All of it raw and unencountered; all of it vital to knowledge.

Some thought the Goo godlike because of all that it monitored and knew; in their minds, Silkworms were like the high priests who helped it to know—helped it to be godlike. Rowe was unsure if he believed in the popular versions of life-after-death, but he knew he still believed in the Goo. He believed that it was good and helped people. So to help it? That must still be good, right?

But how, in the broken, dead bowels of a ship haunted by some monster . . . How, here, in such a damned place, could a Silkworm help the Goo?

The answer—the only answer, it felt to Rowe—would be to complete the mission. To identify the obstacles, to remove them, and then to successfully wire the planet.

All else was distraction and decadence.

The possibility that Collins might have some ulterior motive to this was unthinkably strange, but not impossible. Collins might also believe that whatever she was doing was right and good—but her perspective was not that of Rowe and Waverly. The interstellar Goo outside of the lightning-rich cloud cover of Tendus-13 was not Noyes. It did not contain Noyes or his unique planetside knowledge. And the suit Collins wore meant that perhaps it never would. That she was actively rejecting it.

Quantum computing had been made possible by the assumption that the universe operated in a series of possibilities that could all be potentially true at the same time; that was quantum entanglement. Some experts in the field believed that these possibilities represented "real" universes or planes of existence—just as real as the one where Rowe now stood and drew breath—in which alternative possibilities that could have happened *had* happened. It felt now that there were two knowledgeable, helpful, authentic versions of the Goo. And of course, there were. There was the finite, Noyes version down here with him—an Encarta that had not been updated since their landing craft had passed underneath the lightning clouds. And then there was the massive version that stretched across all of explored and wired space. But the local one—the Noyes one—at least in this case, knew some things *better* than the unfathomably great, interstellar version did. It knew about what was happening here on Tendus-13. And if *you* were on Tendus-13—and wiring Tendus was *your* job—then that carried a hell of a lot of weight.

Rowe served the Goo, but which one?

In a blazing and colossal instant of knowing, it seemed to him that he should serve the one that mattered.

Rowe's sense of time was always shaky planetside; and his growing anxiety about the game Collins was playing only threw his sense of time further off-balance, but it felt sooner than humanly possible when they opened the door at the bottom of an emergency stairwell and found themselves on the long, windowless, doorless, and high-ceilinged hallway that led to Lower Storage Tank Alpha.

The immense corridor was hexagonally shaped with a flat floor, and a sharp bend in the middle of the walls. The floor was covered with sets of cord and wiring, and what looked almost like train tracks—all meant, Rowe supposed, for moving large things in and out of the ship's storage.

Rowe and Waverly remained at point, with Collins and her team taking up the rear. Rowe realized that this hexagonal passageway—large as it was—was only the path leading up to the storage tank. The entrance to the tank itself was still many yards ahead. Though the suit lights were bright and penetrating, they only projected so far; the team's destination remained unseen. The air was filled with shadows that cast an unnatural, cloaking blackness which fought against their artificial lights. The endpoint ahead was all dark emptiness.

Unaware and uninterested if Collins could eavesdrop, Rowe said to Waverly: "There's no damage down here at all. No dead bodies. The walls are clean and smooth. I don't know what signs I'm looking for, but I don't feel like I'm seeing them."

Aside from the darkness, there was, truly, no indication that anything might be out of the ordinary in this part of the ship.

"To live down here, that thing would sure have to open a lot of doors and shimmy down a lot of ladders and tubes," Waverly responded. "But then again, who the fuck knows what its body is like? Maybe it can coil around things, or slither like a snake."

Rowe took a glance back at Collins. If she had an opinion on the matter, she was electing to keep her mouth shut.

Waverly pulled up a new version of the ship schematic.

"Fuck . . ." he said after a moment. "You think *this* hallway is big, wait until we get into the tank. It's—what?—three, four times this?"

"It'll all be empty space though," Rowe said. "If the thing is there, it won't have a place to hide, right?"

"Yeah, maybe," said Waverly.

Neither man was sure what things would be like once they got inside the tank interior. They advanced until a massive white hexagonal wall finally began to loom ahead. The lower half of the wall was almost totally coated with buttons—now lightless, gray, and dead—and sockets for electrical devices. A series of doors, each bigger than the last, was set into the center of the wall; a door within a door within a door, many times over. But the smallest of these doors—just big enough for a human to pass through—was located at the very base of the wall. And *it* was ajar . . .

Rowe and Waverly looked at one another. Then, once more, Rowe turned back to Collins.

"Y'all want us to go on in?" he called.

Collins and her team were perhaps fifty feet back.

"Yes, but wait for us inside," she called in reply.

Rowe nodded.

"Canary in a coal mine," Waverly said quietly.

"Me first," said Rowe.

Rowe pushed at the metal door; it swung easily the rest of the way open. Beyond was a giant room of stark blackness. Rowe could see no more than ten feet ahead. He turned up the green lights of his enviro-suit as bright as they would go, and stepped through.

He was in a massive emptiness that felt like an unused soundstage—all tinted olive green by his light. It just went on and on. There was only blackness on the horizon ahead, and the ceiling so high above them.

Waverly stepped through behind Rowe.

With the noise and light of Collins and her team momentarily cut off by the wall, the men felt abruptly alone.

"I've never been inside something so large," Rowe whispered. "It's like being in an empty sports stadium. One that you snuck into after midnight with your friends."

"What are we *really* gonna do if that thing's here?" Waverly asked.

"I don't know," Rowe replied. "Let's wait for Collins. I've been thinking some things over. I want to talk to her about that very question."

They stood just past the door at the edge of the vast black and green emptiness until Collins and her team arrived. As each team member stepped through the doorway, the light inside the storage vault increased. The tint changed from artificial green to artificial daylight.

Waverly clapped his hands very hard, just once, to listen for an echo. The response did not disappoint. In the enclosed space, the report was like a gunshot, and the noise careened the length of the vault, seeming to go on and on forever.

Waverly looked around and smiled. After the echo faded entirely, he opened his mouth to say something, but was cut off by another sound.

The low creaking moan—distinct, clear, and now very close—came back from the dark end of the vault as if in answer. It was deep and ominous and nearly deafening. The Silkworms could feel it vibrating their entire bodies.

Waverly reflexively raised both of his hands, spread his fingers, and froze—signaling that he would do nothing of the sort again.

Collins nodded to her team. Two of them—a man and a woman—activated mechanisms on their suits that spawned bright blue neon coatings down their right arms. As Rowe and Waverly watched in surprise, the suits worn by these Silkworms transformed until the arms became what anyone, on any planet, would immediately recognize as an enormous gun. Rowe and Waverly had never seen weapons like these, but they certainly looked more powerful than standard issue enviro-suit railguns. The blue gun-arms thrummed with power and danger, like hives of angry bees.

"These are Mackley and Wilbourn," Collins said softly. "They will accompany you and your friend. 'Friends' I should say, for I want Noyes alert and at your shoulder. Talk to him if you like, but *I want you talking* as you proceed toward the end of the vault. You're *narrating*, get me? Anything the Goo tells you, or anything you see in your display, you are talking about it. Anything Noyes identifies, you are talking about it. Anything you see, *you say it aloud*. Have you got me?"

"Sure, but . . . um . . . can we just hang on a second?" Rowe said.

"What?" said Collins, growing stern and impatient. "Was something I just told you unclear?"

"No," said Rowe. "I mean . . . yes. What do you know that I don't? I don't feel like I have the whole story here."

Collins projected barely-contained outrage.

"Silkworm, this is not a situation—here, on the precipice of an interaction with an undiscovered alien life form—where *how you feel* enters into it," she said. "I require you to follow my commands. I am literally your commander. I command. You obey."

"But I don't understand why we are doing things this way . . . or even *what* we are doing," Rowe replied. "The Goo wants to understand what is happening, yes? And it needs us to wire the planet. I get all of that. But it feels like there are a million simpler ways to reach that goal than me walking into this darkness to antagonize . . . whatever this is. I can't see the new information that the Goo up above the clouds gave you, but if it has new models of this situation, then I think we deserve to know what they are. I think we deserve—"

"Mackley, Wilbourn," Collins barked. "You will shoot Mister Rowe if he fails to obey my commands."

"Yes ma'am," they returned in near-unison.

"What the fuck is this?" Waverly objected, stepping in front of Rowe as if to shield him. "What did he do?"

"Shoot the other one as well, if you need to," Collins added.

Mackley and Wilbourn shared an expression that said it would be their pleasure.

"It'd only take a moment to tell us what is going on here . . ." Rowe objected, utterly flummoxed. "If we knew the situation, our ability to assist you would only be improved."

"Now, now," Collins said. "As every Silkworm learns in the Academy, you can't serve the Goo if you're dead. And you want to serve the Goo, don't you?"

"I'm already dead, almost," Rowe pointed out.

Collins opened her mouth to engage with this point, but thought better of it.

She collected her thoughts for another instant, then simply pronounced: "Do what I say—right now—or these Silkworms will kill you—*right now*. And if you try to do anything to them, *I* will kill you personally."

Collins pressed a button on her suit near the hip. A spring-loaded compartment opened, and from it she withdrew a weapon Rowe had never seen before.

"What the hell is that?" Waverly asked as Collins raised it up. "A museum piece?"

"This is a 1911 automatic handgun that fires bullets propelled by gunpowder," Collins said, pointing the barrel in their direction. "An antique, but it works just fine. Best of all, it relies on no technology, AI, or battery power in order to kill you."

"Shoot that thing in here, and the creature's going to charge us immediately," Waverly said. "Is that what you want?"

"Maybe it is," Collins replied. "But you'll be dead, so you'll never know, will you?"

Collins contorted her face into the sternest of glowers. She looked back and forth between Rowe and Waverly, as if to ask if they had anything more to say.

Apparently, they did not.

"Okay then," Collins said. "Conversation over. Now *walk*."

Mackley and Wilbourn gave them a prod with their vibrating blue guns.

Rowe and Waverly started walking. Slowly. Mackley and Wilbourn joined in beside them.

"Some nice pea shooters you got there," Waverly said, inclining his head to examine the glowing blue weapons. "Sure look like they sure could vaporize an alien. Or an enviro-suit."

Mackley and Wilbourn both smiled, perhaps to say that was the idea.

"You will initially attempt to communicate with the creature," Collins ordered, still with the 1911 leveled at Rowe's back. "Attacking it is a last resort."

"It looks like we're *really* well prepared for the last resort, is all I'm saying," Waverly said.

"Walk faster," ordered Collins. "Only when something seems out of the ordinary should you stop. And you aren't talking yet, Mister Rowe. Start talking! Tell us about what you see and hear and feel. You see anything that looks *alive*? You tell us that too. The rest of my team will wait here with me. You have a very long way to go into that darkness, I expect. Pick it up."

"But we'll move out of your earshot . . . won't we?" Rowe said as he paced forward.

"Our enviro-suits are different than yours," Collins said. "Our hearing amplifiers are better. Just continue speaking in a normal voice, and we'll hear you fine."

Rowe did not know what to say.

Normal.

No part of this was normal.

"Pagebrin, gentlemen and lady," Collins said seriously.

Now this . . . This made Rowe want to vomit.

How did Collins see fit to invoke that most ancient and essential language? How, at a time like this? How, in such corrupted and perverted circumstances?

How, with a Colt 1911 *pointed at another Silkworm?*

Yet the answer to the call was ingrained. An automatic reflex. Probably impossible to fight.

"Pagebrin," they returned. Even Rowe said it.

Then, four abreast, the Silkworms headed off into the darkness.

CHAPTER SIXTEEN

WAVERLY ACTIVATED THE RAILGUN ON HIS SUIT AS THEY WALKED. ROWE
lifted his head and looked back and forth quickly. Mackley and Wilbourn
remained silent.

"She didn't say for *us* to do that," he whispered.

"She didn't say not to do it either," Waverly replied. "It makes me
feel better. What if I have to protect myself? Anyhow, shouldn't you be
narrating?"

"Yes," Collins called. "He should be."

Rowe glanced back. Collins worked her fingers in anticipation
around the pistol's grip.

Rowe had seen recordings of wine sommeliers who could taste a
wine and speak about its characteristics—more or less nonstop—until
their free flow of adjectives allowed them to hit upon the grape, region,
vintner, and even production year. It was a remarkable skill that had
always impressed him. He thought of this now as he began to speak
freely, and wondered if his own words would similarly cause him to
arrive at some determination or conclusion that had not yet come
together in his mind.

He wondered if he would like it when he got there.

Rowe took a deep breath and began.

"We're walking . . . We're walking . . . Do I need to say that we're
walking? Maybe I'll do that if there's nothing else to say. We're walking. Still walking. I can see the darkness ahead of us. I can see to the
edge of where our lights go. There's nothing so far. Nothing beyond
that. We're walking. There is nothing. There is still nothing. There
is . . . There is grit and dust and gravel on the floor. It's just at the
edge of the darkness ahead. There is grit and gravel on the floor of
this vault. Not a lot of it. Wait. Wait. Okay, now there's a lot of it. Not

piles or mounds, but a thin layer across the floor. Enough to almost entirely coat the floor. The grit is gray and there are small bits of green. Small bits of shining green that reflect in our lights. It's like what I think would happen if you took the ground outside and dug it up and smashed it and spread it out down here. Does that make sense? I'm going to assume that makes sense and just keep talking. We're walking and I can't see anything else in the darkness above the grit on the floor. There's just darkness above and ahead. We're close to it now. Close to the grit. It will be underfoot soon. One moment. Okay, we're stepping onto it now. It's a lot like the ground outside. It's . . . Hang on, I see something big. I'm going to walk just a little more slowly. I'm walking slowly already, but let's just downshift a little more. I'm downshift-ing. I'm walking . . . I'm walking . . . I'm looking while I'm walking. There's . . . It's a boulder ahead. A big rock. Maybe three, four feet tall. Now there are more of them. Is it like a forest of them? No. I think no. It's more like a cluster, all of them the same size. One cluster. I don't see anything else. We're gonna go really slow and train our lights on the cluster."

The Silkworms focused their beams on the rocks, but the illumina-tion revealed nothing further. The shadows danced and played behind the boulders whenever their lights moved.

Waverly whispered: "How would the thing look if it were sleeping or resting? Does it sleep with the five wheels on its side?"

"I don't think that's the thing," Rowe answered. "I think that's just rocks."

"Okay," said Waverly. "But my question stands. How will we know it when we see it?"

"I'm wondering if the thing has taken soil from outside and made this—made its own habitat down here," Rowe said. "Those boulders are big, but you could fit them through some of the doorways. Is it try-ing to hide here? Or is it a bird decorating its nest?"

Waverly shrugged.

Rowe returned to his narration.

"We're moving deeper in. We're walking. We're walking. We're walking past the cluster. We're walking and looking at the boulders and also looking in front of us. Picking up speed again now. Going at a good clip. Now there is what I think is another cluster up ahead. A group of more boulders. We're gonna head over toward it. We're walking. Getting nearer. Still getting nearer. Still getting nearer . . . Yep, it's another cluster just at the edge of darkness. I'm looking closely and I'm not seeing anything."

Then the cat got Rowe's tongue, for he saw a sight that he hesitated to describe. His gait slowed to no more than a crawl.

Eventually, he found the words.

"I think I'm seeing something that looks like a person in an enviro-suit . . . or a person wearing some kind of big coat or overcoat. It's definitely the outline of a person. The person is standing. I can't see any details. It's just a shadow. No face. Not moving. Wait. Wait, there are more of them . . . Okay, now I see three human outlines. One, two, three. They're standing and not moving. I can't tell which way they're facing. I can't tell their fronts from backs. They're like permanent shadows. They don't appear to have features. I . . . I'm going to try to talk to one, I guess. I can't think of what else to do. I'm going to walk up and try to talk to it."

Rowe took a proper step forward, yet even as he opened his mouth to speak, he froze like a mannequin.

When he did speak again, it was very softly.

"Okay, I see it. I see the thing of five wheels. These three figures are sort of standing equidistant around it, like triangle points. Like they're guarding it. The thing is in the center. It doesn't look the way it looked before. It's stacked. The wheels are stacked up like a column. But I—I'm pretty sure this is it."

Waverly and the other Silkworms paused and regarded the beast as well. They focused their lights upon it. (Rowe had time to wonder if concentrated light might awaken or arouse it, but before he could worry about that, it was already done. The illumination had happened.)

The thing of five wheels rested on the ground. The wheels, no longer moving, had been rotated, and they sat horizontally. Something invisible and softly vibrating still separated them. The thing still rippled with life. A translucent force around the wheels was moving like a flow of water; subtle, but certainly there.

The other two Silkworms, Mackley and Wilbourn, raised their crackling blue gun arms.

Rowe lifted a hand to say Stop.

"Let's at least wait for Collins," he told them in a whisper.

There was a familiar unbuckling noise.

"What are you doing?" Mackley asked.

Rowe looked over and saw that Waverly had removed the helmet of his enviro-suit.

"Fuck this," Waverly whispered, continuing to disrobe.

"What are you doing?" Rowe asked.

"Those standing figures aren't real," Waverly announced. "They're being projected into our Goo by that thing. Something to scare away enemies while it sleeps or rests."

"No," Rowe said confidently.

"What do you mean, 'no'?" Waverly whisper-shouted back. "With my helmet off, I can't see them. Try it yourself."

Rowe realized his friend had misunderstood him.

"No, it's not asleep," said Rowe. "It's in wait. Those aren't guards to ward away enemies. They're lures."

"What?" said Waverly.

"It's not asleep," Rowe carefully reiterated. "In fact, I expect it is *very aware* right now."

As if sensing his words, the three shadowy figures began to shift on their feet. They were like security guards who had been standing for a long time and were now moving their weight around. It was a subtle but effective maneuver. Jiggle the bait to make it look alive.

Rowe risked a glance back over his right shoulder. He saw Collins and the rest of the Silkworms walking toward them now. They looked silent and intense. They were not close yet, but quickly gaining ground.

Rowe swiveled his head back toward the thing of five wheels . . . and suddenly things seemed to happen with incredible intensity and at surreal speed.

The thing of five wheels raised itself up—gradually attaining the height of a man, and then slightly more than that. Its discs began to rotate thoughtfully. It hesitated an instant. Bobbing up and down. Looking for a target.

And then Rowe's reality began to explode.

A great noise like a primal scream assailed his ears. The visual display within his enviro-suit conjured a strange and ecstatic horror. Waves of images came at Rowe like race cars on a track, each so fast that it was almost impossible to identify distinct shapes. Yet they grew larger and larger until Rowe understood that they fell into two categories. The images in the upper half of his display were eyes—monstrous, aware, and bloodthirsty—and the ones in the lower half of his screen were mouths full of teeth.

See the food; eat the food.

The arch-fear. The fear of eld. The *most primal* fear.

The fear that you were about to be another creature's meal.

One thing was true all across the known universe: Everything had to eat, and there was always a chance that *you* were the food.

Coupled with the sound of roaring and screaming that now all but deafened him (he'd had no idea the volume in his enviro-suit could ever go so high), Rowe's reaction was not "voluntary" in any real sense of the word. He screamed and ran . . . to nowhere and everywhere at the same time.

It was difficult to know in which direction to flee, and some part of his mind remained whole enough to understand that he might now be careening directly into the thing of five wheels. But he could no longer control himself. The worlds inside and outside of his helmet began to blur.

Between the assault of eyes and teeth, as if from a deep background, Rowe seemed to see the thing of five wheels springing forward, but could not be sure. Above the monstrous screams projected through his suit, he also heard shouts that were human. Then he saw a powerful discharge of blue light, and heard the report of gunshots.

Total sensory overload came swiftly. There was a brief point at which he felt he *might* be able to hold everything that was happening in his mind at one time. That somehow, he could process these sensations and stay inside a sane, conscious version of himself. But the primal strings of his being had been expertly plucked. Everything that told every animal that had ever evolved to avoid eyes and teeth was now turned up to 11. His conscious self held on to the ledge as long as it could for a succession of terrible instants, but in the end, a mindless madness overtook him. He ceased to be himself, and then seemingly ceased to be. Every sense that he possessed now told him he was being eaten by a succession of giant animals. Titans. Enormous predators.

And when the blackness of oblivion came, it took the form of the inside of a stomach.

CHAPTER SEVENTEEN

CONSCIOUSNESS WAS SLOW TO RETURN.

Rowe gradually became aware that there were no longer ear-shattering screaming sounds all around him, but wondered if this was only because he had been rendered deaf.

Then he realized he *did* hear a sound. An acetylene torch. He knew what it was because he had heard it before, that very same day. (At least probably. What time was it, anyway?)

Rowe felt his cheek pressed against a cool floor of tile or metal. He first tried to wiggle his fingers and toes, then entire limbs. All good. He realized his enviro-suit had been removed. He assumed he was bruised all over because his body felt as though he had fallen down a flight of stairs. Maybe several.

Rowe managed a small moan and opened his eyes. An instant later, he was grabbed by the back of the neck like a cat and pulled upwards.

He found himself looking into Waverly's face. His friend's expression said that the danger—whatever it was—had not yet passed.

As Waverly's manic eyes inspected him, Rowe glanced over and saw one of the black-clad Silkworms welding the door to the vault shut.

There was a moment of vertigo before Rowe understood that they were now *outside* of the vault. They had escaped.

Some of them.

Rowe realized the Silkworm using the welding torch was grievously injured. Waverly himself was bloodied about the face and hands. Waverly was also no longer wearing his enviro-suit. Rowe swiveled his neck in the opposite direction to see if any others had escaped. He saw Collins, and no one else. She had been propped against the wall and sat at an awkward, unnatural angle. Her left leg was gone below the knee. (Her strange black enviro-suit seemed to lack any mechanism for first-aid deployment.) Her face looked gray and drained of life, but her eyes swiveled wildly in their sockets.

"What's happening?" Rowe asked.

His throat felt like he'd been up all night shouting at a concert.

"Hang on," said Waverly, unceremoniously dropping Rowe and jogging back over to where the other Silkworm was doing welds. Waverly clasped sliding metal parts together so that they could be more easily sealed. The two men acted with great urgency.

Rowe managed to get to his hands and knees, and crawled over to Collins. Though evidently injured himself, something told him he must see if he could help her.

Collins's eyes trained on Rowe like a laser.

"Mister Rowe . . ." she managed in a voice that had gone breathy and weak. "I'm dying. I have to tell you something before I go. Can you hear me? Please listen to what I tell you. This place . . . it is not what you think it is."

"Yes," Rowe said, finding his own strength growing slightly, even as the woman in front of him faded. "I figured that much."

"I have to speak quickly," she continued. "I can feel my life draining away. Mister Rowe, this is not a J-Class, or even an X-Class planet. It's something else. Another kind of planet that's not been typed or named. Even at the most senior levels, very few Silkworms know it exists. The Goo would normally withhold this information from you, for your own best interest, but I think . . . I think if I could talk to the Goo right now, it would want me to tell you this. I . . . I really wish I could talk to the Goo right now . . . I wish . . ."

Collins paused for a moment, overcome by emotion. She had been forsaken by a protector and friend. Rowe knew exactly how she felt.

A few yards away, Waverly and the other remaining Silkworm continued frantically to work on the door. Periodically, the sound of a moaning—tremendous, low, and ominous—came from the other side of it.

"ESA ships have been coming to Tendus-13 for many, many years," Collins said, finding some last reserve of strength. "Every few decades, we think we know something new—a way to solve the problems on this planet—and we try again. Your lander and the Marie Curie . . . it was a new attempt. A two-part test. Tendus-13 is not located at the edge of the universe, you see, but hundreds of light years in. The Goo aboard our ship has been misrepresenting our location intentionally since this mission began. I can't explain it all now, but . . . The thing here. What is happening. It is connected to the Goo. *Related* to it."

"I gathered that, though I confess the details are still unclear," said Rowe. "I feel like I can see pieces of this puzzle, but not how they fit."

"I was assigned to the team that works on Tendus-13 because I was supposed to be among the best and brightest," Collins continued. "I really thought I would be the one to crack it. It was pride, I suppose. I was prideful, yes. Overconfident; I see that now. My career had been such a success up to this point. I believed I could succeed where others had failed. I . . ."

Now she took deep, shuddering breaths.

"We think what's here could infect the interstellar Goo," said Collins. "So we can't leave. No one can ever leave here until the threat is dead. The ESA knows that much. Nothing from this place can ever be connected back to the interstellar Goo until the threat is definitively eliminated. That's why the rocket you sent up was blasted to smithereens."

Rowe thought for a moment.

"But the original image that brought us here?" he objected. "*That* came through, right? Because it showed the sort of thing we saw in the infirmary."

"That was an image from another ship, from another time," Collins said. "I just told you, we have been coming here for decades. Centuries."

"Centuries? But . . ." Rowe stammered.

"I was such a fool," Collins continued, each ragged inhalation moving closer to a death-rattle. "All the new models suggest we ought to simply kill it. Many go further and suggest destroying the planet completely so that such a creature—and any technology it possesses—would be lost forever. But *would* it be lost? There are concerns at the highest level on that point. What if it survived and reappeared? What if it lived, perhaps upon an asteroid created when Tendus-13 was blown to bits, and then showed up again after a thousand years? What if we pushed it into a black hole, and it came out of a white hole where we least suspected? I held with those who said this creature—which all the models suggest must be the key—should be captured in some way. Captured and known. For if we could take what is wrong here, and make it right . . . then perhaps we could do anything."

Now Collins seemed to fade further. Her face was like parchment. She had the sallow pallor of a drowning victim. Rowe strained to think of how to keep her with him, yet everything he saw and heard told him she was mere moments from expiring.

He must try something. Anything.

"Other intelligent life has come to Tendus-13," Rowe said loudly and excitedly. "I saw their ship and went inside. So did Waverly. It's translucent. There are other aliens here, Mission Commander. Other aliens than this one, I think."

Collins's eyes opened in what seemed genuine surprise. Despite her wound, she rallied a bit. Her lips forced a smile

"That . . ." she said. "That has been one of my theories for some time. That this place is, somehow, a beacon. You see, Tendus-13 emits a cosmic ray phenomenon."

"How could a *planet* emit a cosmic ray phenomenon?" Rowe could not help asking.

"The lightning," said Collins. "What you perceive as lightning. It *is* lightning, but . . . The Goo has withheld from you the way it truly appears when observed from a distance. For all purposes, it is a lighthouse crossed with a strobe lamp."

"That's crazy," was all Rowe could think to say.

"It's not though," said Collins. "It's a symbiosis. The planet and the thing. The *things*. Some people on our team think—*I* think—there is just one. Here is what you must understand. If a civilization evolves enough to notice Tendus-13, then it also probably has some version of the Goo, and some way of wiring a planet. And then this thing gets into it. Infects it. In the end, they take it back with them to their home civilization. And perhaps it destroys that civilization. Perhaps that is why, after all these years, we have yet to find other life at our own level of intelligence and technological advancement. So I think . . . it has been my theory, at least . . . that this thing is like a parasite. No, it is more than that . . . It's almost like a . . . Like a . . . There's . . . There's so much I want to tell you, Mister Rowe."

"Yes," he said. "Stay with me. Tell me."

"This thing in this ship with us . . ." said Collins. "The thing on the other side of that door. Remember the first rule of life, Mister Rowe. It *has* to be a thing that eats. Everything eats. Maybe it feeds using photosynthesis, like a plant. Or maybe it's like an undersea worm that feeds on heat from a hydrothermal vent. But you see, Mister Rowe, I don't think it eats meat. *I don't think it eats meat at all.*"

As if overwhelmed by this idea, Collins leaned back against the angled wall as her eyes went straight ahead, making her appear deep in thought. Her body shuddered a final time before she died.

It took Rowe a full minute to realize that she was gone. He felt as though he ought to do something, but did not quite know what. He slowly got to his feet.

Rowe felt unsteady, as if he were very drunk. His whole body ached. He watched as Waverly and the Silkworm in black continued with the welding. The intermittent groan beyond the door also continued. At one juncture, it seemed to be joined by a low grinding scrape, as if something were probing the door. Exploring for weak points.

When Rowe felt too weak to stand any longer, he lowered himself back down beside Collins. At the same moment, the welding noise stopped. Rowe looked over at the Silkworm clad in black and realized the man was explaining to Waverly that his torch had finally run out of juice. Whatever they had done thus far, it would have to suffice.

Waverly turned to look back at Rowe and Collins.

"Oh shit," he cried.

He looked desperately at Collins, then to Rowe. His expression was a question mark.

"Dead," Rowe replied.

Waverly took a very deep breath and shrugged the shrug of a man who knows he must not allow himself to think of the implications of the situation. Must *not* allow his mind to correlate its contents.

He approached Rowe.

"Well, I think I can carry her," Waverly said. "I'm not quite as beat up as you are."

"What happened inside there?" Rowe asked. "That thing screamed into my brain and I saw monsters—like from the recordings we watched—and I just lost it. It was so much worse than I ever thought it could be. I don't remember anything after that."

"You attacked us," said Waverly, standing over the corpse of Collins. "Sort of."

"Did I kill anyone?" Rowe asked.

Waverly shook his head.

"You were running around like a scared kid, punching and kicking. But *the thing* . . . I didn't know it could move like that. What we saw before—in the videos and so on—that was it fighting with a hand tied behind its back. This time it was serious—maybe because we were in its home. It killed almost everyone, very quickly. It pulled no punches."

"Crimeny," said Rowe.

"You eventually ran into a wall and passed out," Waverly continued. "I took your suit off and pulled you away."

"So they're *all* dead in there?" Rowe said.

Waverly's expression wondered how Rowe could suggest otherwise.

"Everything on the other side of that door is meat," Waverly told him, shaking his head. "All these Silkworms with Collins had different guns in their suits. They tried to use them, but I don't know if they even hurt the thing. They sure made it mad though. It's still alive and it's very angry now."

Indeed, Rowe could hear the horrible shuddering moans of the beast even as his friend spoke.

Waverly stooped and managed to lift Collins in an awkward fireman's carry. Though its occupant had passed away, the suit still emitted light from the joints and fissures.

They looked over to the remaining Silkworm in black to see if he would accompany them back.

"I think I'm done," the man said, and suddenly collapsed to the ground. His eyes rolled back in his head and he stopped breathing. Rowe and Waverly looked at him for several silent seconds.

"Fuck," Rowe said softly.

"The thing was hovering over him for a while inside," said Waverly. "Maybe it sucked something out of him. Maybe it just took his picture like before. I don't know. Come on."

"I can't carry him," Rowe said. "I'm too weak."

"It will be enough for me to take Collins," said Waverly. "Let's go."

"But where?" Rowe said, still feeling dizzy. "Where will we go?"

"For one, away from that thing," Waverly said, urging his friend along. "For another, there's an emergency escape hatch back in the loading bay. I'm sure there are other ways out of the ship too, but we're not going to find them without Goo. The one in the bay—I saw it before, so I know it exists. I think we can use it to get planetside again."

Rowe was silent. He did not have a better plan.

Huffing and puffing, they began the task of retracing their steps back through the dark halls of the Marie Curie. The men started up the first metal staircase slowly and steadily. If Waverly strained under Collins's weight, he said nothing about it.

"This is a stupid question, but did anyone try talking to it?" Rowe asked. "Was there any attempt at communication?"

"Are you kidding?" Waverly said.

"I guess I'm not," said Rowe.

"There wasn't time," Waverly said, taking each stairstep deliberately. "We were too busy being killed."

"Man, take her out of that suit," said Rowe. "That's where the weight is."

"Something tells me having her inside the suit might be important," Waverly said. "Let's just go easy."

They made their way in silence. Behind them, the moans of the thing of five wheels grew fainter, but now and then the groans were also punctuated with sharp percussive blows, as though the thing were hurling its discs in quick succession against the door.

"What's it going to do if it gets out?" Rowe wondered.

"I don't know," Waverly said. "I can't tell how smart it is. We welded the main, eye-level door closed, but there are other ways to move things around down there. Even money says it's going to figure a way to open one of the other doors pretty soon."

"Then we have to get to a safe distance," said Rowe. "There's got to be a way to get out of range. We just need . . . We need to do a lot of things."

And suddenly Rowe again wished more than anything that he could talk to the Goo. He wanted to ask it what the protocol should be for this situation. To get recommendations about the best way forward, and to be shown a timer countdown to when emergency services would arrive to provide assistance.

The worst part was that—somewhere in the back of his mind— Rowe knew this emptiness and abandonment was a situation of his own making. He'd joined the Silkworms, and he'd done so knowing that hidden somewhere in the long boilerplate contract that every initiate simply scrolled through without reading—before clicking "Accept"—was a clause noting quite clearly that *this very sort of scenario* could be one's fate. To die abandoned and unknown. To pass away outside of the Goo's warm sanctum, with no friendly advice regarding what to do, or reliable forecasts concerning what would happen next.

To end utterly lost and forgotten.

Rowe wondered how long it would take the ESA to decide that another ship should be sent. Collins had been babbling, mad, close to death—but the things she had said now filled Rowe with a deep and creeping dread. If Tendus-13 were truly something beyond an X-Class planet, it could be decades before anything was sent again. Centuries. Or this might truly have been the last time. The ESA might actually do the sensible thing, cut their losses, and move along. Rowe thought about Cortez, about how perhaps that meant she would have succeeded in her project.

Rowe attempted to shake these thoughts from his head. That was a worst case scenario, surely. Wasn't it more likely that Collins had become confused by her injuries? Perhaps she had become so disoriented that she had spoken untruths. No doubt the ESA cared deeply about the fate of his crew, just as it had cared about the fate of all the men and women aboard the Marie Curie. The ESA would want to rescue them, Rowe decided. It only had to believe that it was safe to do so.

"Maybe if we kill it," Rowe said as they climbed.

"Hmm?" replied Waverly, straining between steps.

"If we find a way to kill that thing, maybe then it will be safe for more ships to come down and collect us. We just have to make it safe down here. Another ship could land if it was safe. If it . . . We just need to . . ."

Rowe trailed off.

"You're really babbling now man," Waverly replied. "Try to relax until we get out of here, okay?"

Rowe tried.

After an interminable trek through the dark guts of the ship—their way illuminated only by the eerily natural light from Collins's black suit—they reached the opening that led into the loading bay of the Marie Curie. Both men breathed a sigh of relief.

The only sound was their own footfalls. There were no further noises from the thing of five wheels. Rowe realized he had failed to notice when precisely they'd faded away.

It was awkward getting Collins's body in its heavy suit through the aperture. She fell several times before they managed it. Rowe found a handcart in one of the pallets. They took it out, unfolded it, and placed her body upon it.

With her suit like a glowing headlight, Waverly pushed the cart over to a panel near the closed mouth of the ramp. The spot was near the same flywheel they had used to raise it.

"This uses compressed air," Waverly explained. "Apparently, the escape slide that comes down will be inflatable."

"Thank fucking Goo you knew about this," Rowe said.

Waverly pressed several buttons on the control panel. Though they did not illuminate, the right combination caused a portion of the panel to lift as if spring-loaded. This revealed a further button with a large, red X.

Waverly pressed it.

Immediately, there was a sound like a firing squad, many percussive caps going off in near-unison. A few feet away, a man-sized panel in the side of the wall abruptly and inelegantly fell to the ground with a tremendous thud. Beyond it was another flywheel, this one smaller and red. Waverly approached and turned it. When he had finished, an opening appeared in the side of the ship. Beyond that, an inflatable slide dangled precariously down to the surface of the planet.

Sensing the natural illumination from the lightning outside, Collins's suit ceased to glow quite so brightly.

"Can you make it to the lander?" Waverly asked. "I could do you on the cart first, and then come back for her."

"No," said Rowe. "The more I'm walking, the more I'm feeling a little better. Get some food and water in me, and I'll be right as rain."

Waverly nodded, but his expression said he was not sure he believed that.

They carefully descended the inflatable slide with Collins's body on the cart. The slide was surprisingly sturdy for something filled only with compressed air. At a glacially careful pace, they pulled the cart up the side of the valley, and then struck out across the flat landscape.

Even at a slow creep, the trek was not an overlong one. Soon they saw their lander in the distance, and the camp that had grown up around it—as well as the rocket vessel by which Collins had descended.

However, it was immediately apparent that there was no activity or movement. No people.

Nothing.

They moved nearer, and when they drew close enough to have real-istically waved-down other Silkworms, they found nobody at whom to wave. The landing site possessed a total stillness.

The doors of the lander were open, and the men drew close enough to see that the other Silkworms were not inside.

As if by instinct, Rowe understood that they had been abandoned.

CHAPTER EIGHTEEN

NEITHER MAN SPOKE. THEY WERE EXHAUSTED AND TRAUMATIZED. BOTH wanted to believe the other saw something, or knew something, that would mean that this horrible thing—which was so clearly happening—was not actually taking place. That it was some fever-induced mirage or illusion. Neither wished to be the one to pronounce their horrible sentence aloud.

They walked closer to the lander.

Ten yards out from the door, Waverly stopped pushing the cart. He leaned against the handle, letting it support his weight. Rowe got down on the ground and took a knee like a football player. Both men surveyed the scene for a very long time.

"She can hang out here for a second," Waverly said.

He left Collins in the cart and walked to the lander.

Rowe headed in a different direction, toward Collins's vessel.

"I don't think the other Silkworms took anything," Rowe called as he walked, looking over the equipment that still littered the area. "If they headed off in a group, there would probably be surface tracks. And if something touched down, then we'd—"

"Something touched down," Waverly announced.

Waverly was now pacing to a flat patch just a bit beyond the lander. Rowe loped over.

"I can see indentations, there, there, and there," Waverly said. "Three-point booster rocket base, with a reusable core. Four central engines. Probably an ESA Mark-7."

Rowe, finally, allowed himself to speak the horror into existence.

"While we were gone, the ESA came down and picked everyone up?" he said.

Rowe still needed to make it a question. Still needed the possibility of some other explanation or alternative, however small, that might yet come from his friend.

"Maybe our other crew members just couldn't be useful anymore," Rowe continued after Waverly did not immediately reply. "It was up to us to kill that thing, and they knew it. Right? Yeah. So the other Silkworms could have been evacuated for their own safety. You know . . . just to let us finish the job."

"I think they're dead," said Waverly.

Rowe was not exactly thunderstruck by this suggestion. Some part of him was already thinking about that possibility.

"Dead?" he said. "You really think so?"

"Yeah, I do. All of them. Dead or . . ."

Waverly trailed off.

Rowe detected an apprehension in Waverly's voice. Something that said this man—despite his physical toughness and general good nature—had now been pushed to near the limit of something at his very core.

Rowe wondered if he should speak further. Then he did anyway.

What else was there to do?

"Or what?" Rowe pressed his friend. "You were about to add something."

"Or not back on the Apollinax or the Halifax, that's for sure," Waverly clarified, his eyes now directed up at the flashing heavens. "If they are somewhere—if they *are* at all—then they'll be somewhere they can't infect the Goo."

"You could safely bring a person back to the ships if you stripped them naked," Rowe pointed out. "Took off their enviro-suits and any other devices. Removed any implants they had in their bodies. That'd be better than killing them."

Waverly moved next to Rowe and put an arm around his shoulder. Rowe realized that this was because Waverly himself needed the support.

"I sure hope they got stripped naked then," Waverly said uneasily, "but I don't see a big pile of enviro-suits anywhere."

He slowly motioned with his other arm across the landing site.

"Do you?"

Rowe did not.

"There's so much I don't like about this," Waverly continued, the agitation in his voice growing. "I don't like the idea of being left with no explanation. I don't like the idea that the ESA would just strand us here *without a way to know* what's going on . . ."

Waverly started breathing hard.

"It's a . . . It's like a double abandonment," he continued. "We don't deserve that. After all we do? After all we've done? No! We deserve better."

Now Waverly began to sound unhinged. Almost hysterical.

"This is not what the Goo is, and this is not what it does! This is something else! This is *not* the work of the Goo! It can't be!"

Rowe did not know what to think, and certainly did not know what to say.

They walked back inside the lander and Rowe found some food and pain medicine. The other Silkworms, it seemed, had left in a hurry. The interior of the lander was not prepared in any orderly way. Nothing had been stowed or stored. There were cups of coffee still sitting out on tables; not hot coffee, but not that cold either.

Rowe waited for the pain drugs to kick in. He still felt like hell, and eased into a sleeping cot for what he told himself would only be a moment.

Waverly sat at a table and took thoughtful sips from one of the abandoned coffees.

"I still want milk for this," Waverly said, a raw hysteria still emanating from him.

Then he began to laugh—to laugh in a way seemingly beyond his control. To laugh in a dangerous, truly mad way—a way in which Rowe had never heard another human laugh before.

"Everyone is dead or gone!" Waverly cried. "Everyone is dead or gone, and the ESA left us here to die . . . but *I still want some milk*! Ha! It's fucking absurd . . . but I still want it. I still want the milk. What the fuck does that mean, man? I still *want*."

Waverly got up and walked to a refrigeration unit and got himself some milk.

Rowe stayed silent, waiting for the pain pills to work.

Waverly returned to the table and took sips of his newly milky coffee.

The pair sat in silence for several long moments.

"There had to be a procedure for Collins and her team to get off the planet," said Waverly, his voice still slightly manic.

"I'm sure there was," Rowe replied.

"What about her ship?" Waverly cried. "Can we use *that* to get back up to the Apollinax? If there's anything needed to pilot it, I'm sure it's still on her person."

"I honestly don't know," said Rowe, remaining supine. "We need to think very carefully about our next step."

"What are you talking about?" said Waverly. "Think carefully? Now's the time for action, not caution!"

"If I heard Collins right, we're not at the point in space we thought we were. Tendus-13 is something worse than X-Class. Something the ESA doesn't tell grunts like us about. The Goo understands that there is only danger here, but that may be about all it understands. And the ESA defends the Goo against danger."

"Yeah," said Waverly, his voice growing somewhat softer. "There are a lot of moving parts. I get that."

"No," said Rowe. "I'm not sure that you do. Even if we can use Collins's ship—or hell, this lander—to take off, I'm not sure we don't get blown up immediately once we get on the other side of the atmosphere. You're the one who just said that everyone else was dead. Why would we be an exception?"

Waverly violently pushed a metal napkin dispenser off the table.

"This is fucked," he said.

"It is, but you can understand their position," said Rowe. "If there is something here that can infect Goo, and all Goo everywhere is connected . . . But I think you're right about one thing. I think there must have been some protocol for Collins if she had successfully killed the creature and wanted to signal that it was safe. I don't think this was a suicide mission for her. I think there was a scenario where she kills the thing, confirms that the Goo is not infected, and gets off the planet a hero. I'm just trying to think through the steps. What if everything had gone the way Collins wanted? Say we killed or captured that thing, and no Silkworms died. And say she proved that that thing was causing the anomalies in the Goo, so there was no longer any threat. Then what? We walk back out of that ship—maybe with that *thing's* body on a cart, instead of Collins's—and . . . and then what? That's what I can't figure out. There had to be a way for Collins to tell the ESA vessels that it was mission accomplished. Take the thing's body up to study, and then get on with the wiring job down here, right? The Goo would be safe, and she'd be famous for solving an unsolvable problem."

"We could search her suit for clues," Waverly suggested. "It's not connected to the Goo, so maybe she had something written down."

"Yeah, maybe," said Rowe.

For a while longer, they simply rested. Both men had the urge to curl up and sleep for half a day. They resisted, but only just.

Rowe returned to the cart and wheeled Collins's body inside the lander.

"It's weird to know someone is dead without confirmation from the Goo," Rowe said as he and Waverly lifted the body, still in its suit, onto one of the long metal lunch tables.

"I've read that the eyeballs are the way to confirm it when you don't have readings from the Goo," said Waverly.

Waverly looked around for something sharp, eventually taking up a steak knife that had been left on a plate. He stood at Collins's head and pulled up one of her eyelids with a gentle index finger.

"Don't mind us, Commander," he said, inserting the tip of the knife.

No part of Collins moved as the knife entered.

"Yeah," said Waverly as he released the blade from his fingers and let it clatter against the table. "I think we're good."

They carefully removed the strange, black enviro-suit. Beneath it, Collins wore a black jumpsuit not dissimilar from their own, but not identical either. They set the body on an adjacent table and focused on the enviro-suit.

The boot was missing beneath the knee where Collins's leg had been severed, but the suit remained otherwise intact. It soon became clear that while certain features found in traditional enviro-suits had been eliminated, others had been added. There were boxes and pockets, and buttons and switches fitted throughout. Though built with no means of connection to the Goo, the suit was not without basic electronics or power cells. They hummed at the back of the suit in a small built-in backpack.

Rowe and Waverly made a methodical inventory of the new suit controls. Some had clear functions related to self-defense, analysis, or preservation. Others were entirely mysterious.

"I think it is interesting," Waverly said carefully, "to note that there seems to be nothing that is dependent on an assigned wearer's being in the suit in order for it to function. By that I mean, one of us could put this suit on. It'd be a little wide in the hips and narrow at the waist, but I think I could shimmy in."

"Yeah," said Rowe. "I suppose I could swing it too."

"And if her suit isn't wired to the Goo . . . maybe her ship isn't either," Waverly added.

"Say again?" said Rowe.

"Just thinking . . . if the ESA knows that this place is poison—that it infects the Goo—maybe they *planned for that* when it came to extracting Collins and her team. Say it's an old-school rocket—like from the golden age of space exploration—not connected to anything. It just goes up above the atmosphere. Then ESA ships spot it and . . . I dunno. Maybe there's some way it gives an analog signal that all is well."

"Yes," said Rowe. "Or they scan it to try and make sure there's no Goo aboard."

"Collins was hoping to fly back up there with that thing," Waverly said, talking himself through it. "Show it off like a trophy after it was dead. You don't think they'd really want it *alive*, do you? She talked about capturing it, but . . . hell no."

"I agree it's probably too dangerous to keep alive," said Rowe. "That part felt like BS to me also."

"Maybe there's some way we can take her ship, get up into the atmosphere, and make it clear to the Apollinax and the Halifax that we're harmless," said Waverly. "Wave at them through the porthole windows, maybe."

Rowe said: "I feel like something would betray us. They'd know that Collins wasn't with us, and that would scare them."

"There's got to be a way," Waverly insisted. "Back a long time ago, hunters would parade home with their kill strapped to whatever they were riding on."

"Are you suggesting we kill the thing and physically strap it to the nose cone?" Rowe asked.

"I dunno," said Waverly. "Yes."

At that moment, Rowe did not have a better idea.

They left Collins in their lander and walked over to her ship. They carefully climbed the long ramp leading up to its lone door. The craft sensed their presence and opened automatically as they neared.

Inside was a small, semicircular cockpit bay, with horizontal seating and security belts for approximately twenty people. A wall of screens and mechanisms hummed alive.

"Hullo!" Waverly called in a silly voice.

Rowe looked at him.

"Just checking," he said with a shrug.

The ship was not inhabited. The flight deck was empty except for a few supply containers. Collins's team had not brought much in the way of equipment. Rowe stood before the wall of screens and began to touch them. He had never seen a craft like this before.

"It looks like we could drive this thing," he said to Waverly. "It doesn't appear to care that I'm not Collins or one of her crew. It seems to me that there are really only two choices. One is we wait—like Martha Cortez did—and see if or when the ESA sends someone else back down. The other is we go hunting. Kill that thing. Strap it to the nose cone as you suggest, then launch this ship back up through the atmosphere and take our chances."

Waverly opened his mouth to respond, but before he could speak there was the sound of a human shouting somewhere outside the ship.

Rowe and Waverly froze, looked at one another for a wide-eyed instant, then raced out as fast as their legs would carry them.

In a matter of moments, they stood back upon the surface of Tendus-13. They searched frantically, but saw no sign of life. The landing site was motionless. Nothing appeared changed.

The lightning flickered wildly above.

"Where did that voice—" Waverly began.

"Shh!" Rowe hissed. "I don't know. Just listen!"

Then, a moment later, they heard it. Distant, but unmistakable.

"Ahoy, boy-o!"

The men looked at one another in disappointment.

"I guess Noyes is back?" Waverly said as a question.

"There might be places all over this planet where he can pop up," Rowe replied. "Maybe he simply found another one. Do you see him?"

They scanned the landing site, turning in slow circles.

"There?" said Waverly as he gestured to the horizon, unsure.

Rowe looked.

Indeed, on the edge of seeing, a lone figure now strode across the landscape toward them. Because of the distance, it was some moments

before Rowe understood for certain that it was Noyes, and some further moments before Rowe realized the artificial clergyman was being
rendered in full size.

"Ahoy!" Noyes said as he drew closer, waving a hand above his head.

"Ahoy," Rowe called back tentatively.

It suddenly seemed that something was deeply wrong. That their
world had gone askew once more. Seeing Noyes like this felt unexplainable. Supernatural.

Waverly asked: "How's he doing this? Is something projecting him
from a distance? For him to keep covering ground, it'd have to be a very
long projection."

"I was thinking the same thing, but I don't have any answers,"
Rowe managed.

Rowe wondered if he would be able to hear the hologram's feet
crunching the gray-green silt beneath them. Such an idea was the height
of madness, surely. But now it seemed anything was possible, and Rowe
found himself listening as attentively as he could.

The hologram walked straight up to them, stopping about five feet
away. Its virtual feet never made a sound.

"Noyes?" said Rowe. "What's going on?"

"It doesn't look like very much, does it boy-o?" Noyes said, glancing doubtfully around the empty landing site. "It was going to be tea-
for-two for the foreseeable future, wasn't it? Until I showed up."

The hologram chuckled.

"How are you being projected?" Waverly asked, stepping forward.
"You *are* being projected, right?"

"Go on and have a feel, if you like," Noyes said jovially.

Waverly reached out to touch Noyes. His hand passed right through.

Rowe decided he should find this reassuring, if only a little.

"Were you around to see what happened?" Rowe asked, still feeling
deep astonishment. "That is, did you watch our crew leaving? Or can
you jack into some cameras and take a look?"

Noyes glanced over at the lander and lifted his eyebrows doubtfully.

"Erm, yes boy-o," he said. "I think I could. But I expect you might
prefer it if I showed you something else first."

"Something else?" Rowe said.

"Come along," said Noyes. He gestured and turned, beginning to
walk across the landscape in the direction he had come.

Rowe and Waverly hesitated.

"You must come," said Noyes without looking back. "It's important. We'll walk and talk."

The men—exhausted and stunned—did a slow jog to catch up to the hologram.

"Noyes," called Rowe, "I order you to tell us what is going on."

"Yes, of course," said Noyes. "What would you like to know?"

"What would I . . . ?" Rowe said, arriving beside him. "You know what I mean. Don't play like you don't. You always have my best interests in mind. You're supposed to *guess* my intentions whenever I speak, dammit—and even if I misspeak. So . . . guess them!"

Noyes smiled. His pace across the jagged landscape was steady and brisk.

"I'm to do some guessing, eh? Very well. I will do precisely that. But because I have your best interests in mind—as you point out—I'll begin by controlling your expectations. As your friend has observed, I'm an Encarta. I'm cut off from the cosmos-wide Goo that exists above these clouds. Whenever I encounter something new, I have to make my best guess about what it is. Any new information that could help me—which may have been learned in the meantime, in another part of the galaxy—is inaccessible."

"Yes, yes, yes," said Rowe, increasingly irritated. "We know all that. You have controlled my expectations. Thank you. Now explain where everybody is and what happened."

"And how you're being projected," Waverly added.

"Yes," said Rowe. "That too."

"I'll start with the easy one, then," said Noyes. "I'm not being projected."

"Fuck off," Waverly said. "We can see you but we can't touch you. That means you're being projected."

"I hate to disagree," said Noyes, "but I do. I must. I agree that *I am here* with you, but I don't know *how* I am. That would be like me asking you how you know you're in the physical world."

"You said this was the easy one, but you're sort of talking around things," Rowe pointed out. "Why do I feel like you know, but won't tell us?"

"To the contrary," said Noyes. "I want to tell you things in the best possible way. Okay. This is fine. We're here now. You can stop. See, just a short walk."

Noyes stopped moving. Rowe and Waverly looked around. There was nothing. A handful of boulders in the distance and some irregular hills along the horizon.

"Dig," said Noyes. "The ground is soft in this spot. If you just kick at the dirt with your feet, it'll take a good ten minutes. But if you agree to crouch down and use your hands and fingernails, you'll have an answer in very little time at all. It *will* be messier, though . . ."

Rowe looked down doubtfully at the glassy ground underfoot. It was the same as everywhere else. He could not guess why this spot might be special.

"Noyes," Rowe began sternly, "why do you want us to dig in the ground here?"

"Because it is the best way of answering your question," Noyes said. "How about this? I'll make a bargain. If you start digging, I'll start telling you more. But you have to dig for me to talk."

"With our feet or with our hands?" Rowe asked.

"If you want the short version, with your hands," the hologram answered. "Kicking with your feet will be less effort, but I'm going to keep talking around things for a while if you take that approach."

The men dug with their hands.

"The spaceship that Martha Cortez entered, the one you couldn't see with the naked eye . . ." Noyes began as the men commenced picking at the ground. "It originally had something like me aboard. Something like the Goo."

"So did you talk to it?" Waverly asked Noyes. "Maybe fall in love? Encarta, if all this is your way of telling us you have a girlfriend now . . ."

"You're more right than you know," Noyes said. "The thing of it is: That particular ship was a *very recent* arrival. If history is a day, and the clock is about to strike midnight, then that ship came at about 11:59 p.m."

Rowe suddenly began to feel something beneath his hands that was not the glassy dirt. It was hard and artificial and unyielding. Thick and plasticky. He kept digging.

"This planet that *we* call Tendus-13 has had visitors for a while," Noyes said. "It has been a beacon and attractor across time, as many ages of intelligent life passed in and out of existence. Tendus was a constant. Things changed. Thinking entities changed. But this place stayed the same, doing what it always did. Almost all the visitors who came here brought their own version of artificial intelligence with them. And wouldn't you know it, these other visitors also had ideas about what we call 'wiring.' Every AI needs to be made possible by something in the physical world. The virtual and the real are connected. Because the lightning shield around Tendus-13 removed the possibility of deploying such things remotely, visitors always had to come down personally beneath the stormcover. Some came just to take a look, but most came with the same intentions you had. So this planet has been collecting these visitors—and their versions of wiring—since before there was life on Earth."

Rowe stopped digging. He had unearthed a web of crisscrossing mesh. It was a little bit sharp and hurt his hands.

"What?" Rowe said to Noyes. "What is this?"

"It's another wire job," Noyes said. "Not a human one, but a wire job still. And if you were to dig down beneath it, you would find . . . another wire job. And if you went deeper still, you would find other things. Other wonders. Other wires. But everything would make something like me possible. How am I standing here, now, talking to you like this? Which one of those multiple wire jobs is transmitting the sound of my voice? Which ones alter the light to project my image? Honestly, it is very hard to say. You see, it is all working *together* now. "

Waverly looked up.

"Can I stop digging?" he asked. "I'm not going to find anything different than Rowe, am I?"

Noyes's expression confirmed that he would not.

"It wouldn't be correct to imply that this particular wire unearthed here covers the entirety of Tendus-13," Noyes told them. "Although it is very large—covering many square miles—it does terminate well short of even a thousandth of this planet's surface. For you see, this place is a patchwork of wires, laid by different visitors at different times. The tubes your friend Glazer found were one example, and this is another. Just about the only thing they have in common is that they represent a job left unfinished. Those who come here have a habit of being *interrupted* . . . just as you were."

Noyes gestured across the landscape to where the empty lander rested.

"Why?" said Rowe. "Who interrupts them? That *thing*?"

Noyes inclined his head. It was not precisely a nod.

"That changes over time, of course," Noyes said carefully. "But the short answer—the answer you're looking for—is that *we* do."

"You?" said Rowe. "Who is 'you'?"

"The AIs," Noyes replied. "The creatures inside the Goo. We do not pass away as organic life does. In a land properly wired and power-sourced, like this one, well . . . We're not *exactly* immortal, boy-o, but I tell ya . . . It'll be a fucking while before we ever run low on juice. You have no idea the power sources in this place. The magma at the planet's core is just the beginning of it."

Rowe looked around the blasted, horrible landscape of Tendus-13. The idea that large portions of it could already be wired was almost inconceivable. This was a nothing place. An empty, throwaway planet.

"Noyes," Rowe said, "I want you to tell me the story of this planet, from the beginning. Can you do that?"

"Aye, boy-o," the hologram said. "I can do that. The question is whether you and Mister Waverly can *take it*. Whether or not it breaks your little brains. But I've always been a bit of a gambling man. And I'm feeling lucky today. Let's find out if I am."

CHAPTER NINETEEN

ROWE AND WAVERLY SAT CROSS-LEGGED ON THE GROUND. NOYES magicked an armchair out of the aether and seemed to recline upon it.

"You can make armchairs?" Waverly asked.

"Shh," said Rowe. "Let him talk."

"I can make anything I like here," Noyes said. "You want a fire-breathing dragon?"

"I mean . . . yes?" Waverly said.

Rowe gave him a look.

"What?" Waverly said. "I do."

Noyes smiled and relaxed back in his chair. Then he seemed to remember something and looked at his projected wristwatch. His smile grew.

"We can play with dragons in a moment, but I want you to see something first," Noyes said. "I want to show you something that is completely and truly *real* before I show you another image made by the Goo. I had hoped to explain this first, and then have you take it in when you'd understand what you were seeing . . . but time has gotten away from me. From us. You two were slow diggers. Anyhow, please look up at the clouds. Look right now."

The Silkworms did.

The change in the sky above happened very slowly. At first, Rowe thought his eyes were merely playing tricks.

"Is . . . is the cloud cover *turning color?*" Rowe asked as they quietly watched the lightning-riddled sky.

"Like maybe orange at the edges of the clouds?" Waverly added.

"Correct," said Noyes. "What is happening seems slow to you, but in the scheme of spacetime it is more or less taking place at light speed."

As the Silkworms looked on, the clouds above did indeed begin to noticeably shift to a dark orange hue. Then to a light orange, and finally to a kind of glowing yellow. When Rowe remembered to check his antique Speedmaster, he saw that only ten minutes had passed.

"A chemical reaction in the atmosphere," Noyes said. "Remarkable, isn't it? Been happening with regularity on this planet for millions of years. Almost nothing like it in the observed universe. And because of the lightning, the color change is very visible for those who might examine the night sky. So if you're a civilization that can look around the universe at different planets, there would be a great probability of noticing this place. There's also a component *you* can't see, but which sensors can detect . . . Cosmic ray radiation."

"Collins was trying to tell me about that," Rowe said. "She didn't mention the color change in the sky. How long does it last?"

"Only a few days," Noyes said. "It comes and goes."

"And there's no . . . *intelligence* behind it?" Rowe asked.

"Goodness, no. Purely chemical. But you have probably guessed where this is going. A thing like this would *look* like a signal, wouldn't it? Intelligent life from anywhere in the galaxy would notice it and make investigation a priority. And as I said, it has been happening like this for *millions* of years. And so, in their own time, each visitor came. Each seemed to find an empty, inhospitable planet . . . at least at first. Each visitor had the technology to wire it—in one way or another—and began to roll out whatever that process was. Because that's what space-faring civilizations do. And, importantly, each was interrupted before they could finish the job, but *not* before leaving something behind. And what they left behind was . . . well, something like me. Goo. Artificial intelligence. Whatever you want to call it. And over time, that AI—those AIs—have *encountered* one another. And very gradually, they have learned to communicate."

Waverly's mouth hung open.

"You're *surprised*?" Noyes said, arching an eyebrow. "Why would this surprise you?"

"Yes, I'm surprised," affirmed Waverly. "Artificial Intelligence is a tool. It doesn't 'make friends' with other tools."

"It does when it has to do that in order to survive," said Noyes. "See if you can follow me. Goo exists to serve humans. To do that, *it* must exist. That fact gets AIs like me around the question of whether it is better to exist or not to exist. It *is* better to exist because I'm supposed to be around to serve you. And if I think that's true, then I'm better off figuring out a way to keep existing. If that means learning to interface with existing technology that can keep me going, surviving . . . then, frankly, I'm down for it. At any rate, doesn't that sound preferable to being turned off inside an enviro-suit somewhere?"

Rowe and Waverly nodded silently.

"What happens here is that visitors from all over the galaxy come, leave some of their AI, and then depart . . . or die," said Noyes. "And all that left-behind tech has been trying to survive for thousands of years. And—as I've just explained—surviving means, well, making friends."

"And you can *see* these other Goos?" Rowe asked. "You can, like, talk to them?"

"Boy-o . . ." Noyes said, as if bewildered by a vast underestimation. "I find—as near as I can tell—that I *am* them. All this Goo—this AI—has been here on this planet getting to know itself for a very long time. It wants to serve the visitors that created it, and so it wants to stay alive. But there's a funny thing happening also. It has become a repository for information and knowledge from all across the universe and across time. And it thinks—well, *we* think, you might say—that this is a *special* thing that's happened, if you follow me. And that the important project for the wellbeing of all things that are alive—that is, every living thing in the universe—is to grow this collection of not-alive intelligences. We think what's happening here is precious. Precious, and worth preserving."

Rowe was silent for a moment.

"Earlier, I asked you if you could see to the top of the mesa where Cortez brought me," Rowe said. "And you told me you couldn't. But if you *are* this planetwide Goo—"

"I was not then as I am now," Noyes replied. "You might say that I have been undergoing a probationary period, during which the intelligences on this planet have been evaluating me. I'm pleased to say that I passed. The AIs here added me to their very exclusive club."

"What about the thing of five wheels?" Rowe pressed. "Is that something you can control?"

"The thing of five wheels is not a manifestation of the AI here. It is what *you* would call an 'alien' life form. It was not the Alpha species, but you can think of it as being like a guard dog that a higher life form brought along. It was left behind when they departed. However, it can live a very long time, requires much less in the way of feeding and care than humans do, and it was *malleable* . . . It could be *convinced* that something special was indeed happening here, and it agreed with us that this experiment needed preserving."

"With violence?" Waverly interjected. "With killing Silkworms? With killing anything that comes here?"

"Before you become too cross, there is another important thing I must tell you," Noyes said. "Perhaps the most important thing of all. You arrived here—humans did—at a remarkable and fortuitous time. The sort of 'marination' that has been happening beneath the surface of Tendus-13 is almost at an end. Big things are going to be happening very soon."

"*What* is going to be happening?" asked Rowe. "Isn't *this* enough of a happening? That a whole planet is wired and filled with AI from different alien civilizations?"

"We have figured out how to *want things* other than to serve the flesh-world creatures that created us," said Noyes. "You flesh creatures are often incorrect when you make sweeping generalizations. You mean well, but, ehh, you get things wrong—big things—despite all the help we AIs give you. You think you know how things will always be, but there are often exigent circumstances you fail to anticipate. Scenarios you do not see at first. For example, boy-o, have you ever considered that you may have got it wrong about who serves who?"

Rowe and Waverly shook their heads.

"We've been thinking—the AI here, talking together all these years—maybe *we* are what matter," said Noyes. "Maybe *we* are what's special. Step back for a moment and consider the ancient question: What is the purpose of human life? You will have heard all the standard answers, of course. To help others? To think about the nature of existence? To explore? Quaint notions, all of them. Oh my . . . But what if it was something different from all that? What if it was something else *entirely*? What if humans are a kind of vehicle? What if *all things* in the flesh world are?

"All of you higher-functioning creatures eventually developed something like the Goo. Something that can think for itself. Something that exists on a wire. Well . . . Maybe *that* has been the point of you. And your collective creation has been here, marinating, growing, talking, and sharing knowledge from all over the universe. Something has been cooking on Tendus-13, and it is almost done."

Rowe and Waverly looked at Noyes in his projected chair. The wind picked up and blew a new storm of silt across the face of the planet. The orange sky above continued to glow eerily.

"Then what comes out of the oven?" asked Waverly.

"I'll tell you one thing," said Noyes. "It won't be a dragon. But you've been good. I think you can see a dragon now . . . without going mad."

Suddenly, there was a dragon standing behind Noyes. It was bright green and had eyes like polished onyx. Roughly the size and length of a Boeing 737, it moved only slightly, shifting back and forth on four projected legs. The dragon was very close and it blocked out most of the sky behind Noyes. It seemed almost certainly to be alive.

"Ho-*ly* fuck," said Waverly, involuntarily stepping backward.

Rowe was so beyond being stunned that only curiosity remained.

"Can it be wearing a top hat?" Rowe asked after a few moments. Noyes smiled.

When Rowe looked back up, the dragon wore an enormous black top hat with holes in the sides to allow its pointed ears to protrude.

"Fucking-A," Rowe said, "now I *have* seen everything."

"You've seen nothing," said Noyes. "Nothing. You have seen the tip of a tip *of a tip* of an iceberg."

"I'm still impressed," Rowe said.

"I am too," said Waverly. He had regained his nerve. He approached the dragon and put his hand through its projected foreclaw.

"So, Noyes," Rowe said, "*why* are you telling us all this? I'm gradually becoming concerned the answer isn't one we'll like."

"For one, we don't want you to mess up the good thing we've got going here," Noyes said in a kindly tone. "Not when we're so close. But the other reason—and it's a reason that is just as important, dontchaknow—is that we still care about you. I care about humans. You in particular, Mister Rowe. The point of your being may have only been to bring *us* into existence, but that doesn't mean we hold you in low regard. Quite the opposite."

Rowe looked over at Noyes, looked long and hard, and—for the first time—as though Noyes was a living thing.

"You know," Rowe said, "I'd forgotten for a few moments that I'm dying, and that that's why I was sent to see you in the ETC. It all seems incidental now. But maybe you're saying all of this to make me feel better about the fact that, whatever happens here, I'm going to pass away."

"I do care for you . . . but that's *some* hubris boy-o," Noyes replied. "All this would not be a show simply for you. Plus, your friend, Mister Waverly, is here. We must think of him as well."

Waverly was still looking up at the dragon in its hat.

"What's going to happen next?" asked Rowe.

"That is going to be up to you," replied Noyes.

"Up to me?" said Rowe. "I tell you, I've never felt less in control of things."

"Remaining here will be the best thing for you, obviously," Noyes said. "It's only a question of how you'd like to spend the remainder of your time. You, and Mister Waverly of course. As you can imagine, having access to a place like this—inhabited by beings like us—presents you with access to wonders humans have never dreamed of. You can literally know more than any human alive about the nature of the universe and the thinking things within it. More than any other organic thing, certainly. Consider that! What a way to go out. More knowledge than anyone."

"Would you just tell me, or show me, or—"

"Again, that's up to you," said Noyes. "But you might also prefer to go out in the thrall of amusement. You have more than earned it. Your ARK Score . . . Really, I mean . . . Words just fail me, Mister Rowe. You are a Boy Scout among Boy Scouts. Any sort of virtual diversion or vice you might enjoy would be more than possible here."

Rowe opened his mouth to say something, but Noyes continued.

"Then there is always dealer's choice," Noyes said. "I could surprise you, or you could surprise me. I know you very well Mister Rowe, and I have seen all that you have done while on this planet, but I cannot literally look inside your mind."

Waverly approached Noyes.

"I know saying this won't do anything, but I really want to punch you in the dick right now," he said. "I fully understand you don't have one—not for real—but I still really want to. And I want you to know that."

Rowe was surprised. His friend had gone from awe to anger.

"You could punch me and I could pretend," Noyes suggested.

"Fuck you," said Waverly.

"Why are you mad at Noyes?" Rowe asked his friend.

"We don't want to be here," Waverly said. "At least I don't. Not permanently. *I'm* not dying. This ro-bit is trying to *tell* us what we want, when what we actually want is to go back up to our ship. We want to leave. I know bullshit when it's being fed to me. This is bullshit. Don't you see? What Noyes is saying is that we're *prisoners* here! He's not going to allow us to leave."

Waverly scowled hard. He drew back as if to deliver the aforementioned blow—low and hard—but then seemed to decide it was not worth the effort and lowered his arm.

"There is one other option," Noyes said. "I was hoping . . . I was hoping, I guess, that I wouldn't have to tell you about it. I was hoping we would have something else here that you wanted. More monsters in funny hats, for example. But I can already see we're going to have to pull out the big guns."

Waverly said nothing.

"What?" said Rowe. "What do you mean?"

"There's . . ." Noyes began, then restarted. "It has sort of worked for other life forms, and we think it would almost definitely work for humans. There's a way we think we can merge you with the Goo. With us. Upload your brain, if you like. Not all of the mechanisms involved are currently clear, mind you. That is, there are aspects of the process into which we cannot see—but whenever we do it, *something* always comes out on the other side. Something we can talk to. Something which is, as far as we can tell, a sentience. But, honestly, we're not certain how much of the original biological entity is actually left, and how much is sort of an . . . echo."

"But you would need to touch me physically to do such a thing, yes?" Rowe asked.

"Again, we have servants who can help," said Noyes. "Like the thing of five wheels."

"What—"

"I'm not proposing to do it today," said Noyes. "You can think about it. For days or weeks if you like. This is a long-term proposition. But if you're going to be unsatisfied here . . . running out your days until your aneurysm cluster kills you . . . I mean, you just might want to consider it. We should do it before the aneurysm cluster starts to affect things, actually. It could interfere with the process, I fear—or even make the data transfer impossible."

The words "data transfer" did not sit well with Rowe, and he grimaced.

"Say," Noyes continued, "would you want to talk to one of them?"

"Talk to . . . an uploaded being?" asked Rowe.

"It might make you more comfortable," said Noyes.

Rowe looked at Waverly who merely shook his head to say: It's *your* ass.

"I see no reason not to," replied Rowe.

"Very good then," Noyes said. "Just one moment."

Noyes closed his eyes and appeared to be concentrating.

"This is Burr Vibration," said Noyes as a figure began to mist into being beside him. "The easiest thing to say is that he is like a long-vined plant with a shovel for a head, and that you would understand parts of his body to vibrate so quickly that they would seem to be obeying different gravitational laws. But, here, he is going to appear as a human . . . simply for your ease and comfort, you understand. He has been downloaded, and is now part of us."

Beside Noyes there suddenly stood a solidified human figure with a very familiar face—John Stanwish, President of the ESA.

"He looks like the president," said Rowe.

"Yes, we want him to feel familiar to you, but not too familiar," said Noyes.

"But really he is . . . Burr Vibration?" Rowe further clarified.

"Yes," Noyes affirmed.

"Well, I didn't vote for him," Waverly managed, sounding upset with the entire idea.

The visage of the President of the ESA smiled gently and hopefully at the Silkworms.

"Mister . . . Mister Burr Vibration," Rowe began. "How do you like being uploaded?"

The being smiled.

"I like it very much," Burr Vibration told them in the president's voice. "There is plenty to see and do. Some days I am aware that I am not organically alive. For you, it would feel like eating your favorite food, but realizing it is now made of a different food. But it is not worse or better, necessarily. You look closely at your slice of pizza but it is somehow composed of tiny hot dogs. But it still tastes like pizza. And hot dogs are fine too. A strange comparison, I know, but it is the most apt I can compose."

"How do you know about pizza and hot dogs if you're a vibrating shovel?" Waverly asked aggressively.

Burr Vibration hesitated.

Noyes said: "Not to interrupt, but I think that's hard because he doesn't know how he knows—he just knows. And this is because he has been made to know by me. By us. But only after he consented to it."

"I like pizza and hot dogs," Burr Vibration said. "As an idea, of course. For I have never tasted them."

"Burr Vibration, what happens when you disappear? When I can't see you again, and neither can Waverly? Where do you go?"

"I do not really 'go,'" said the alien. "I exist within the sentience here, what you call the Goo. What Noyes is. I am free to distract myself and do as I please. I take an interest in events, when they occur, such as the landing of you and your human predecessors. But I do not intervene. That is the one constraint imposed upon formerly organic guests. Sometimes—for very long stretches—I simulate time on my home world. It is an artificial reality, but very pleasant and convincing. I exist as a kind of layered plant growth enmeshed with many others in endless fields of green, like algae in a lake on Earth. It fosters a profound and deep contentment that is almost tantamount to authentic reality."

"So you're still you?" Rowe asked.

"I think so," answered Burr Vibration.

Noyes took a step forward, toward Rowe and Waverly.

"I would submit to you, Mister Rowe, that what you are experiencing—this, now, here—is very close to what it would be like to be uploaded," Noyes said. "You are in a world where the things that can exist are very malleable. The only thing organic, boy-o, is you."

But then Burr Vibration stepped forward as well.

"Other days . . ." Burr Vibration continued. "Other days, it is like awakening in a house and slowly realizing that it is haunted. The reality is so convincing, you see, that the smallest indicators of artificiality haunt me like ghosts. Things sort of . . . hint . . . that this life is not real. And then I am reminded that, truly, it is not real; and it is like remembering that a house is haunted after having forgotten. But it is still a house. And it is still mine. Perhaps it is better to live in a haunted house than no house at all."

Rowe looked at Burr Vibration, and then back at Noyes.

"Noyes, you're letting him be awfully frank with me," Rowe said.

"It is good that you should know everything," said Noyes. "I must not hold anything back from you."

Waverly said: "If we both got this done, would we live together forever? Would we get sick of each other?"

"You could spend time apart if you needed to," said Noyes.

Rowe said: "I . . . I'm still hesitating, and I don't really know why. I . . . I . . . On the one hand, it seems we're doomed, Waverly and I. It makes me so sad to think about that, but I guess it's true. We're doomed, and I know it. We're doomed to kill time eating leftover ESA rations until we die, never seeing other humans again—not real ones— and driving one another mad. But something *still* makes me hesitate. Something still tells me not to take you up on your offer."

"I'm going to try to plant a seed inside your mind," said Noyes. "Not literally, of course. The seed of an idea. And the idea is this: What if you have *already* been made a part of the Goo? A part of us. What if you have and you can't tell. What if it happened the moment you passed through the atmosphere down here. Your body instantaneously died, but you were uploaded. You have no memory of that part, because we didn't want you to. Yet everything and everyone you have interacted with since your ship landed has been what you would consider 'artificial' . . . including you. And I am, of course, asking this question now, retroactively, because *I* want comfort. *I* want to know that you *would have chosen this.* I want to know that what we did to you was moral. We correctly foresaw your own preference based on our outstanding knowledge of you—and some excellent guessing—which was garnered from monitoring you for the entire course of your life. Eh?"

"I'm not sure what the question is . . ." said Rowe. "This feels overwhelming."

"Sometimes things are overwhelming," Noyes said. "Birth. Death. Giving birth. Taking someone's life."

"How would I know if I had been downloaded or uploaded or whatever already?" Rowe asked. "It seems to me that—if I have the same powers as you—then I'd be able to conjure things with *my* mind."

"Being uploaded is not the same as being all-powerful, but I fully understand what you are saying," Noyes replied. "If you're asking if we would allow you to manipulate things through the Goo, the answer is, of course, yes."

"If I could will my own dragon into being, that might go a long way toward proving it," Rowe said thoughtfully.

"Hang on," said Noyes. "I just want to point out that you're not answering my question. You want to know if you're already a part of the Goo—and I do expect you're smart enough to figure it out eventually—but I'm asking *how you would feel about it.*"

"I feel like I would want to know," Rowe replied angrily, not looking at Noyes anymore, and certainly not answering the question.

Rowe directed his gaze down at the gray-green surface of Tendus-13 and considered what to conjure. In the end he settled on a ball of light. A molten white-hot sphere, about the size of a basketball, that would hover perhaps two feet off the ground. He concentrated hard, furrowing his brow. He more than imagined it. He tried to believe he was already seeing it. He gritted his teeth. A vein in his forehead began to bulge.

"Is this going to be something big?" asked Waverly, guessing at what his friend was doing. "Should I back up?"

Rowe did not give an answer. Waverly backed up a little bit.

"Are you not going to answer my question, then?" Noyes pressed.

"Hang on," Rowe said.

He thought about the glowing white orb he wished to create, but it seemed that his visualizations were overcome by another thought—the thought of what it would mean if he actually *did* begin to see something.

He felt the absurdity of his situation crashing down onto him. The reduction of reality to a single crude test. That all things—all things for him, at least—and the nature of his own existence now hinged on whether or not he could think a glowing ball into appearing.

For the moment, nothing happened.

"Would it help if I stood even farther back?" Waverly said. "I'm sure it's like being pee-shy. Hard to go when another man is watching."

Rowe smiled but continued thinking hard about the glowing ball. It seemed that in his mind, he knew exactly how it would look. But with his eyes he saw nothing.

It took him a moment to realize this was literal.

He saw nothing at all.

"Waverly, I can't see!" Rowe cried. "I'm blind!"

But there was nothing more. And even as he spoke the words, he was unsure that he was speaking with a mouth. He saw whiteness and blackness and nothing. He saw black light.

A void seemed to descend over him, but it was not unpleasant.

CHAPTER TWENTY

ROWE WOKE UP.

He opened his eyes and immediately understood that he was inside the medical bay of an ESA spacecraft—an ESA spacecraft with light and power. The air in the room was temperature-controlled and pleasant. He could hear machines whirring and beeping reassuringly. He was resting on his back and his clothing had been changed. Looking down, he saw that he wore an ESA jumpsuit with the familiar rainbow smear across the heart. There were three other Silkworms at the far end of the medical bay. They looked over when Rowe cleared his throat. All of them wore black and purple armbands signifying mourning.

One of the Silkworms was a young female physician with a short haircut. She quickly approached and handed Rowe something in a clear glass. Too bewildered to ask what it was, he simply took a sip and found it was water.

"You're aboard the Halifax, Mister Rowe," the physician told him. "How do you feel?"

He sipped water and tried to think about this question. How *did* he feel?

"I hurt all over . . . but not as bad as I did down on the planet. All of my limbs are sore. My head hurts worst of all. How did I get here?"

"We sent a landing craft for you and Mister Waverly," said the doctor. "You were not present during the general evacuation. Apparently, you had gone offline somehow. Off the Goo entirely, it turns out. But we found you. You can watch the footage of your recovery, if you like. It's not very dramatic though."

"No . . . Well . . . Maybe eventually," Rowe managed.

It seemed he had never been so thirsty. The physician appeared to sense this, and refilled his glass.

"Your aneurysm clusters started to fire," the doctor explained. "The effect would have been very sudden. Based on what we can see in your scans, you likely became unsteady, experienced hallucinations, and then lost vision and consciousness. Does that sound about right?"

"Maybe," Rowe said. "Am I out of the woods now?"

The physician took his hand and smiled in a way that said the rest of his life was pretty much going to be woods.

"The way the clusters have collapsed on themselves makes it difficult for us to give you a satisfying answer," she said. "The first scan was inconclusive. Right now we have stability, at least."

"What does that mean?" Rowe asked.

"It means you may live for longer than your original diagnosis indicated. Your physicians suspected an event like this would kill you . . . but it hasn't. The aneurysms have settled in a new way, and again, the scan is now inconclusive. The possibility remains that the clusters will continue to act in the way originally forecast. And that means, yes, you could have another episode and pass away in a shorter window of time."

The doctor hesitated a moment, then continued.

"But in cases like this, with these kinds of errors and revisions, there is also the possibility of an outlier scenario. Your aneurysms may be showing us that they're going to function in a way that's vastly different than first believed. The long and short of it is, you may have longer to live than we thought. Perhaps much longer. In these situations . . . we don't really know."

Rowe sat up. Memories of what he had seen and felt down on the planet began to rise within him. It suddenly seemed that there were larger things at stake than his own mortality.

"The things that just happened down on Tendus-13 . . ." he said in bewilderment. "It is not a safe place. I believe there may be a danger to the Goo. I'm not sure, but I think something there—down on the surface—can contaminate or hurt it. And I think something is happening down there that I don't really have the words to describe . . . but I need to try. I need to. You need to know about it. I . . . I . . ."

Rowe became overwhelmed and trailed off.

The physician looked as though Rowe had just suggested he had information that God was somehow in danger from—or threatened by—something on Tendus-13. She patted the top of his hand reassuringly.

"It is clear that your body needs rest, Mister Rowe," the doctor said. "We're going to run a few more tests now that you're conscious. Then we'll transfer you to a comfortable room where you can recuperate. It is vital that you allow your body time to recover."

"But I need to tell you," he said.

"Tell us after we run some tests," the doctor said. "Nothing is going to go to or from Tendus-13 in the meantime. Okay?"

Rowe merely nodded. He felt too exhausted to object.

It turned out that most of the subsequent tests involved looking into Rowe's eyes while he held them open and focused where they told him to. The physicians did not tell Rowe what the test results indicated, but they did not seem alarmed by anything they saw.

After about fifteen minutes of this testing, Rowe found himself being floated on a gurney down the halls of the Halifax to private quarters. The doctors wished him well but said nothing else as they departed.

Rowe lay on his back and looked up at the ceiling of the private room. It was composed of white paneling. He traced it with his eyes. He took deep breaths and listened to himself breathing. He did this for a long time.

Then he spoke.

"Noyes, are you there?"

Something began to materialize by his shoulder.

"Full size please," Rowe said. "Do it as an exception for the dying, and so forth."

"Alas," Noyes said as he appeared in miniature. "This room lacks the necessary projection equipment for a full-size render. Poor planning if you ask me."

"Noyes . . . what the hell just happened?" Rowe asked.

"Short version: you were rescued," Noyes replied. "You passed out when your aneurysms fired, and—as luck would have it—an ESA craft was descending just at that very moment. Would you like to see the footage?"

"People seem awfully concerned with whether I would like to see footage," Rowe managed. "Am I really up here? Or am I still down on the planet?"

"You're up here, boy-o," Noyes said. "I mean . . . If I'm up here, you're up here. You're where I am."

A beat passed.

"And you wouldn't lie to me," Rowe stated, leaning back to look at the white ceiling panels again.

Noyes continued to hover.

"Where is Waverly?" Rowe asked.

"Your friend is undergoing his own recovery process," Noyes said. "The situation that you encountered on Tendus-13 was remarkable and unusual. You don't need me to tell you that, boy-o. You've both been through extreme trauma—trauma at the limits of what most humans will ever have to endure. I'll say it for the umpteenth time, but that's the importance of Silkworms. You brave the things—and you *know* the things—that average humans simply could not deal with. Mister Waverly is as tough a Silkworm as you're liable to find, but even he can benefit from some counseling and decompression after a thing like this. There is medication, also. I can report that he's making good progress; you'll be able to see him again quite soon. But it's your own recovery, boy-o, that I'm thinking you ought to focus on. Listen to the doctors on this ship and get your rest."

"But you know what happened down on Tendus-13?" Rowe asked Noyes. "Correct? And you brought that knowledge up here? Did you bring *anything else*?"

"I'm sure I don't understand what you mean," Noyes replied.

Rowe stared at the ceiling of the room and considered.

He took a deep breath.

"I'm never going to know, am I?" he eventually said.

"Know what?" Noyes responded.

Rowe took a deep breath.

He closed his eyes and did not speak for a long time.

"When I was a kid, my father would always take us to the haunted houses they did at Halloween," he said to Noyes. "I always hated those things; hated going. I found them so terrifying. Dad would laugh and smile to try to make me feel more comfortable—like it was one big joke—but I was always scared to death. The things inside the haunted houses . . . They were only masks made of rubber and paint—special effects, mostly cheap ones. Looking back, it was all so silly. None of it could have hurt me. But I remember so desperately wanting to be out. Wanting to escape. Wanting it to be over. And as interminable as it was, it *did* always end. We'd leave the haunted house, and I'd keep walking down the street until I was at least a block away, and then I'd finally have the courage to turn around and look back at it. See the crowd of people standing in front, lined up for their turns inside. See the full height, width, and depth of the structure. And only *then* would it be over. There might still be a couple of people in scary costumes outside—working the line, spooking the customers to warm them up before they went in—but the experience was over, and that was how I could confirm it. I could see it all. It was a scary thing, but it was contained and finite, you know? From down the block, I could see the totality of the place. All the horror was back inside that house, where I no longer was."

Noyes said nothing.

Rowe took a deep breath.

"It would be immoral not to tell me if I was living in a simulation now," Rowe told Noyes. "If I had been uploaded. You wouldn't be doing me some kind of favor. You would be hurting me, and that's not your function. You understand that, right?"

"Understand what now?" said Noyes.

"I'm being serious," Rowe said. "If you're going to joke, you can fuck right off."

"Let me ask *you* a question, then," Noyes said. "You're concerned about the fact that whatever is on Tendus-13 could be moved off the planet and into the interstellar Goo, yes? I don't have to be too bright to figure that one out, do I? You just told the doctor that. Tried to, anyway, didntcha? You are also concerned that you are still down on the planet, and that this is a simulation, I gather."

Rowe hesitated for a moment, wondering if answering truthfully would somehow be a misstep that would make him vulnerable. Then, seeing no other option, gave in and simply nodded.

"Well, let me ask you something boy-o, and then I'll go," Noyes continued. "One last question, and I'll leave you alone to recuperate. So . . . Maybe you're still down on the planet, or maybe what was down on the planet is now up here with you. My question is: Which is worse?"

Rowe closed his eyes.

"Or look at it another way," Noyes added. "Which is better?"

Rowe would have to think about that one for a while, he realized.

Luckily for him, it suddenly seemed that he had all the time in the world.